"**Flight of the Sparrows** is mixed with action and love, a pair of emotions rarely hammered together. Baumbach is as much of a teacher as she is a writer. Her book includes good lessons about things readers can relate to. Things people encounter in everyday life in the real world. Flight of the Sparrows has an interesting beginning and a heartwarming end. It's lively and lovely, both at the same time. Most important of all, however, is Baumbach's uncanny ability to write a rare kind of story. To write a book that is both a literary gem and a blockbuster novel."

Reviewed by <u>*Rocky Reichman*</u> *...TCM Reviews*

Erotic Tales by Laura Baumbach

A Bit of Rough
Out There in the Night
Details of the Hunt
Roughhousing
Mexican Heat
Walk Through Fire
Enthralled
Sin and Salvation

Coming Soon:

The Lost Temple of Karttikeya
Genetic Snare
Entranced
Monster
Ripples on the Moon

Laura Baumbach

Flight of the Sparrows

Published by MLR Press, LLC
3052 Gaines Waterport Rd.
Albion, NY 14411

Cover Art by Deana C. Jamroz
Edited by Sandra Hicks

Printed in the United States of America.

ISBN# 1-934531-10-3
ISBN# 978-1-934531-10-5

First Edition
2007

Flight of the Sparrows

Chapter One

From the outside, the old warehouse looked abandoned, its paint peeling, the colors fading with each year of tortuous, wet weather it endured, leaving tattered reminders of past occupants on its pitted surface.

Inside, the glow of half a dozen dirty, bare light bulbs dimly revealed the heavy film of grit covering the thick glass windows arching up the three-story walls. Untold numbers of two foot wide venting pipes crisscrossed the flat ceiling, suspended from miles of rusted chain and strips of metal braces. The rustling of a waking body cracked the silence.

"I'm up."

The quiet phrase tinged with just a bit of triumph startled Kevin and Liam McCabe from their monitor induce stupor. Kevin sprang from his seat and bounded over to Quillan Tarquin, the youngest in their trio. Quill knew the others though of him as an anomaly, a born computer wizard who actually *thought* in terms of bytes, the basis for machine languages.

Several tabletops were burdened with more computers, all tied together in a rat's nest of thick, black power cords, multi-colored cables, and countless power strips. There wasn't a single computer that had been allowed to keep its metal protective casing. Their circuit boards and cables were displayed, half-gutted and laid bare to the room.

Three tattered mattresses topped by old, colorless blankets lay propped up on crates in one corner. A single electric space heater hummed away between two tables in the center of the work area. Paper wrappers from the local fish and chips stall were strewn from table to floor and the smell of fish and vinegar hung in the air.

Content to stay in the background as usual, Liam watched his friends from his tattered armchair. His eyes darted back and forth between the other two.

Quill re-confirmed his chain of custom virus-infected zombie PCs were online with a few keystrokes then launched a specially crafted packet into the local Brixton Police Station's public web server connection. The answering server predictably couldn't respond properly to Quill's packet and the server instantly crashed, allowing him to take control of the machine from a remote relay at the end of his zombie chain.

"And I'm in." Quill's soft voice had a lilting tone to it, gentle like its owner. His appalling south London Cockney accent was evident only when he was angry or upset.

Scanning the police network directory, it took Quill several attempts before finding an available machine that was accessible to him. One marked "Server5" opened to his command. He began downloading anything he could access, channeling files, and folders through multiple anonymous PCs his virus program had infected and gained control of all over the British countryside. The information bounced from point to point until it ended up on his computer, waiting to be stored on his hard drive.

Nine minutes and two hundred seventy-two megabytes of data later, Quill backed out of "Server5" and returned to the police network to find another accessible machine. This time "Disc380Z" opened to his persuasive, legitimate commands. Ten seconds into the next download, the connection severed.

Disgusted, Quill pushed back from the computer. "Shit! Someone in the chain powered down. Bastards!" The program didn't have a chance to send his clean up in for the server log. The relay's address would still be in its memory.

"Fuck!" His face twisted into a dark scowl, he managed to look more hurt than angry, the unpredictable event taken as a personal failure.

He raked both of his hands through his unruly curls, tugging at the stray strands that insisted on tangling in the odd assortment of silver rings on his fingers.

Kevin glanced at Liam then slapped at the back of Quill's head. "Cool it, mate! It's just a zombie a hundred miles from here. Don't sweat it. They'll never trace it back to us. That's the whole point." He squeezed Quill's shoulder in sympathy.

"I know it, you wanker. I wrote it." He folded his long legs up under his lanky frame and hunched down into the arms of his swivel chair, instantly feeling guilty for his outburst. "I just like to keep everything clean. No reason to take risks, Kev. That's how people like us get nicked. Don't fancy doing time in any prison."

"No one's going to prison, so chill out. Who'd you get?"

"Gimme a minute." Quill copied data from one directory to another, glancing through the file to get a feel for the nature of the stolen data. Strangely, all of the file names in one folder were of animal species. Maybe they had hit the Wildlife and Countryside Directorate. That would be disappointing.

"Shit. The file's huge. Where the bloody 'ell were you?" Kevin split his attention between the screen and draining the last few drops from his beer can. Liam tossed his brother a fresh can the moment he finished drinking. It was fortunate their favorite brand was also the cheapest beer on the market.

"I *said*, gimme a minute." A few more keystrokes and an individual file opened on the screen. Quill's eyes flew over the text, his breathing turning rapid and shallow as he tabbed down the page.

"Ah. . . bloody hell," he said.

Kevin abandoned his beer and took another look at the monitor. "What?"

"Looks like…um…MI5," Quill said.

Letting loose a whoop of celebration, Liam shot out of his chair to dance around the table. Stunned, Kevin downed his beer in several huge gulps, then joined his brother in the uncoordinated victory dance. They worked their way around the room, ending up back at the computer where Quill sat ignoring them, his sole focus on the text on the screen.

Quill felt the first stirrings of tightness in his chest warning him to relax. Taking several slow, measured breaths, he worked at convincing his body he was calm.

One nervous hand strayed to the inhaler lying in wait beside his keyboard. Long nights, too little sleep and the heavy dampness of the last few days were playing havoc with his sensitive lungs. Quill had no idea how long this latest inhaler would last him. He had already used it three times and he had no idea how full it had been when he nicked it off a luncheon counter weeks ago.

Oblivious to the younger man's growing unease, Kevin clapped a vigorous hand on Quill's shoulder, jarring his slight frame in the chair. "Shit, you jammy li'l sod! I can't believe you broke into MI5."

Quill nodded at the compliment, swiping at a bead of sweat running down the side of his face. He blotted at the offending trickle with the frayed cuff of his sweater, then rubbed at his burning, gritty eyes with a heel of one hand, cradling the precious inhaler in his other. Grabbing the closest beer can he could find, he finished off the last swallow, tossing the empty into a nearby box already overflowing with trash.

"Fucking 'ell, I need another one." Quill launched himself out of his chair and over to the small fridge. "Bollocks! Last frigging can and I need to get pissed after that one."

Liam stopped his insistent dancing in place and turned to look at Quill, something close to worry settling on his bland face. "Pissed? You? You don't drink more than two cans at a time. That's what makes you such a good roommate, mate."

Hands clutching the cold can, Quill turned his back to his friends. He rubbed at his weary eyes again. "Yeah, well, maybe it's time I caught up to you two louts." Even as he said it, Quill grimaced at the thought of the bitter taste the cheap beer always left in his mouth. Drinking made him feel more like one of the guys, but it wasn't his idea of a good time. It made the dreams come too often. He didn't need his feelings of loss and abandonment magnified. They were huge all on their own.

"Hey, if that's what you want, that's what you get," Kevin said. He checked his pockets, making sure he had enough cash to support his offer. "You've earned it. Not many can say they busted into MI5. You're something else, boy, must be that photographic memory thing you've got."

"It's not photographic," Quill said. "It's called eidetic. I can't remember everything I see. Just...most of it."

"Whatever, mate. Long as it works." Kevin nudged Liam to gain his attention, jerking his head toward the outside doorway. "Come on, Liam. Let's get the lad some refreshment." The heavy door clanged into place as Kevin and Liam headed out.

Sighing in relief, Quill set the unopened beer can down and wandered back to his seat, an old, vinyl-covered office chair he'd found abandoned in one of the warehouse's back rooms. It was his favorite spot, even though the chair squeaked and protested under his slight weight. It was comfortable and roomy, cradling him through hours at the computer and days and nights of endless searching.

Still trembling and wheezing a little from the earlier adrenaline spike, Quill began looking through the stolen data. Usually they copied the information onto discs, one copy for a potential buyer and another copy so they could examine every entry when time permitted. This time, he wanted to see what they had right away.

Quill habitually spent endless hours pouring over the tiniest piece of data they'd hacked from government agencies looking for specific information.

This MI5 file was an unexpected boon of wealth to the information-starved young man. This just might have the answer Quill was looking for, the information that, in his mind, justified his illegal actions, the thing making it worth all the risk. Kevin and Liam might be working to right the wrongs they felt the government inflicted on the powerless masses, but Quill was doing it for less altruistic reasons.

He skimmed through the open file looking for something of interest. Code-named 'RedDogOne,' this file appeared to be a dossier. He studied several photographs of the same man. One showed him in full dress uniform and medals, others were in more casual poses, like photos taken by a friend or relative. The last page was a brief one-line statement declaring the man's demise on the third of last month. He had died in the line of duty. It struck him as odd that it didn't mention where, how or by whom the death occurred.

Continuing his usual meticulous search through the mountain of data, thoughts of Kevin, Liam and six packs of Carling Black faded away along with the rest of Quill's awareness of the outside world.

* * * * *

Miriam Walker was an organized, punctual woman and prided her good work ethic as MI5's System Administrator for the computer files section. Right on time as usual, she began her day as she always did, reviewing the logs over the period of time she'd been away from her beloved computers. The hours of 6pm last evening until 7am this morning -- the precise times she was off the premises -- came under her methodical, uncompromising scrutiny.

Glancing through the log, Walker wasted a whole three seconds in thought before placing a call to the Brixton Police Station. Waiting for the call to be answered, she rechecked her files to be sure their computer's detection alarm system hadn't been triggered at any point it the last twenty-four hours. Finding no evidence of tampering and the system in perfect running order, her mood darkened, her voice taking on a bit of a sharp tone by the time an officer on the other end of the phone line picked up.

"Brixton Police Station. Seton speaking." The man's tone was polite, but somewhat harried.

"Sergeant Seton. Good morning." Walker forced her twitching fingers to refrain from fussing with the phone cord while she talked. "This is Miriam Walker with MI5. I'd like to speak with your Chief Superintendent immediately please."

The sergeant's tone and manner shifted at the mention of MI5. "Yes, ma'am. Chief Superintendent Davies is a bit tied up at the moment, but I'll see if I can get him for you. We've had a bit of a problem here during the wee hours of the morning and his attention's been directed there."

"I see, Sergeant. This problem he's facing, it wouldn't have anything to do with your computers would it?"

"As a matter of fact, ma'am, it would," Sergeant Seton said. "Some bloody berk took down our server early this morning. Crashed the whole lot and took over the system to boot. The Chief Super has half the department's computer lads working on it."

"Ah, I see, Sergeant. Could you put me through then? I may have some information for him regarding his current problem."

While she waited, Walker began searching through her computer's download directory to see just what data Brixton's midnight visitor had obtained from MI5's database. Twenty minutes later, she was on the phone again, this time with MI5's second in command.

"Deputy Director Richmond. Walker, sir. System Administrator on level four, Security's Computer Data

Section. We have a situation, sir."

* * * * *

Walker didn't dare shift her gaze away from Richmond. If one didn't remain focused on the man's every facial twitch, one tended to miss the tiny clues as to what he was thinking. Richmond's features had settled into a mask of granite the moment she explained the situation.

Walker knew her own face was flushed with the embarrassment of having to report the fact that their high-powered, very expensive, virtually impenetrable security system had been hacked. Worse, the intruders hadn't even triggered the system's detection alarms. Using neither a virus nor a backdoor, they had waltzed in through a legitimate open police link and downloaded an entire folder of confidential files.

Privately, Walker thought the job had been masterfully done; professionally she was livid.

Richmond rolled a small, silver-toned lighter around in his hand, distracting Walker's gaze. When she averted her eyes he let out a shallow breath, seemingly relieved to be out from under her gaze.

She knew Richmond disliked forceful women. Miriam Walker was an aggressive woman by all accounts, even hers. But that didn't make her fearless. The sooner she was back at her post in the underground levels, the better she'd feel.

"What have we learned from Brixton so far?" Richmond asked.

"Well sir, they've been able to trace the unauthorized connection to its source by its server log, but it only leads to a schoolboy's computer in Warwick. The boy's father noticed the computer running in the middle of the night and shut it down shortly after the download from our files was completed. The computer's logs have verified that. He's probably the only reason the server log wasn't erased. No time for the intruder to send a cleaner program through."

Walker looked up expectantly at her superior officer, flinching at the grim set to his lean face. "They did find a virus on the boy's computer, one set up to link it into a series of other computers, crafted to disguise the source of the original connection. It works quite well, sir."

Richmond shot a rather pointed look, leaving little doubt to what he thought about her grudging compliment for the culprits' skill.

"Gather up all the information you can on this. Director Davenport expects a full report within the half-hour. I want the exact physical location of these intruders found and I want to know exactly what they took. Everything, even if it's someone's shopping list. He has undoubtedly left something behind as well -- a virus, a backdoor, a time bomb. Make sure you look."

Walker felt a large measure of the responsibility for fixing the mess settle onto her shoulders. "Yes, sir. Brixton was able to narrow down the geographical location by the Internet Service Provider, so there is at least a starting point for ground agents to work with."

A grudging note of admiration tinged Walker's voice again. "Whoever they are, they are very good, sir, or very, very lucky."

"No doubt savage terrorists at work." Richmond's tone was laced with disgust for the whole affair. Miriam knew a clear face-to-face war was more to his liking and he had no respect for the nameless, faceless foes of cyberspace.

"Save your professional awe for the officers who will hunt these criminals down and put a stop to this kind of underhand warfare." Richmond turned in his chair, dismissing her.

"Yes, sir." Walker fled the room.

Chapter Two

MI5 specialists assigned to unearth the complete details of the intrusion were torn between being pissed off at the hours eaten up in the phantom chase and admiring the simplicity of the job.

Admiration eventually won out due to a number of factors. MI5 ran a Ministry of Defense Intrusion Detection package designed specially to ferret out this type of unauthorized access. The intruders must have managed to convince the program this was a normal access by overloading it with bogus "valid' packets until the package had to allow some traffic through unmonitored. This method had been thought impossible until now.

Hailing the work as that of a genius, they reported the emergence of a new, formidable foe in their midst. A brilliant hacker or hackers had targeted MI5, successfully penetrating their best shields. The possibility of it being a lucky accident was discussed and then discarded as too wild and unpredictable a chance ever to have happened.

Terrorism was taking on a startling new image in the form of the geeky computer nerd, a computer mouse in one hand and an explosive device in the other.

Several hours and untold strings of obscenities after Richmond and Walker's conversation, MI5 undercover officers met with their informants all over the London and Brixton areas. Between the combined effort of pinpointing the location with the ISP company logs and billing records, supplemented by the information coming in from street sources, a name emerged for a possible suspect. A group of hackers known as *FalconHawk* had become a player in the trading of government secrets.

* * * * *

At 4:22pm, two agents from MI5 knocked on the door to the Cain flat. One solid lead had emerged and a unit of agents arrived at the home of Mrs. Olive Cain, housewife, mother and sister of the McCabe brothers. Not only did Mrs. Cain have BT Openworld for an ISP, but this was the last known address for Kevin and Liam McCabe, alleged members of the soon-to-be infamous *FalconHawk*, hackers-turned-terrorists group.

After several minutes, a young woman carrying a toddler opened the door. Slithering out of his mother's arms, the child wandered off to sit in the middle of a group of pots and pans on the floor behind her. Flashing the child a weary look, the young woman wiped her soapy hands on the worn dishtowel tucked into the waistband of her jeans.

Turning back to her visitors, she sighed the same sigh everyone gives when confronting unwanted door-to-door salesmen. Impatient, she asked, "Whatcha want then?"

Being a father himself, Inspector Jamieson read the situation in a heartbeat. How many times had he listened to his own wife complain about the bothersome interruptions from unwanted visitors at their door when she was busy with the twins? Turning on his most charming smile he worked on setting her mind at ease.

"Olive Cain? Good morning, Miss." Jamieson had found the use of the youngish title of Miss never failed to please any woman over twenty-five, especially the married ones. 'Ma'am' closed more doors than an insurance salesman. A small smile lifted the corners of her mouth and the Inspector knew he had her attention.

Dark eyes darting from one man to the next, Olive allowed her posture to relax just a bit, her voice remaining tentative. "Yeah, I'm her. And it's Mrs. Who're you?"

"We're friends of Kevin's. Business acquaintances really. He did some programming work for us awhile back and we'd like to get in touch with him about doing another job. This is the address he gave us back then." Jamieson turned the charm on full volume. "We were hoping to find him at home." She moved a little farther out the door, lessening the din of the toddler banging away on his pots and pans interrupting their conversation. "Our Kev don't live here anymore. Him and Liam moved out when the baby come."

"Liam?" asked Jamieson.

"Our younger brother. Year younger than Kev. Miss the rent money they kicked in, but can't say I wasn't relieved." Olive twisted her face into an exasperated expression. "I can only look after so many little boys at once, you know? And now that there's three of them… well, let's just say I'm glad they moved all of their computers and junk into their own place."

Concern flashed across her oval face. "Not that I'd call that dirty old warehouse a home, but they like it and it's big enough for all of their 'toys'."

The concert from inside the flat reached new heights off the music scale. Olive sneaked a quick peek to be sure everything was fine with her son before turning back and adding, "I don't miss that either. Computers don't make as much noise as pots and pans, but they make just as much mess, with all the covers off and such.

Too dangerous around a baby, y'know?"

Jamieson shot his partner a knowing look. "I agree. Now that you mention it, Kevin did say he had a brother working with him. Sorry, I never knew his name. You must be quite a sister. Not every young woman is so devoted to her younger siblings these days."

Olive fiddled with the ends of her long hair, flashing an embarrassed smile at Jamieson. "Nothing any sister what loves her brothers wouldn't do. You have to watch out for 'em these days. They're too young or too simple to watch out for themselves and some dirty old perv or pimp will nab 'em straight away, they will."

Olive's tone took on a possessive, protective edge to it, adding, "That's why I hooked young Quill up with 'em. That poor child woulda been easy takings for one of them sorts. Too smart with computers and too bloody innocent with everything else. Prefers 'em to people, he does. Wasn't going to last two days alone, poor bugger. Weren't safe."

Jamieson asked, "Quill? Is that Kevin's third partner you mentioned? Are we looking at three potential programmers for hire?" He let just the right amount of hopefulness creep into his voice, encouraging her to tell him more.

Olive gave an uncertain laugh, running a hand through her long hair.

"Well...I know I should've told Child Services where he was back then, but the poor sweet boy'd been through so much already, what with his mum up and disappearing like that. Been almost two years now. But I just couldn't, his mum being a friend and all. Quill was shattered when she disappeared and once that wanker of a landlord found out Sheila was gone, he threw Quill right out on the street. Poor kid didn't have no place to go, now did he?"

Jamieson nodded sympathetically. "The street is no place for a child."

"Especially one what looks like he does. Wait a min, I'll show you a snapshot of him. He's a beautiful boy, turning into a right handsome young man." Slipping just inside the doorway, Olive picked up a frame off a small table. Handing it to Jamieson, she said, "Took it at his birthday bash two weeks ago. Quill's the cute one in the black leather jacket. I got it for him as his present." Olive ran a finger over the glass protecting the boy's image. "He got all choked up when he opened it, nearly cried."

Jamieson studied the photograph, taking in the sharp, classic cut of the teenager's young face and the too-thin lines of his slender frame. Clothed in a tattered, fraying sweater, scuffed, worn boots and faded jeans, the boy looked to be barely in his teens. Frowning, Jamieson thought there was a touch of sadness around the teenager's eyes that shouldn't be there in someone so young.

Olive pointed at each of her brothers in turn. "That's Kev, and Liam is the one in the army jacket. The three of them hit it off like brothers. Quill's been living with them ever since. Kev says he's brill with computers. I wouldn't know about that. I only use ours for shopping on the Internet."

The Inspector couldn't help the smug, tolerant smile that tugged at his lips, breaking the spell of his charm. "Shouldn't be carrying on so about personal things, now should I?" Olive stepped back inside the doorframe, taking the photograph with her. "Even business acquaintances only needed to know so much about a body."

"Listen, I really have to go. It's time to put the baby down for a kip. I'm sure Kev'll be pleased to hear from you if it means work," she said.

Jamieson smiled and tried to recapture a bit of the ease of their earlier conversation. "We understand. If you don't mind giving me his new address, I'll drop by his place today."

His smile wove its charm again and Olive blushed for the second time. "Blimey. Forgot about that. Mind's on the baby and all."

The smile increased, becoming both sympathetic and disarming. "Does Quill have a last name? In case he's the one that answers the door when we drop by."

Flustered, Olive grabbed a pad and pen from the side table and scribbled an address on it. "Course. It's Tarquin, Quillan Tarquin. His mum was Sheila. Can't remember what his dad's name was…Quill never talks about 'em, not even if you ask." Olive shrugged her shoulders in a 'what can you do' gesture.

"I'd give Kev a call to let him know you're coming." Jamieson's smile turned a little brittle at her offer, but relaxed as she finished with, "but he doesn't have one yet. Bloody phone company's taking months to fill orders out in that area. You can catch him there most any time, though. Sleeps during the day and works on those computers all night, they all do, 'cept maybe Quill. That boy seems to be up all hours of the day and night. He always looks knackered."

A soft, motherly expression came over the woman's face as she added, "Now and then, he'll come over to watch the baby so I can run to the supermarket on my own, you know? And every blessed time I come home, there they'll both be, tucked up together on the sofa, dead to the world."

An ear-splitting screech from behind her drew Olive's attention back inside the flat. "Listen, Mr., um..."

"Jamieson," the Inspector answered. Olive's eyes darted to his silent companion. Jamieson hurried to calm any wariness that might be stirring in the talkative young woman. "My partner, Mr. Gabriel."

The easy offering of names seemed to reassure Olive. She picked up where she had left off. "Mr. Jamieson. If you see Kev, remind him about dinner Friday night. Baby's birthday and all. With presents." Olive gave the agent one last blushing glance and slipped back inside her flat to the sound of peals of delighted, nonsensical chatter from her son.

Jamieson and his partner walked toward their car. Gabriel commented, "Good-looking lad," as they crossed the busy street.

Jamieson said. "Yeah, he is. Too bad it'll only give him grief in prison."

Expression grim, Gabriel nodded and got into the car.

* * * * *

Notified of the breach of security at the onset, the report's final findings came to the desk of MI5's Director General James Davenport. Along with the report came Deputy Richmond.

"Well, Anthony, what do you think?" Davenport asked.

Richmond closed the office door and walked to his usual seat in front of the imposing oak desk. Once seated, Richmond faced Davenport and frowned. "I think we have a serious problem on our hands, sir. We haven't had a breach like this in years, not since before the last round of firewalls were installed. I think we're facing a serious threat to government security. If this group of terrorists can get into MI5 this easily, who knows how often they've been doing it or where else they've gone?"

Davenport responded. "I felt that since a large portion of the data contained materials of a very sensitive nature involving past and future combined British and American covert missions, the Americans need to be informed of this security breach. They have just as much at risk as we do."

Richmond knew the protest was nothing more than a token. Davenport had already made up his mind, but Richmond felt the need to object. He believed MI5 should take care of its own internal problems without involving another country. "Sir, that really isn't...."

Davenport continued as if Richmond hadn't said a word. "I have already contacted Ambassador Farish and the US Army's liaison officer here in London. They're diverting a small team of experienced men already close by to join ours in the retrieval of the stolen data. They're to be given full disclosure and cooperation. This is to be a joint effort between British and American forces."

"Certainly, sir." Richmond forced his lips into a grim smile of acceptance. "I'll inform our assault team personally. I'm sure they'll extend a warm welcome to the Americans. When are they expected to arrive?"

"Within the hour. I believe they were...close by."

Richmond dropped his gaze to the floor before pulling in a resigned breath to ask the one question he'd been dreading most of all. "Are we familiar with the team, sir?"

Davenport smiled. "Old friends, Anthony. Daniel

Burke's team, Sparrow Four, is doing us the honor of joining us again. I'm sure you remember them from the last time they were through."

"Yes, Sparrow Four. How delightful, sir." The sarcasm was barely contained. Richmond stood.

Davenport's eyes narrowed. "You do realize Burke had nothing to do with the press leak two years ago. The secretary in records acted entirely on her own."

"So they say, Director." Richmond was unwilling to let the Americans entirely off the hook for an event that led to the most embarrassing moment in his career to date. "However, there is still the matter of the missing piece of evidence, sir."

"Oh, come now, Anthony. Surely, imagining that ones likeness graces the walls of one of the world's finest art collectors isn't all that bad." Richmond watched as Davenport fought to keep a smile from showing. "We don't honestly know he has it, after all."

"If all the pointed innuendo he and his men kept dropping afterward are anything to go by, he has it. I'm sure of it. Probably hanging on the walls of his private collection right now, every crude friend and servant the man has gawking at it and telling tales. You'll have to excuse me if I don't appreciate that dubious honor, Director."

"I doubt that, Anthony. Daniel Burke isn't the kind of man to take personal pleasure from another's misfortune."

Davenport cut Richmond off as he made to object. "Not that I'm saying he wouldn't keep something as a private memento, but he wouldn't put it on public display."

Richmond accepted the fact he wasn't going to

sway the Director in his assessment of Burke's character. Davenport and Burke's family had been friends too long for that. "You would know best in that regard, sir."

He knew he wasn't hiding his displeasure from Davenport as the man asked, "You're not contemplating asking for it back are you?"

Richmond went from outraged to horrified in the space of a heartbeat. "And bring all that attention and press back down on our heads again? Most decidedly *not,* sir. It took weeks for Thames House to get back to normal, what with reporters and gawkers hanging about the exits. It was insufferable."

"I'm pleased to hear that. As to the hackers, do we actually know it is terrorists? Has there been some type of press leak or demands made I'm not aware of?" The skeptical tone to Davenport's voice wasn't difficult to hear.

Richmond shifted uncomfortably in his chair. "No. There hasn't been anything like that—yet. But I'm convinced it's coming, sir. You don't break into MI5 as a schoolboy's lark. Besides, there isn't a schoolboy around who could accomplish it. We have the best safeguards in existence, and they weren't good enough. It has to be the work of professionals and that means, nine times out of ten, terrorists, sir." Richmond hissed the words out.

Davenport sighed. "I want you to show more restraint here. You're probably right. It would have taken an extraordinary talent to accomplish a breach of this magnitude. We can't be too cautious." He drummed his fingers on the desk's smooth, polished surface.

Richmond broke the uneasy silence saying, "I've called for an assault team to be assembled. As soon as the meeting with this *FalconHawk* takes place and their identities are confirmed, as well as the information they're selling, the team will do a complete and thorough cleansing of their location. I'm confident we can recover everything if we move swiftly."

"I've been looking into the data they accessed. Not the actual files, mind you, too many of them really, but the nature of the content."

Richmond shifted his weight on the padded surface and willed his mouth to remain shut, knowing what the Director was going to say, but dreading to hear the words spoken out loud.

"This incident will have repercussions all the way to Parliament and beyond. I have a meeting scheduled with the aide to the Prime Minister in two hours. We need reliable information on this very soon."

Sensing a dismissal, Richmond moved closer to the door. "I'll report back as soon as we hear anything concrete, Director."

"You do that, Anthony. I'll be available." Richmond flinched when Davenport gave a tiny poke at his pride. "Wouldn't want to miss the Americans' arrival after all, would we?"

Richmond's stiff reply bordered on a growl. "No, sir. We wouldn't." He sailed out of the office, closing the heavy door behind him with exaggerated caution. His posture stiffened even more at the muffled snort of laughter coming from behind the closed door as he walked away.

Chapter Three

The numbing chill of the forty-degree weather coupled with the dense mist in the rain-heavy air greeted him like an old friend. Colonel Daniel Burke, U.S. Army Special Forces, was used to unexpected shifts in assignments in different locations and the abrupt weather changes that came with them. Less than three hours ago he and his men were sweltering under the heat of a blistering Moroccan sun. The English rain was a welcome sight.

Ready to disembark the recently landed transport plane, the strong winds swept the rain over Burke, ruffling his blond hair and pelting his sunburned face, making the flesh sting with each new gust. The driving rain bounced off the black tarmac like bullets ricocheting off concrete

"Those clouds are as thick as pea soup," he said. "It might rain for days."

Behind him, his second in command, Master Sergeant Jackson Burr grumbled something obscene about the weather.

Burke turned his head to one side and laughed. "It's not that bad, Jackson. Besides, when have you known it to be anything *other* than raining when we've landed in this country? It's enough to make me think I'm not welcome here."

Burr straightened up from checking his duffel bag, shooting his team leader and best friend an unhappy glare. "I know it. I just wish we could break the cycle for once, Daniel. I'm not even sure what the sun looks like, shining down on this rock."

Snorting in amusement, Burke said, "You're just complaining because we had to leave Morocco and all those beautiful, veiled ladies you kept attracting."

Burr puffed out his impressive, muscled chest. "What can I say? They know a prime specimen of manhood when they see it." A short bark of laughter from deeper in the plane answered this remark, along with Burke's own amused snicker.

"You three are just pissed because I don't have a sunburn." More snickers echoed from the back of the plane as Burr smoothed his cheeks dramatically. "Go ahead and laugh, but deep down I know you're all just envying my creamy, dark, burn-free complexion."

The color of milk chocolate and bald as a cue ball, Jackson Burr stood six foot three inches tall, the same height as Burke. Burke was leaner at two hundred and twenty pounds, but Burr's additional forty pounds in weight was all muscle. Broad-shouldered with a thick chest and slim waist, the sergeant was a fine cut of a man. Intelligent and quick-witted, he'd been a pre-med student before joining the army. Once in the service, he changed his major to mathematics and found the joys of probability factoring. He was an excellent strategist and detail coordinator.

Where Burr was dark, his best friend was light. Daniel Burke's fair hair and blue eyes, as well as his Scandinavian heritage, guaranteed a fair complexion, which, unfortunately was dark pink and painful at the moment. The sharp angles of his face defined his cheekbones and jaw. Faint lines caused by years of harsh weather and tough climate cracked the skin around his pale eyes and chapped lips like tiny road maps. Each wrinkle was born of a hardship or a moment of laughter, engraved on his face by sorrow or joy. It was a face that could be caring and charming or hard and unyielding in the space of a heartbeat.

At forty-one, Burke was beginning to feel his age. His choice to stay in covert ops for the last fifteen years had begun to spark twinges of regret over all the things this rewarding, but uncertain life had denied him. In moments like this — when he returned to the one place were she lived–the one woman he ever truly loved, or when preparing for a new assignment where his life expectancy was, again, questionable, his thoughts turned to the missed opportunities.

Burke was dedicated to the Army. He would never regret the years of service he gave to his country, but he was beginning to wonder if he still had time in his life for a family, children, and a comfortable, loving home to come back to each night. But all that meant a civilian life. Covert ops and children just didn't mix in his book. In the world according to Burke, no child should grow up without loving parents who were a present, positive influence in their children's lives, like his parents had been.

"I don't know about you fellas, but I'm kinda glad to see the rain. Sorta comforting to know some things never change. First time we show up here and it's not raining, I'm staying on the plane until it starts."

The source of the voice emerged out of the shadows of the hold. The empty space of the open walkway disappeared. Both of the other two large men looked small in comparison to swarthy Ethan James.

Burke looked up at the tall man. "I hear ya, Ethan. A sunny England? Wouldn't be a good omen."

Sergeant Ethan James, an explosive specialist, hunched to keep from hitting his head on the ceiling of the plane. At six foot seven inches, three hundred and ten pounds, few spaces looked large enough to contain the beefy man. Wavy, brown hair framed a rugged face dominated by a pair of deep brown eyes. His polite, western manner, along with a swagger only a lifelong horseman could acquire, rounded out the picture.

Even in army attire, James made people automatically think of cowboys, cattle and horses. The ever-present cowboy boots were merely a concession to the fact that finding a pair of nineteen triple E's in any kind of footwear was a challenge, even to the US Army. James had his boots custom made back home in Texas, where super-sized anything wasn't such an abnormal request.

James' impressive physical attributes were equaled by the man's intelligence and gentle heart. Adept at keeping his emotions under control, a necessity for his career, James was still a very caring, tenderhearted man. One of twelve children, he was a born nurturer. When one of Burke's team was ill or injured, it was James, not Burr the ex-medical student, who fussed and mother-henned the invalid to distraction, speeding the poor patient's recovery time with the sheer need to escape the caring attentions.

"It's still damn uncomfortable when you don't have any hair to keep it off your neck. It just rolls right down my skull into my collar. You see me shivering, it's because cold, English fingers are dancing down my spine. Damn unpleasant, unlike the women here."

Clapping a hand down on Burr's shoulder, Burke said, "It's only a little water, Jackson. Be a man."

"Come on, one of you give me a cap. Mine's back in that crummy cantina in Morocco." Burr made a halfhearted attempt to swipe the black skullcap off James' head. The taller man just straightened up, easily moving out of Burr's arm range.

Burr and James stepped to opposite sides. A fourth man insinuated himself between them, invading their personal space. As he passed between them he leaned in close to Burr.

"You're not brown sugar Jack, you won't melt. No matter how sweet the ladies think you are." Grabbing the olive green bush cap off his own thick, brown mane of hair, Spencer 'Ray' Weston, set it on top of Burr's head.

Burr accepted the gift, sending a mild sneer of disdain at his other team members. "Thank you. At least *someone* cares about my health and well-being," he said, pulling the hat down with a tug over his smooth dome.

Ray shouldered his way to the front of the plane to stand beside Burke.

"No, I don't. You're a big boy. You can take care of yourself. I just don't want to listen to you bellyaching the whole time we're here. It ruins the whole *ambience* of the trip." The look of innocent wonder on his face was undermined by the bright sparkle in his eyes.

"Ambience?" Burr gaped. "What the hell kind of *ambience* does this wet, dreary stub of a rock have?"

Weston waved his hands in a wide as if creating a large circle in the air. "Oh, come on, Jack. Don't tell us the mystery of the last minute reassignment, the excitement of foreign intrigue, and thrill of international travel have become old hat for you?"

Playfully poking the younger man in the chest, Burr rocked Weston back on his heels, knocking him into Burke's huge hands. "You're so full of shit, Ray, I can't believe you can find a deodorant that covers the smell."

Before Weston could reply, Burke waved his hands in front of his face. "No, Jackson, I think *that* smell is his new after-shave."

As they descended to the tarmac, Weston rushed to defend the latest addition to his personal hygiene regime. "My sisters sent me that from Central America. It's supposed to be irresistible to females."

"Females? Of what species?" James' deep tones pierced through the howl of the driving winds.

Burr stepped up to Weston's side and threw an arm across his shoulders, confiding in a loud stage whisper, "Ray, Ray, Ray. Never trust a nun to pick out something sexy for you. And certainly not *two* of them, even if they are your older sisters. It's unnatural. For crying out loud boy, they think holy water is a turn on."

Ray's expression took on a thoughtful, bewildered look. "I'll admit, there *has* been a fundamental problem with their more, shall we say, intimate attempts at gift giving."

They all shook their heads and burst out in howls of laughter.

"Nope, afraid not." Weston pursed his lips and frowned at the image in his head. "I just can't go there, gentlemen." With a meaningful glance at his companions he added, "And I'd prefer it if none of you did either. My sisters, the *Sisters*, have no place in that particular scenario. I'll toss the after-shave."

"Wise decision, Ray, very wise." Burke picked up the pace a little as the rain slackened to misty drizzle. "The next time your sisters are back in country, I'll be sure to tell them how much you appreciated their gift."

"You can't lie to a nun, Daniel. It's a sin." Lingering bewilderment still colored Ray's distracted tone.

"It's not a lie really. You do appreciate it. It's the rest of us who are objecting to it." Burke tilted his head to one side and glanced up at the heavens. "And if it's a sin, God can just add it to the list I have to answer for already. Maybe your sisters can put in a good word for me when my time comes to see Him."

"Well, not if you lie to them, Daniel. Nuns have very strict rules about things like that." Weston stopped, chewing on his lower lip for a moment before adding, "Then again, maybe that was a sisters' rule." He shook his head. "No. No, I'm pretty sure that was both a sisters' *and* a Sisters' rule. Either way, you'll never catch *me* lying to them. Not worth the penitence."

Laughing, Burke pushed Weston's shoulder. Passing under a protective awning, they sauntered toward a soldier waiting for them just inside the tower building. Burke returned the salute the soldier snapped off.

"Lieutenant Commander Burke, sir." The man's voice was crisp and formal, just like his salute. "Sergeant Willis, I'm your escort to MI5 headquarters, sir."

"Sergeant."

Willis handed Burke a large sealed, manila envelope. "My orders are to give this to you and see to it you and your men are transported to HQ at your earliest convenience, sir."

Skeptical but polite, Burke nodded. "Our earliest convenience? I assume that means we should be there by now." He knew it had been meant as a politely worded command for Burke and his men to move their collective asses as soon as they arrived.

The sergeant nodded. "Yes, sir. You're familiar with General Weiss's terminology. That will make things easier for all of us."

Sergeant Willis extended his hand to the dreary weather outside the door. "There's a car waiting, sir. If you and your men are ready, we'll proceed directly to Thames House. Deputy Richmond was especially pleased to have you and your team called in to assist his men with this assignment."

Willis shot a nervous nod at Burke. "Sir."

A look of satisfaction settled on Burke's face. "I'll just bet the idea made him all sweaty with anticipation, Sergeant."

Turning his head a bit to hide the smirk forcing its way onto his face, Willis nodded his agreement in prudent silence.

Willis opened a door to the waiting car, gesturing the foursome into its interior before taking the position behind the wheel. The dark sedan eased out into the pounding rainstorm and heavy London traffic and was quickly swallowed up by the thick, gray fog.

Chapter Four

There were drawbacks to having an eidetic memory. Quill hit the return button on the keyboard. When an event or object was tied to his emotions and etched deep into his heart, it seemed to be permanent, engraved in his memory, often resurfacing when he least wanted it.

A burst of loneliness and isolation overwhelmed Quill, bringing to mind the last time he saw his mother. Her golden-brown hair hung long and full around her tired, youthful face. The sound of her voice telling him she'd just be a minute, to save her a biscuit or two for when she got back made him choke a harsh sob out.

Another memory of a month ago when he'd literally stumbled across a homeless man, maggots and water rats competing for a meal off his decaying corpse.

Quill shuddered, trying to wipe the horrific vision from his mind. He had learned over time he could push aside images if he studied something new in enough detail. They didn't disappear forever, but they would no longer dominate his every thought and it gave him a sense of control over his 'gift'. Thought he wasn't entirely sure 'gift' was an accurate name for it.

There were far too many things in his short life Quill would like to erase from his eidetic memory.

Everything he read about photographic memory told him medical science was convinced it didn't really exist. It was supposed to be just a highly organized way of remembering things that would fade as he grew older and other cognitive skills took over but it was a parlor trick, a sham.

None of these 'scientific facts' held any truth for Quill. If anything, his memory was improving as he grew older. Computer programming was getting easier and visualizing the intricate patterns of the machine language was becoming second nature to him. Because it was so easy for him, it became his preferred method of communicating.

A simple evening of casual reading more often than not turned into a marathon session of speed-reading and effortless memorization, often giving him instant recall of every detail of the material.

Quill found trying seemed to make it harder to remember details, so he never tried. He could never be sure how well something had been retained until he tried to access it later. Sometimes he would be caught off guard when a memory he didn't even realize he had would surface uncalled for. They weren't always pleasant surprises.

His superior memory had allowed him to stay in school while doing very little actual work. By the time he was thirteen, he was skipping entire weeks off school. At fifteen, he didn't even bother trying to show up for anything besides the exams. Overburdened and understaffed, Social Services made only token gestures at enforcing the laws requiring him to attend.

Sheila Tarquin worked any shift she could at several different low paying jobs. School officials lost track of him when he moved to the streets after her disappearance.

After the adrenaline rush of last night's spectacular

breach into MI5's computer files and twelve hours of sorting through the stolen files, Quill felt drained. He had already read through the smaller files, cataloging their content and sorting the material into similar categories, leaving the largest file for tonight. The file, code named 'Overkill', was huge. It would take him all night to digest it and he had yet to find the information he'd been hoping for.

Quill yawned and stretched, flexing the stiff muscles of his neck and shoulders. His body was starting to complain about the endless hours hunched over the keyboard and he needed to go for a run and spend some time outdoors. His sleep-deprived mind felt like it had been wrapped in cotton and buried in sand, his head empty and heavy at the same time.

The warehouse door clanging shut shook Quill out of his contemplative daze.

Kevin and Liam clamored into the room, voices raised and spirits high. Liam swayed over to Quill's workstation and with an exaggerated flourish, presented him with a large, greasy box of takeout.

The aroma from the box made Quill's stomach growl, his mouth watering in response. "Barbecued Ribs! Wow! Thanks, mate, I haven't had these in ages. What's the occasion?" Quill dipped his fingers into the box and began to devour bits of the tangy meat, licking the thick sauce off his fingertips as he chewed.

Kevin grabbed a couple of beers out of the refrigerator, tossing one to Liam as he walked over to join them. "We're celebrating, mate." Kevin said drunkenly.

Quill shifted back in his seat to avoid the beer fumes from Kevin's breath. Not taking the time to swallow, he talked around a mouthful of food. "Of what?

Just had my birthday."

"Something better'n birthdays." Kevin clapped Quill on the shoulder and pulled a crate over to sit on. "We're going to rake in the coin on this one, mate. Dropped a few hints around about having some new top-notch info to barter and we've already got us an interested buyer," he said. "This stuff's going to make us a bloody fortune Quill."

The skeptical teenager choked down a half-chewed mouthful of food. "Bloody 'ell Kev. We don't even know what's in the stuff yet. I haven't read but half of it. Haven't even looked at the biggest file yet."

Kevin grinned and rubbed his hands together in anticipation. "That's the beauty of it, mate. No one cares. All the buyer had to hear was 'MI5' and they were in. It's like magic." Kevin snapped his fingers.

Smiling, Liam nodded in agreement with his brother, taking another long, satisfying swig from his beer can.

"Seems a bit odd, Kev." The ease and rapid timing of the deal made Quill a little wary. "You sure 'bout this?" His tone was questioning, but more than a little hopeful at the same time. They really could use a bit of good fortune right about now. Their pocket money was almost gone for the month.

"It's one of our usual contacts — Fisher. It's cool, Quill." Kevin stood up, running his hands roughly through Quill's already messy curls. "You worry too much, Sunshine."

Quill batted at the offensive hands until both Kevin and Liam laughed and moved away. He pulled their attention back to him by asking, "When are you planning to meet with him?"

"Don't know yet. Fish's going to make the arrangements. Tonight, I hope. Going to meet him soon as I grab a clean shirt. Careful, the ribs're messy, man." Kevin gestured at the dark stains on his own plaid shirt.

"Come with us, Quill. Make a night of it and cheer up for a change." Liam said.

Quill watched as Kevin pulled on the faded tee shirt with the words 'explicit content contained within' written across the front of it in peeling white letters.

"No thanks. I'm no good with people, mate. I'll stay here an' finish up. You handle it like usual." Glancing down at his own frayed cuffs, Quill fussed with one of the sweater's mismatched buttons before hunching down further into the mock embrace of his armchair. "We could use a bit of cash."

"Suit yourself." Kevin raced past Quill, rubbing both of his hands over the younger man's head again. "Don't wait up." Grinning, Liam grabbed a rib from the box at Quill's elbow and followed Kevin out the door.

* * * * *

True to his word, Director General Davenport met Burke and his team just as the four soldiers sauntered into the conference room on the fourth floor of MI5's headquarters. Davenport and Burke had developed a friendship based on mutual respect and admiration for each other's integrity and intelligence over the years.

Commander Richmond kept to the background. Burke resisted a smile, knowing the pompous man was letting his refusal to surge forward in enthusiastic greeting of the Americans speak for itself.

"Lieutenant Burke, how very nice to see you again." Walking over to join the men as they entered, Davenport shook Burke's hand, nodding a greeting to each of the other three men in turn. "Gentlemen, I wish your visit could be under better circumstances, but it rarely is."

"Good to see you again too, sir." Burke and his men returned the handshake in kind. "My mother will be pleased to hear I had the chance to see you this trip."

A warm sparkle lit the older man eyes. "Your mother and I have plans for the Eifman ballet next month when she visits. She's vowed not to miss one of the five times they perform, not one. Under those circumstances, I can predict that neither shall I."

"She can be a very persuasive woman, sir."

"Norris Burke is a force of nature not to be denied by a mere man. At least, by one that doesn't want to bear the formidable consequences of his actions for months to come."

"As someone who's been on the receiving end of those particular consequences more than once, I'd have to agree with you, sir."

Davenport chuckled. "The Russian ballet times five, it is then."

"I'm afraid so sir."

"Ah well, such is life. I'll just have to suffer the indignity of having a beautiful, intelligent and delightful woman on my arm for each and every performance." Davenport waved a dismissive hand through the air.

"I'm sure you'll both enjoy every moment of them, sir. If I were free I would join you, but I doubt I'll be back this way again so soon."

"Most unfortunate, but I must say, everyone here was pleased to hear it would be your team that would be coming to assist us in this little venture today." A small smile twitched at one corner of Davenport's mouth.

Flight of the Sparrows

"Everyone?" Burke said, letting exaggerated disbelief color his words. "Had a run of amnesia in the ranks, sir? I don't remember our last trip being *picture* perfect. I think, we may have left *behind* a few bruised egos."

Placing a slight emphasis on those two words Burke poked at Richmond, reminding the man of the caricatures that were, even now, secreted away in a MI5 evidence vault beneath their feet. All except that one elusive, missing sketch. Shifting his eyes to meet Richmond's, Burke allowed his amusement to show in the laugh lines around his clear, blue eyes.

Behind him, Burke's men settled on to the ample armchairs placed around the conference table. With his choirboy smile Ray Weston slipped past Richmond to sit down, adding, "We're hoping this mission goes as smoothly as a well-oiled machine."

The sound of Richmond taking in a deep, controlled breath rewarded him. Weston eased down into his seat, his eyes never leaving Richmond's chiseled face.

Richmond stepped forward to join the conversation.

"Gentlemen. I see you have arrived safely. What a relief. I was concerned there might be some difficulty with your flight considering the turn the weather has taken. But I see your usual run of luck has won out yet again."

Burke frowned at Richmond's implication that the American team's history of excellent success was a result of mere fate, not skill.

"We're so pleased to see you're all well."

Refusing to be cowed, Burke's smile grew bigger and he said heartily, "And you're looking well yourself. The last picture of you I saw was less than complementary. I believe the *London Times* ran a story about you concerning the changing role of MI5 and its need to meet the escalating internal terrorist threat." Burke shook his head in mock sympathy. "Terrible picture of you."

Richmond's eyes grew hard, but his tone remained unflappable. "Yes, quite. Abysmal photo, I agree. But then the press tends to look for the least attractive angle on anything involving authority these days." He smiled, just a little. "I suppose it's the fate of citizens like myself, those of a certain social or moral standing, to suffer abuse at the hands of those of a lower station in life."

A smirk played over Richmond's normally bland features in satisfaction of having the last word, but his pleasure was short-lived.

"I wouldn't know. I try not to put myself above my fellow man," Burke said. "It makes it too tempting to play God then. And that's not something we can afford to let happen in this job." Relaxing his hard tone he continued. "But then, as a public servant in the service of one of your government's law enforcement agencies for many years, you already know that."

"Quite so, *Colonel*," Richmond replied, "But then, there are many difficult obstacles placed in the paths of those trying to bring some sense of order and justice to today's decaying society. Ego is just one of them."

Burke didn't try to suppress a small snort of disbelief. "Like this latest threat? A group of egotistical college boys?"

Amused by the by-play, but mindful of the pressing issues at hand, Davenport interrupted the verbal sparring before it could escalate. Gesturing to the open chairs surrounding the conference table he said,

"Gentlemen, now that we have the pleasantries out of the way, let's join the remainder of the Colonel's men and sit down."

Taking his seat at the head of the table, Davenport pressed a button on the intercom at his elbow. "Sterling, please have Lieutenant Crowe and his men join us in the conference room as soon as they arrive."

"Yes sir, Mr. Director. They're already here and waiting, sir," replied a soft, female voice.

All eyes turned to watch the door on the other side of the room open. Four men dressed in black battle uniforms, minus armor and guns, entered. All of them were fit, athletic, intelligent-looking men who carried with them an air of self-confidence and restrained power experienced warriors acquired over time. Confident of their place of dominance on their home turf, they flowed into the room, taking up the remaining four chairs beside Richmond.

After a respectful nod at both Davenport and Richmond, their leader took the initiative, extending his hand across the table to Burke.

"Lieutenant Eric Crowe, Special Projects Team, SAS. You must be Lieutenant Burke of the infamous *SparrowFour*. My team is *JackRabbit*." Though his words were friendly, the man's grip was too firm, his eyes offering to Burke an unspoken challenge for control from this point on.

Sighing over the schoolboy antics that tended to dominate the military mindset, Burke took the offensive, returning the pressure of the handshake. "Yes. But I'm afraid I can't answer in kind, I don't believe I've heard of you or your team before."

Irritated, Crowe pulled back from the handshake

and sat down. Glancing at each man in turn, he introduced his team. "This is Warrant Officer Roy Fitzpatrick, my second in command."

Fitzpatrick nodded, extending his hand to Burke. There was nothing overt or challenging in the man's grip and his eyes held none of the anger Crowe's did. Burke liked him.

Continuing with the introductions, Crowe moved down the line, not giving either of the other two men time for more than a brief nod of greeting. "Corporals Trevor Blake and James Nelson."

Each of the Americans acknowledged the men in turn, then Burke gave his own introductions.

"Now that the introductions have all been made, let's get down to the business at hand shall we gentlemen?" Davenport opened the file lying in front of him. An identical folder was before each of the other men. "You have all been given a file detailing the incident of this morning's security breach into the Brixton Police Department's computers and subsequently MI5. Most of the high level, confidential files were unavailable to our thieves, but they did manage to obtain one sensitive folder. It's not so much the lost data that is the problem, although seeing restricted information bandied about isn't conducive to a high degree of ally and public confidence. It isn't the end of the world either. Commander Richmond has reassured me that the contents of the files do not pose a great risk to the countries or the agents involved. On that basis, I think it's best we turn our combined attentions to the 'how' and the 'who' of the problem."

Davenport waved a hand at Richmond. "Commander, if you would please give them the rest of the details."

Flight of the Sparrows

Richmond eyed the group of men surrounding him with a cool, appraising stare. "We already have a team of computer experts working on the 'how'. There is a unit of skilled street officers tracking down leads to the 'who'. As you know, we have suspects already within our sights. It will only be a matter of time before we have their whereabouts."

Crowe's ramrod straight spine grew more rigid in response. "My men and I are ready, sir. We'll be on those sodding buggers before they even know what hit 'em. If there's even a whisper of fight, it'll be the last time they take a breath. No mistake about that, sir."

Frowning, Burke sat forward in his seat to lean his elbows on the table top, shortening the distance between Crowe and himself.

"Wait just a minute here. Are we talking about the same suspects outlined in the report I received? Because if we are, you're talking about taking out two college-aged computer geeks with a penny-ante scam selling day-old, low-level, police and government secrets."

Crowe shot back at Burke, disdain and anger heavy in his words. "All the evidence gathered so far points to a sophisticated group of hackers, probably operating with the help of militant subversives. None of us will be forgetting the bombing incident of last summer. That was supposed to be a harmless group of computer savvy, political activists protesting the most recent government action on monitoring Internet connections. That group of 'computer geeks', as you call them, opened fire on police and twenty-three people died. Now we operate under the assumption that deadly resistance from this kind is a given."

The Americans exchanged a quick look of unease.

Burke shook his head, disagreeing with Crowe's assessment of the situation. He reached across the table to tap Crowe's copy of the file with a callused forefinger.

"'This kind'? Neither of these two boys has a history of violence or anything more anti-social than an unpaid parking ticket. You can't use one highly unusual, unconnected incident as a basis for evaluation of a new target."

Jackson Burr joined in. "Look at the facts provided. They're novice hackers. They aren't even any good at peddling what they steal." Burr leaned back and frowned. "The word from your own informants is that nobody has seen them with anything more deadly than two six packs of that warm pis–stuff you call beer. What kind of resistance are you expecting? Uzi's and dart guns? If they have them, you'll probably find they go with their laser tag computer games. There's no indication here these kids are a lethal threat to anyone besides themselves, *Sir*."

Richmond mirrored Burke's aggressive stance by leaning into the other man's personal space as best he could from across the table. "It is MI5 policy to approach unknown targets with extreme caution, Lieutenant. We have no idea what these men will do when cornered. I won't lose a single man because of the mistaken notion these computer hackers are harmless geeks. What they've done is treason. They have to know that and as such, they must be aware of the consequences of their actions. They will know MI5 will respond with deadly force and be prepared for it, every Brit would. I agree with Lt. Crowe's assessment of the situation and advise we act accordingly."

Burke said, "I disagree. I think we should approach with reasonable caution, but lethal force shouldn't be the first thing on our minds."

Monitoring the interaction between the two very different teams he had brought together, Davenport considered both sides of the argument. While Richmond and Crowe had policy and recent history in their favor, Burke and his sergeant had valid points that were more in line with the details of the case.

Richmond's penchant for aggressive use of force as a first line of defense was well known. His attitude was reflected in his choice of assault teams. Crowe's record for successful missions was over-shadowed only by his excessive body count. However, the man was a loyal, devoted soldier who had never lost a team member. Causalities on the British side tended to be very low when he was leading an anti-terrorist mission.

But what about suspects who could be nothing more than a bunch of kids? Davenport's brows furrowed. "I suspect this will be a bit of a complex decision, gentlemen. Both sides have valid offerings, but...I'm inclined to agree with Lt. Burke's suggestion of caution and re-evaluate the situation once the suspects have been identified and located."

Richmond began to sputter an objection, but Davenport cut him off with the stroke of a hand. "But the use of lethal force will be permitted if evidence of equal resistance is shown. I don't expect anyone's guard to be down because these young men prefer computer keyboards to bombs. Terrorism is terrorism and treason is treason, no matter what the instrument of assault used." He gave both Burke and Crowe a stern look, relying on his long years as a commanding officer to settle the conflict.

"As the ranking British officer, Lt. Crowe will be in charge of any suspects apprehended." Taking in the smug smile twisting up one corner of Crowe's mouth he added, "However, as the highest ranking military officer present, Colonel Burke is in overall charge of this mission." He felt a small niggling of satisfaction when Crowe's smile slipped a bit. "I'm sure you gentlemen can work out something amendable to our combined goals."

Any further conversation was vetoed by a knock on the conference room door. Fresh from the questioning of Olive Cain, two plain-clothes officers entered the room. The younger of the two stepped forward to address Davenport with an air of casual familiarity.

The man nodded at his senior commanding officer. "Deputy Richmond. We have a confirmed address, all three names of the suspects involved and a meeting set up as new buyers with them in two hours."

"Three names, Agent? We were led to believe there were only two young men involved," Davenport said.

Richmond used the opening to press home his point of view. "I told you there was more at work here than just a duo of computers nerds. The third man is probably part of a terrorist group, their connection to a larger group of subversives."

"I beg your pardon sir, but I doubt that," Jamieson responded.

"Pray tell why?" Richmond wasn't easy to dissuade.

"Because he's a kid. Sir." Jamieson let a sour expression cross his face, like he had just tasted lemons. "Tells people he's nineteen, but if the picture I saw of him is anything to go by, I'd say he's closer to sixteen, maybe younger."

Frustrated, Richmond pressed on. "That doesn't change a thing. If he's part of this group, he's equally guilty of the crime no matter how old he is. Or isn't."

Richmond shifted the focus of the discussion to the additional information Jamieson had obtained. "We have a confirmed address, gentlemen, let's solidify a plan of action and put it in motion immediately. Time is our greatest enemy here," Richmond said. "You're dismissed, Mr. Jamieson."

Before turning to leave, Jamieson let an appraising glance linger over the assembled team of soldiers, aware of what their purpose was in this situation. Knowing the American team's reputation as one of straight dealing, he caught Burke's eye. "If you're going in after these three blokes, make sure you pack a nappie, mate. I'm betting these kids will wish they'd worn brown trousers after the likes of you burst through their bedroom windows."

Chapter Five

Letting a small breath escape, Quill settled himself in front of his monitor screen. Opening the MI5 folder, he couldn't fend off the need to squirm in his seat.

Trying to shake off the uneasy, lingering chill, he chided himself out loud. "Bloody wanker. Scared yourself right proper last night, you did." His eyes darted around to the layers of darkening gray shadows in the corners of the empty warehouse. The strong winds and the cold rain hitting the metal roof sounded ominous. "You'll be seeing bogeymen carrying guns next. Just cool it and get back to work. You've a whole, great, bloody file to get through tonight."

Drawing his legs up underneath his slender frame, Quill began to read through the directory. If nothing else, the folder's name was intriguing. What would a place like MI5 consider to be 'Overkill'? All of the combined British forces hunting down one lone, lost soul looking for home?

Quill snorted at a mental image of E.T. in front of Buckingham Palace, long misshapen finger extended to touch the unflinching, stoic Royal Guardsman on duty. The sounds of his own laughter helped dispel a little of the gloom surrounding him. Maybe MI5, the bastards, would make it a combined British and American mission like the ones he had just been reading about in the file.

Spirits a bit perkier, he settled himself back into his seat. With a few deft keystrokes, he opened a custom program of his own making and sent it off to sort through the massive file, its sole purpose to find any references to one particular man's name. A file by the name 'SparrowHawk' popped up seconds later.

Quill began skimming the file, details fixed into his mind, whether he wanted them there or not. He paused at the picture of a blond man. The man still looked so much like the photo Quill had. A little more weathered, a little older, but still very much the same. He kept the picture in his wallet, hidden behind a photo of the McCabe's toddler nephew.

For a brief moment Quill wondered what the man in the picture's voice sounded like. If he heard it, would it pull the rest of the partial memory he had out into the light? He could remember so many, many details about so many things, why couldn't he recall this?

What would happen if he did remember? What then? This man, his father, wouldn't want him. Nobody wanted him. He was never going to be a part of a family again, outside of Kevin and Liam. He was destined to be alone. Sheila's disappearance had proven that.

Maybe it was a bizarre kind of trade off for his 'gift'–he could have a perfect memory of his parents, but not them. If that was the case, he'd been short-changed in the case of his father. He couldn't grasp one memory tightly enough to hold on to it.

Quill shook his head to clear away the confusion and forced himself to move on to another familiar picture. Ethan James was huge. Even in the photographs, Quill could tell he was extremely tall and broad, muscled and very powerful. The American had a handsome face and kind smile. Quill imagined the big man to have a good sense of humor.

Realizing he was getting lost in the details of this one file, Quill read through the rest of it, hungrily memorizing the faces of two more men and facts about each of them until he reached the end of the dossier.

The last page forced him to sit sharply forward in his chair, half eaten ribs dangling forgotten from his sticky hand. He dropped them onto the dusty tabletop.

Quill re-read the page, then read it again and again. By the end he was hyperventilating.

This can't be true.

The plan laid out to be put into action in a few weeks had to be a mistake, an error, a piece of misinformation badly filed. MI5 didn't plan these kinds of missions. It was wrong. It was illegal. It was murder, assassination at the very least. With American soldiers, these American soldiers. But there it was in black and white, waiting to be put into action—soon.

Trembling, Quill opened another file and began skimming its contents, his skin turning clammy. His lower lip was peeling from being raked over by his teeth as a release for his growing anxiety.

At twelve sixteen in the morning, two hours after he began reading, Quill Tarquin had a pretty good idea what '*Overkill*' was, and it scared the hell out of him. After three more hours, in a full-blown flight or fight panic, he began gathering every printout and disc in the warehouse.

Tossing the papers into an open burn barrel at the far side of the room, he doused them with lighter fluid and set them on fire. Between the effects of the burning trash fumes and his uncertainty over the future, Quill found himself needing to use the inhaler twice to fight off an impending asthma attack. He continued clearing out the warehouse, making sure to shove the coveted medicine deep into his jeans' pocket.

Eyeing the microwave on top of the refrigerator,

Quill started loading it with CDs and pressed the ten-minute timer.

Without a second thought to the cost or the ruin he was lavishing on their only means of support, Quill began wiping the hard drives in every computer in the warehouse, starting with his own.

He fervently wished he could erase his own memory too. Quill was beyond desperate to know where his missing roommates were.

* * * * *

"We're not mental enough to bring a copy with us, mate. If we strike a deal, one of us'll go get it, bring it back here. But we need to see the cash. We're not new to this game. Fish'll tell you that. So don't be thinking you can get something for nothing. This here's a business meeting, straight on the up and up." Kevin McCabe tried not to squirm in his seat, a combination of nerves and excitement willing his body into restless movement.

Beside him, Liam tugged the dark ski cap covering his entire upper face down a bit lower. He couldn't see anything above the level of the table by now.

"You're selling stolen goods, how straight can it be?" Amusement was plain in the man's voice. Playing the clandestine role of information broker and buyer, Inspector Jamieson smiled at the two naïve young men seated across the booth from him and his partner.

Kevin tapped on the glass bottle in his hand. "Well...It's an honest deal, even if the merchandise was nicked. We can be trusted. Never done business with you, don't know where you stand. Don't want any trouble man, just a fair price and a clean deal. Whaddyer say?"

Kevin began peeling the label from his beer bottle. "I say...show me the goods, let me see the quality of what I'm buying for myself and I'll show you the readies. Sounds fair to me."

"Need a price range first. Not offering a sample to find out you're talking beer money, mate. We want to know it's worth the petrol to-in' and fro-in' to make you happy."

Jameison glanced at Gabriel as if getting his approval of the deal. "If the quality's good–ten thousand quid for the lot. More if it's higher quality."

"Ke —," Liam gasped.

Kevin reached out a hand, griping his brother's knee under the table, saying, "It's better 'an good, mate. It's MI5 itself. A whole folder full of files, over two hundred and seventy megabytes. It'll be worth every penny, I promise. If it's not worth it to you, it'll be worth it to someone else."

"I'd rather see proof than hear promises," Jameison replied. So far their meeting with the two senior members of the soon-to-be infamous *FalconHawk* had gone well. The two young men were eager to sell, and outside of a few amateur attempts to cover their tracks and hide their identities–the ski cap really was ridiculous–they were playing right into the police officers' hands.

"Okay. My partner'll go get a partial copy of it and a laptop. You can look at it and decide, but I want to see the money, too. If you're happy with the bugger and we're happy with the cash, we'll trade up to the real thing. Deal?"

"A laptop won't be necessary. I have my own out in the car. You don't mind, I'm sure." Jameison's smile was less charming, more predator-like. "Just so there's no problem with the disc's ability to be read or computer compatibility and such."

Kevin nodded his head, a tight jerky motion. Jameison wondered if he was making the young man nervous.

"That's cool, mate. Your own hardware's fine by us." Kevin relaxed a little as the man's smile widened and the charm returned.

Nudging his brother, Kevin said, "Go on. Get the copy. I'll entertain the gents for a bit."

Liam shot him an uncertain look, but slid from the booth, then trotted out the pub door without looking back.

Back at the booth, Kevin flashed both dark-suited men a hesitant smile and Jameison knew he was trying to ingratiate himself a bit. "Can I get you a jar while we wait? Won't take but a bit."

Gabriel excused himself from the booth to stand beside Kevin. Jameison smoothed out his jacket, leaning towards Kevin from across the small table. "No, thank you. We're not here to drink. Why don't we take advantage of the free time and show you how serious we are about things?"

"Serious? Show me what?" Kevin said, an apprehensive look on his face.

"The money, of course. What'd you think I meant?" Jameison's cool, deadpan delivery did nothing to allay the younger man's growing unease.

"Well, ah, nothin'." Kevin tensed. "Nothin' at all, mate." He brushed his gaze over Gabriel's penetrating stare then shifted to Jameison's more welcoming expression. "Yeah, I'd like to see it. That'd be ace." Kevin slipped out of the booth.

Gabriel, silent as usual, gestured toward the door and Kevin followed Jameison through the thin crowd of pub patrons. Once they reached the street, the three of them walked around the corner to a black sedan parked three cars down. Jameison opened the back door and slipped into the dark interior with Kevin following.

Kevin had already settled down onto the seat before he realized there was no briefcase or laptop in the car. The door shut and the sound of it locking cracked in the sudden stillness of the insulated car.

Kevin looked out through the dark tinted windows but was unable to see anything recognizable. He trailed one hand over the face of the door searching for the handle. His subtle groping turned into frantic pawing as he realized the inside of the door was completely smooth, free of any controls or handles.

"Fucking 'ell."

Turning back to face Jameison, Kevin expected to see a gun in the man's hand, instead he saw a badge. Quill had been right, the jammy sod, MI5 was onto them. Christ, he hoped both Liam and Quill had sense enough not to panic when they grabbed them.

"Sit back and enjoy the ride, son. We're going to meet up with some of our friends and then pick up some of yours. It'll be just like a surprise party...at your house," Jameison said.

Driving off in the direction of the docks, Gabriel radioed the assault team that they were on their way.

* * * * *

Driving into a narrow side alley half a block from the warehouse, a large truck cut off Liam's path home. He was hauled from his car and pushed spread-eagle across its hood, body-searched by two black-clad men, then bundled into the back of the large green, army-style truck. Liam never uttered a sound of protest, docile and dazed, letting the soldiers manhandle him as they pleased.

Flight of the Sparrows

Lt. Eric Crowe congratulated himself on apprehending the suspect. This was going too smoothly. Neither prisoner had offered any resistance. The younger one hadn't uttered a single sound. He was either very cool or very frightened. Crowe didn't really care which. Two terrorists down, at least one to go, maybe more.

Who knew what they would find in the warehouse? It could be a rat's nest full of conspirators. He just had to find the right opportunity to carry out the remainder of his orders, without witnesses.

* * * * *

Arriving at the warehouse moments behind the assault force, Agents Jameison and Gabriel waited until the team radioed them before leaving their car. No need to get doused in the rain. Dragging a cooperative, but verbally protesting Kevin McCabe with them, they formally turned the suspect over to the assault team.

Despite his orders, Jameison gave a weak objection to the arrangement. "My partner and I could run both of these lads down to headquarters for you. This one's been cautioned properly. We'll get the processing started on them, get them out of your way 'til this part of the adventure's done."

Crowe grabbed hold of Kevin's upper arm and pulled him away from Jameison's protective grasp, handing the suspect off to Fitzpatrick. "No thanks. This isn't just about capturing *FalconHawk*. We're here to find out everything we can about their operation as quickly as possible and that means keeping the suspects together. I follow my orders, you and your partner just make sure you follow yours."

Jameison pulled the collar of his overcoat up higher against the drizzle and stared at Crowe's hardened face, deciding on the value of debating the issue any further. There was something about the man that reminded Jameison of a coiled snake just waiting for the opportunity to strike its next victim. Crowe's reputation for violence accompanied by a high body count was well known. However guilty of hacking into MI5 as these boys might be, Jameison didn't think they deserved to suffer the kind of abuse Crowe was reputed to dish out to his prisoners.

His conscience got the better of his judgement. Jameison reached out to take Kevin back. Before he could get a proper hold of him, the boy was pulled from his reach, straight up into the open back of the army truck. Burke's face appeared in Kevin's place, an apologetic smile on his lips.

Throwing Crowe a warning look, Burke nodded at Jameison. "He'll be fine, Inspector. I'm sharing guard duty with Lt. Crowe at the moment."

Crowe gave Burke a disgusted sneer. "We're capturing terrorists Burke, not babysitting school boys. Lower your guard, someone'll pay for it, Yank. But it won't be me or my men, remember that." Crowe climbed up into the truck and disappeared from sight.

Peering after Crowe, Jameison could see the jabbering older McCabe perched on a bench across from his pale, silent brother. Crowe and his men lined one side of the truck with Liam, while Burke's men lined the other. The brothers sat at the very front, one on each side of the truck, corralled in place by the soldiers.

Jameison gave Burke a resigned nod, then walked back to the car. He drove to a more secluded spot down the street. They would stay close to provide back up to the team if it was needed. Chances were, the terrorist assault team would be more than able to handle the situation, but it never hurt to have a plan B. Besides, Jameison was anxious to see the fabled *SparrowFour* in action, even if it was from a distance.

* * * * *

Inside the truck Kevin was trying to reason with the soldiers. "Listen man. There's just Quill in there. He's by himself, maybe even sleeping. You don't have to break in. You nicked the keys from my pocket." He could tell his request was falling on deaf ears. His anxiety level upped a notch. "You go in there like this," Kevin's bound hands pointed at the various men's weapons and dark clothing, "and you're going to scare him half to death. He's just a kid, a teenager." His efforts were met with only cold, hard stares from Crowe and his men, and silent, neutral glances from Burke's men.

Desperate, Kevin waved his tied wrists in the direction of the warehouse. "Look, you don't have to break into the flat and shoot things up. Quill's not dangerous. You have the keys. Take me and Liam in with you. We'll explain things to him. We'll give it all back." Sensing this was a really important issue, Kevin lied with the best poker face he'd ever attempted. "No one's even looked at the stuff yet." Kevin ignored the small, surprised jerk of Liam's head. He covered it with a heartfelt plead, moving forward into Crowe's personal space. "Please."

Crowe shoved Kevin back down onto the bench with more force than necessary, bouncing the back of Kevin's head off the truck wall. "Just do yourself a favor and shut the fuck up. As far as MI5 and the government are concerned, you're all terrorists who've engaged in an act of treason. There won't be any 'taking it easy'."

"Quill's only–"

Crowe cut off the rest of his retort with a brutal slap to his face.

"I said shut up or I'll shut you up." He towered over Kevin's hunched body, arm back to deliver a second blow. Before he could follow through, a whimper made Crowe turn his attention to Liam, cowering across the narrow isle.

Crowe sneered. "What a group of bloody cowards. Tough enough to threaten the national security of your own country, but not tough enough to take a little knockin' about."

"That's enough Crowe. Leave 'em alone. Save it for someone more your own size." The soldier didn't move from his seat beside his trembling, younger brother. "Unless a course, you'd like to tumble with someone *not* your size." The American's voice carried enough conviction to let the Crowe know he would be happy to back up his unspoken threat and keep Liam safe.

The Brit shot James an angry look. "Don't forget your place either, *Sergeant* James."

"The Sergeant has my full support regarding his actions, Lieutenant." Burke cut short Crowe's attempt at intimidation. "And I'm sure Director Davenport would agree. We can't get answers from a suspect who has to be hospitalized."

Kevin watched American as he checked his weapon and glanced at his watch.

"Speaking of which, it's time we got into position. Jameison and Gabriel have had time to relocate and we're gaining nothing by waiting out here. Let's move while we have the rain for cover."

"I think this calls for a minor change of plans. We'll take these two in through the front door. It might lessen the level of resistance and lower the body count." Casting a meaningful glance at Crowe he added, "and I think everyone would like that, wouldn't they, Lieutenant?" Burke continued without waiting for an answer. "We can clean the place faster with their help. And they have offered to help. Plus there's a chance they can secure the cooperation of their accomplices inside."Faced with seven other witnesses, Crowe declared, "I won't risk any of my men, Burke. If there's even a hint of resistance, I'll take down whoever's in that building, teenager or not. You know as well as I do, if they can walk, they can fire a gun or pull the pin on a grenade."

"I haven't forgotten anything, Lieutenant. I'm recommending we use a bit more restraint than usual." Burke nodded. "We split up into three groups and cover all three sides of the building from the street. Ray, you and Blake bring the boys here through the front door once I give the all clear from the front. Burr and Crowe, the door on the north side. James and Nelson, take the windows on the south. We go in with full intent, but use restraint if the only thing we find is a scared unarmed kid. Understood?"

His no-nonsense 'I'm in command here' tone of voice followed up by a glare brooked no argument from anyone.

Dissatisfied, Crowe warned, "If this goes badly, Burke, it's on your shoulders. My objections are on record. These young men are still dangerous. They've committed treason. I can't believe the legendary leader of *SparrowFour* would let the possibility of one orphaned kid impair his decision making."

Burke shook his head. "Maybe that's one of the reasons we're legendary, Crowe. We think through a situation and alter plans to meet the mission's circumstances. Maybe if you tried that, fewer people would pay the price during yours. Face it, MI5's own sources couldn't find any evidence of an outside party involved here. There probably *is* only one kid in there. We're not going to take any chances." Burke exchanged a meaningful glance with one of his men. "The most resistance we're realistically looking at will be a foul mouth and a bad attitude."

Kevin nodded enthusiastically. For Christ's sake, it was just Quill in there, not a resistance force.

Giving Crowe one last hard glance, Burke jumped down from the back of the truck. "I'll take full responsibility for everything that goes down here as long as you and your men remember to stick to the plan," Burke cautioned. "Let's move out. Fitzpatrick, you're with me."

Filing out of the truck one by one, they fanned out to take up their posts. Years of training and experience were evident in their smooth, measured body movements. Even without the cover the rain afforded them, they were silent, their motions flowing through the dark like the powerful river just beyond their warehouse, Kevin thought.

It took Weston and Blake longer to reach their positions, each dragging a clumsy, rain-drenched McCabe alongside them. Once in position, each group radioed into Burke who in turn gave the signal to go ahead. On the silent count of four, all three teams stormed the warehouse.

Chapter Six

Turning to the hard drive from the last computer to need his attention, Quill yanked it from its protective cage, picked it up and crashed it on the concrete floor into a growing pile of metal debris. Kneeling down next to it, he swung the hammer, and whacked the whole pile, mangling the thin metal casing beyond recognition. Three more blows and the drive was nothing but shattered bits. He added three more hits to be sure the data would be unsalvageable by any means he knew of. He had already performed a series of low level overwrites to make the data irretrievable.

In the background the hiss and sizzle of a microwave arcing off metal snapped, drowning out the sound of the heavy rain landing on the metal roof of the building.

Lost in a state of panic, none of the noises registered with Quill. So focused on the task of destroying every shred of data *FalconHawk* had accumulated, past and present, he almost didn't notice when loud crashing sounds exploded into the warehouse. The sight of several black-clad men in body armor carrying automatic weapons pushed through his single-minded efforts to remove all evidence of what they had been doing. It was then the real terror took over.

A harsh voice barked out, "Drop the weapon and lie down on the floor! Hands behind your head, face down!" He felt compelled to repeat himself even as he sighted in his rifle. "Do it. Now!"

Laura Baumbach

Mindless of the shouted instructions and their implied warning, Quill did everything he shouldn't have. Tossing the hammer in the direction of the bellowing man with the gun, he scrambled to his feet and ran. Stumbling over his own mess of devastated hard drives was the only thing that saved him from Crowe's first shot. Quill saw Burke knock Crowe's rifle up so it fired into the air saving him from the second shot. The gunfire stopped. Only the sound he could hear were running footsteps over the pounding rain on the metal rooftop.

Spurred on by the earlier gunfire, Quill raced for the only section of his home not sporting a pair of armed intruders. He dived for the small window that opened to the river below. Quill was willing to take his chances with the Thames as opposed to the rumored assassination units of MI5. He counted his chances of surviving either experience to be next to none, but the thought of drowning won out over being shot to death. Panicked even further by sounds of heavy footsteps gaining on him from behind, Quill launched himself at the window. Just as his feet left the ground, a hurdling object impacted with his back, sending him crashing to the concrete floor. His breath was forced out of his chest in one huge whoosh. Quill's rib cage creaked, muscles spasming under a suffocating weight. Crushed against the unyielding concrete, he scraped his cheek raw on the rough floor attempting to turn his head far enough to look over his shoulder to see what held him down.

Stern, amused brown eyes set in a sunburned face topped with wavy brown hair looked down at Quill. Too close to focus on his attacker, Quill tried to pull his face back an inch or two, but all he succeeded in doing was scraping his already bruised cheek. Rain droplets from the man's hair dripped onto Quill's face, running down his quivering jawline to mark the cold, gray flooring. The chill from the big man's wet clothing seeped through his worn sweater and jeans, making him shiver.

A low drawl, more fitting coming from an American western film star than an armed soldier, brushed against the side of his face. "Take it easy, son. Settle down, do what you're told and everything'll be just fine. Fuss at me and I'll have to get stern. Ya won't like it much if'n that has to happen." The soldier eased his considerable weight to one side.

Terrified and struggling for even a shallow breath, Quill exploded the instant the weight eased, using the only weapon left available to him–his mouth. "Shit! Get off me, you bastard. Great fuckin' troll! Bloody huge tosser! Motherfuckin' wanker! Get the hell OFF ME!"

Ethan James appeared stunned by the rush of foul words coming out of the boy's mouth, but hearing the tight, unnatural wheezing accompanying them, he shifted again until the youth could take a deeper breath. "Watch your tongue, son. There's no need for that kind of talk."

Quill was surprised when the man obeyed and the pressure eased, but he didn't get a chance to regain his equilibrium before he was lifted off the floor and set down on his feet, both wrists grasped in one meaty fist of the giant who had tackled him. Staring up at the dark tower of a man holding him upright, finally able to bring the man's face into focus, the teen forgot to struggle. Quill recognized his assailant. He was one of the men from the stolen dossiers — from the assassination file. He was one of Daniel Burke's men.

Before he could stop the words from escaping, he heard himself whisper through chattering teeth, "James.

Explosives expert. You're here."

Bewildered, James pulled the stunned youth closer and murmured, "How in Pete's name could you know that?"

Realizing his mistake, Quill renewed his struggles, trying to cover it with a stammered variation of the man's name.

"Jam-jammy sod! Bastard! Leave off, you wanker!"

Darting a frightened look around the room, Quill's heart increased its pounding in his already aching chest. Everywhere he looked an armed, black-clad man stood with a rifle pointing in his direction. It was just like his earlier doom-filled daydream come to life. All that was needed now was for E.T. to walk through. Instead of the mature reaction of becoming compliant and remorseful, he struggled harder to break the relentless hold on his wrists.

"Fuck! It was a bloody mistake, an accident. I didn't know where I was until it was too late and then it didn't matter, it was done. I know we shouldn't have tried to sell the stuff."

Quill looked past the mountain who was cutting off the blood supply to his hands to glance at the other five grim-faced men staring back at him.

Panic rising again, his tone so like a frightened child's, Quill asked in a hushed, small voice, "Where's Kev and Liam?" His searching gaze darted from man to man. Realizing he recognized at least four of these men, his breathing tightened. The sudden burn of nylon wire ties tightening around his wrists snapped Quill back to the present.

His knees weakened and James drew him closer, supporting most of his sagging weight. Taking advantage of the closer contact, the soldier did a rapid body search for weapons, coming up with only two pens and his cylinder inhaler. James tossed the pens and pocketed the inhaler, ignoring his indignant protest of, "I need that."

Shying away from the dark-haired man who had shot at him, Quill settled his expectant gaze on the man he felt he knew so well from having spent countless hours poring over so many hacked and pilfered computer files with his name on it–Daniel Burke, team leader of *SparrowFour*.

"What's happened to them? They're not dead are they?" Quill drew in a shaky, tight breath that made him tremble with the effort. "*Please tell me?*"

"They're fine...for the moment." Daniel Burke pulled out his radio and sent an 'all clear' signal to the team waiting outside. Seconds later, Weston and Blake walked through the door with sulking, dripping wet Kevin and Liam McCabe in tow.

"Kev! Liam!" Quill surged forward as far as James' restraining arms would allow, which wasn't far. He twisted around, keeping both of his friends in sight as they were moved into the room. Kevin gave him a weak grimace, while Liam only tilted his head in sad acknowledgement, looking like he was stoned.

"Thank God." Quill was unsure whether to cry in relief or in fear for things yet to come. A few rebellious tears leaked down his cheeks before he managed to get them under control. He had no idea what these men–these trained assassins–would do to them. If the MI5 press releases were to be believed, the three of them would only face arrest and interrogation. If the files he had just read were any indication, the three of them wouldn't live through the night.

Burke moved closer, his voice low and soothing. "Listen to me. Cooperate and things will go just fine. Resist, try to escape or lie to us and things can get very unpleasant. The choice is entirely up to you three."

Distressed by the man's caring tone, Quill stared off into the distance, willing the older man to go away. He didn't want to like these men, not yet. He wasn't ready for this to happen. He needed more time.

Kevin piped up. "You got it, mate. Anything you want, it's yours. The files, the discs, our computers, it's all yours. We never meant any real harm. You know–fight off Big Brother, loosen the collar of government watch dogs, that kind of thing. Freedom of information and all."

Crouching down until he was only inches from the older Kevin's face, the shooter sneered at Kevin. "I don't think performing acts of treason against your country will get you much sympathy from those 'little people' you're talking about, mate. Unless the little people you're referring to are Irish leprechauns."

Startled, Kevin jerked his head, darting his eyes around the room of annoyed soldiers. He managed to squeak out a faint, "Treason?"

"What do *you* call breaking into your government's military security agency, stealing confidential files, and then attempting to sell them? Internet shopping?" Sarcasm filled his equally sarcastic choice of words.

"An unfortunate, but understandable mistake?" Kevin replied, a hopeful tone in his voice.

Quill watched in shock as Crowe grabbed Kevin by the front of his shirt and shoved him into a chair. His gun never wavered more than a few inches from his friend's face. "Not likely. It was a premeditated act of terrorism designed to disrupt and undermine the British way of life and our freedom. Treason, *mate*."

Kevin paled, unable to manage more than a wordless sputter in answer to Crowe's unexpected condemnation.

They weren't terrorists! Anarchists maybe, but not terrorists.

Liam's slack jaw dropped even further at Crowe's accusation. With less force than Crowe had used, Blake deposited Liam into a chair. The young man raised his hands to cover his face in a gesture that spoke volumes about his level of despair.

Quill was lost in thought, trying to find a way of convincing them they weren't the terrorists they were accused of being, and concentrating on regulating his breathing.

James half-carried Quill over to the nearest armchair and folded him, still shaking, into it.

With all the suspects contained, the soldiers began a thorough search of the warehouse, poking into every corner and under every stack of paper in the space. Quill thought the room looked like a hurricane had hit as the soldiers trashed the place in a methodical, patterned assault.

Nelson kicked a pile of unwashed clothing over. A sharp, metallic snap broke the air and the soldier dropped into a crouch, rifle raised. Every man in the room swung around to face him, rifles trained on the pile of clothing.

Kevin stammered and gave a little nervous chuckle. "Rat trap. Big as terriers by the river here."

One of the soldiers shifted through the clothing heap with the barrel of his rifle to find a sprung trap caught on the end of a shirttail. Disgusted, he tossed it, shirt and all, into a corner causing two more traps to fire off in rapid succession. He shot Kevin a harsh glare.

Crowe continued to hover around them until James volunteered, "I'll keep an eye on 'em." His words were as soft-spoken, but the hard glint in his eyes conveyed his true feelings. Crowe wasn't going to be entrusted with their well being.

With a shrug of his shoulders, Crowe wandered off to look around, crouching down to examine the pile of twisted metal Quill had been hammering on. A sharp snap fizzled through the air at the same time the lights dimmed and flickered, drawing his attention to the small kitchen area. The faint smell of burning plastic drifted into the room when he popped open the mircowave door. A hissing mass of computer discs tumbled out onto the floor forcing Crowe to jump back out of the way of the still melting mess.

Burke glanced over at the smoking lump, then turned his attention to Quill, the only person who could have been responsible for creating the mess. "Let me guess. Those were computer discs with stolen data on them, right?"

Shifting in his chair, Quill kept his eyes glued to the floor by his feet, ignoring Burke and his question. He reached up to rub the center of his chest with the heel of his hand, trying to ease the growing tightness under his ribs, each breath more labored than the last. He concentrated on forcing air through thin, tight lips.

A shadow fell over his chair, making Quill jump. A large hand came down to cup his chin, tilting his face upward. He managed to keep his gaze averted for a few long, uncomfortable moments, then guilt and fear made him bring his eyes up to meet Burke's.

Quill swallowed hard, squirming in his seat,

unnerved by the intensity of the man's stare.

Burke studied the boy, taking in the labored breathing and the pounding pulse under his fingertips. Attributing Quill's discomfort to anxiety and fear, Burke decided to notch up the youngster's uncertainty a bit more to insure his cooperation. He kept his voice level, words crisp and sentences slow and menacing.

"I guess you didn't hear me, son. I asked if those mangled lumps over there were part of the data you stole?"

Burke watched his soft, quiet attitude unnerve Quill more than all of Crowe's shoving and shouting had. Whether from terror or cold, a hard shudder racked the boy's slim frame, almost jarring the youngster's face out of his grip. Tightening his fingers to hold the boy still, Burke was startled by the tight whimper the small gesture produced.

Tears spilled down the bruised cheeks, the boy choking on the ones running down the back of his throat, irritating his already labored breathing. All eyes in the room turned at the sound of Quill's next breath, its strangled wheeze of distress audible in every corner of the room.

Quill flinched as Kevin pitched forward in an effort to slide out of his chair, but a heavy hand pulled him back into place. Using more nylon wire ties, James secured him and the chair to one of the metal support posts in the room. Though Liam hadn't moved, he too, was anchored to the beam.

Kevin shouted at Burke. "Leave off, mate. He's got asthma. You can't push at him like that. He can't catch his breath, you soddin' bastard! He needs his inhaler. Let me help him. Please!" Kevin struggled against the restraints, cursing and begging for his release.

Burke captured Quill's upper arms and pulled him upright, his threatening attitude evaporating, replaced by genuine concern. He saw the dark rings under the youth's eyes were an unhealthy shade of gray and his complexion had turned pasty.

Burke signaled Ethan James, knowing he would want to go to the kid. Coming from a family of twelve children, James was a natural caregiver and nurturer despite his threatening size. No one argued with him either. If Ethan said sleep, you slept. If he said eat, you ate. End of discussion. Ray silently moved to take his place beside the McCabe brothers, intuitively filling the role assigned to James.

Kneeling beside Burke, James slipped the inhaler he confiscated from Quill out of his pocket and glanced at the label He shook the cylinder a few times before popping the cap off and placing it up to Quill's mouth.

The boy grabbed onto the devise with both hands, fingers fumbling in his haste to hold it. He inhaled with the first puff, holding the vapor in as long as possible before the need for another breath forced him to exhale. He held the second puff half as long as the first, his body desperate for oxygen. He slumped forward.

Next to the kid, James was murmuring nearby. His meaty hand traveled up and down Quill's back, attempting to coax the teen's tight muscles through their spasms. His breathing eased a bit and it appeared his immediate terror subsided as the medication took effect. His hunched posture relaxed and Quill dropped back into the large arm of James supporting his back.

Burke was aware that Crowe and his men watched the events with a mild degree of interest, but they kept to the background, allowing the other team to handle the unexpected medical crisis. It gave them more free time to examine the room's contents without interference from the Americans. Crowe intended to take full advantage of it, signaling his men to continue exploring the warehouse as the little drama unfolded.

Quill, risked a look up at his audience.

A shudder ran through his body and Burke couldn't help but wonder if thoughts of being exposed and dependent on these strangers embarrassed him. When he dropped his eyes to the floor again, Burke used the same firm grip from before to tilt Quill's face back up. "Better?"

Quill nodded.

"He'll be fine, Daniel. Sugar's always having these things when she's upset. I know how to handle it. He's coming 'round pretty well now, but we'll need to keep an eye on him, just in case."

Quill croaked out, "Sugar?"

Ethan James studied Quill's color and breathing pattern as he talked. "One of my kid sisters. She has asthma too. Real name's Christina, but we call her Sugar."

"Because she's so sweet." Between wheezes, Quill managed to force sarcasm into his words.

James grinned. "Nope, 'cause she thinks she's a little princess. So sure she'll melt if'n she gets the least bit wet or sweaty. Always slacking off on chores to stay clean. Even at twenty-six, Sugar's not sweet. She's an ornery rascal."

Burke was pleased to see a small smile touch the boy's pale lips.

"He's still shiverin' Daniel." James called out to his teammate. "Jack, could you find me something to wrap 'round him? The boy's wasting energy on trying to keep warm he should be using to breathe."

"No problem. Give me a second." Jackson Burr rummaged through one of the piles on the beds, pulling a thin, well-worn blanket out of the heap. He tossed it at James muttering, "Mother hen," then turned his attention back to searching the room.

Burke knew Jackson would keep a watch on Crowe's team as they picked through the debris.

"Quill? Quill, are you okay mate?" Kevin tugged at the nylon wire ties again, leaning out to the limits of their reach, trying to get a good look at the teenager. "Is he all right? Is he? Get him a drink of water, will ya? His throat gets real dry when he's like this. How's he look?"

Ethan wrapped Quill up in the thin fleece, adding a comforting arm around the boy's body. Burke heard Kevin heave a small sigh of relief when Quill let his head drop down to the big man's shoulder.

Quill answered his friend in a thin, reedy mumble muffled by the blanket. "I'm 'kay, Kev. Just need a minute." It was obvious to Burke even the short response sapped his depleted energy.

"'Kay, mate. As long as you're handling things all right. Liam and me are right here."

During the exchange Crowe had wandered back over to the two brothers. Ignoring Weston's warning stare Crowe lashed out, cuffing Kevin on the back of his head. "Shut up. If you were really interested in the lad's health you wouldn't have gotten him involved in acts of treason against his country. Unless maybe, he's the brains behind all this."

Giving both brothers a measured look he added, "I'm not convinced you or your brother are smart enough to have pulled this off on your own."

Weston moved closer to the younger men, but held his tongue. Breaking down a suspect's resistance and gaining the full truth of the situation was one of their goals. Intimidation worked wonders, especially on naïve and inexperienced criminals like these three, but Burke knew Weston wasn't going to let excessive physical violence play a part in it.

The only one who wasn't cooperating was Quill and most of his attitude was an adolescent, knee-jerk response to authority. Being scared breathless hadn't helped the youth's opinion of them much either.

"Quill—Quill and Liam are just along for the ride. I —I did the hacking." Kevin stuttered. "I engineered the break-in. Was all my idea to sell it, too. Was me what made the deal with Inspector whatever-his-name was. No one else."

"Kev don't—." It was the first thing the younger brother, Liam, had said in Burke's presence. His voice was rough, raw with disbelief at his brother's attempt to shoulder the full burden of guilt for their actions.

"Shut up, Liam. It's the truth, ya know it." Kevin shot his brother a dark, meaningful glare, then turned back to face Crowe. "I'm responsible for all of it. Me. The others just–"

Crowe cut him off with a slap to his forehead. "Don't bother. Your sister told us who the real computer genius in the group is. Baby Boy over there is in just as much trouble as you two, maybe more. So shut up, no one's going to believe you anyway."

Crowe cast an appraising glance over Quill's fine-boned features half-hidden under the faded blanket. A dark sneer settled on his face. "Once in jail, his ass will be like a fucking dartboard." Crowe leered at Kevin and Liam. "Not that you'll do any better. They like the young ones best, but it doesn't much matter what your face looks like when you're on your knees all the time."

Liam blanched white. Weston pushed between Crowe and the two brothers, a disgusted expression on his own face. "I respectfully suggest you *fuck off*, Lieutenant. They're still just suspects at the moment and this isn't accomplishing any of our objectives."

Burke materialized at Crowe's side, adding his own special brand of commanding presence to the exchange. "Ray's right. The boy needs to be checked by a doctor before he can answer any more questions. Face it Crowe, there's no one here except these three kids. No terrorists, no group of anarchists, no hordes of explosive devices, homemade bombs, or automatic weapons to overthrow your government. From the looks of it, the only weapon of mass destruction here is the microwave." Burke cast a final look around the place. "We're spending too much time here. It's time we loaded up the hardware and took this party on the road."

Burke favored Crowe with a hard stare until the other man nodded.

"Fine. We'll load everything into the van. It looks like it'll all fit in one trip. I'll take the suspects back to headquarters in the truck." Crowe smirked at the beginnings of a negative head shake from Burke. "You can send a couple of your men with us, if you like."

"Oh, I will Lieutenant. I will."

Crowe flashed an insincere grin, then turned away. "You heard the Commander, men. Let's get this place cleared out. Fitz, you stay with the prisoners." He shot Ray an amused, but insincere smirk before correcting himself.

"Excuse me, Corporal, the *suspects*."

Ray merely nodded, giving Crowe the condescending smile Burke knew he reserved for what Ray called DNA-challenged, mentally deficient beings from the low end of the gene pool.

Crowe's smile slipped a bit, rewarding Ray's irritatingly forgiving attitude his older sisters had nurtured during his formative years.

Crowe moved off and Fitzpatrick took over guard duty from Weston.

Working his way back over to Kevin and Liam's side of the room, Crowe pulled off his gloves and placed his rifle down on the table beside them, shielding his actions from the rest of the room with his body. He tossed a leer at Liam, then moved off again.

He saw the older brother eye the rifle only a few feet from him. He hoped Kevin wouldn't try to resist the thoughts of escape it fostered.

The younger one shook his head 'no'.

I'm not that daft." Kevin whispered.

Too fucking damn bad. It would have made things so much easier.

Burke walked over to James and knelt down beside him, eyes fastened on Quill's face. He ran a hand over his sweat-covered brow and into his tangled curls. "How is he, Ethan?"

Tucking the blanket closer around Quill before answering, James said, "Better. I gave him another couple of puffs off his inhaler. He needs to stay quiet. If'n it gets worse, he may have to go to a hospital, Daniel."

James examined Quill's inhaler, rolling it around in his oversized hand. "It's kind of strange, there's no label on this, nothing that'll tell you who his doctor is or how often to take it. There's always one on the box, but back home, our druggist puts one around the inhaler too. Helps when there's more'n one person taking the same thing in the house."

He looked down at the face resting against his shoulder, giving Quill a thoughtful frown. The boy's eyes shied away from his own, watching his hands as James pocketed the inhaler. "Huh. I guess they must do things different here than back home."

"I'll have to take your word for it, Ethan. Never had to use one," Burke said.

In an effort to avoid looking at James, Quill met Burke's concerned gaze. Burke ran his hand over the youth's head again and Quill had to stop himself from leaning into the contact.

These American's were a very physical group of men. Ever since the giant had tackled Quill to the ground, someone was always touching him. Whether it was a strong arm for support or a tight grip to hold him still, Quill hadn't been touched this often in years.

Sure, he and Liam traded slaps on the back and Kev was fond of rubbing his head until his hair was so tangled he couldn't get a brush through it, but it wasn't considered manly to hug or hold another guy. But this, this was nice. The warmth of the arm wrapped around his back seemed to seep deeper into his flesh.

The muted, ragged wheezes still struggled in Quill's lungs. Burke pulled away from him and glanced at Quill's wide-eyed face tucked between the folds of the blanket.

"Leave him here and let him rest. Sergeant Fitzpatrick seems trustworthy enough, despite Crowe's influence. Let him keep watch while we get this place cleaned out. I want to be out of here ASAP."

James nodded. "Whatever you say, boss." Leaving Quill curled up in the oversized armchair, he joined the methodical evacuation process.

Quill lay all but hidden under the blanket, only a few tuffs of gold-streaked, dark hair escaping out at the top. His wrists burned where the nylon ties pressed into his skin and his body longed to strain against the tight confines of the blanket, but it would take more strength than he had left. Even moving around enough to catch a glimpse of Kev and Liam was proving to be too hard right now.

He slumped into the arms of the chair and closed his eyes against the sight of his home disappearing again. This time as a direct result of something he had done. This made two homes he'd lost. Maybe fate was trying to tell him he didn't deserve one. He didn't think prison was going to be too homey.

Chapter Seven

Within ten minutes every piece of potential evidence in the warehouse was packed and being loaded into the van. Daniel Burke set the box he was carrying down on the floor of the van. He helped Jackson Burr settle a stack of open metal casings on top of it. Both men stepped away from the back of the van to make room for the next deposit, watching Weston struggle a bit with an overloaded carton of his own. Just before the younger man made it to the back of the van, the bottom of the carton gave out, showering the wet pavement with hundreds of smashed computer pieces.

A man of perpetual calm and reason, Ray resigned himself to the small disaster even before the first metal shard hit the ground. He stood stone still listening to the jingle and clunk of the parts splashing down around his boots and into the various puddles in the street, the mere closing of his eyes the only indication he might be affected by the mishap. When he opened them again, all three of his teammates were grinning at him.

Pursing his lips in exasperation, Ray cocked his head to one side. "That's all right, guys don't put yourselves out. Just stand there and watch."

"Okay, thanks, we will." Grin widening, Burr crossed his arms over his chest and leaned back against the transport truck parked alongside of the van. His stance mirrored that of both Burke and James, who were already lined up against the truck.

Ray heaved a sigh worthy of only the righteous

few destined who suffer in the presence of infidels. Bending down, he began to pile the fallen objects back into the carton, restrained frustration in his every movement. "Of course, if it had happened to any one of you, I'd be the first one to help out, but..." he held a hand up, palm out in a gesture of complete understanding and total martyrdom, "it's all right. I'm o-kay with this."

A chorus of mild snickers answered him. Weston didn't even bother to look up, refusing to acknowledge the trio of satisfied smirks. He continued tossing items into the box, innocently voicing the one challenge the other men never failed to answer, no matter how dumb the reason behind it was.

Letting his voice reek of insincere concern he said, "After all, it must be nearly impossible to bend down like this at your ages."

Three indignant protests rained down on him.

"Why you little—"

"Are you sayin' I'm old, son?"

"How'd you like me to 'bend' you over and acquaint your backside with the palm of my hand, boy?"

Laughing, Weston tossed the final item back into the box. All three of his antagonists reached out as one and tried to stop him from rising.

"Ray, stop--"

"I wouldn't do that, if'n I were you, son."

"Did that sunburn scorch your sense along with your pasty-white skin?"

Still ignoring the teasing jibes, the youngest member of the team rose to his feet, box grasped in both of his arms. And once again, the bottom of the battered box fell open. This time Weston just kept his eyes closed.

"Oops," he said.

Taking pity on his teammate, James pulled a half-empty carton from the van and began loading the fallen computer parts into it, cradling its straining bottom on his stooped lap as only a man of his huge size could. Sighing, Weston squatted down and joined in with the clean up.

Burr cuffed Weston on the back of his head and said, "Better old than daft, Ray."

Burke couldn't resist smiling over the entire sixty-second by-play that was so typical for them. These men were more than just teammates or best friends. They had spent the last several years together, fighting for the ideals and values of their country. They had seen each other through numerous life and death situations, both professionally and on a personal level. They were closer than family.

Casting a glance towards the warehouse, Burke wondered what was keeping the rest of Crowe's crew.

* * * * *

Crowe waited until the last load of equipment was on its way out of the door with Burke and his men, then ordered his own men out.

"Blake, Nelson. Take these boxes and make sure everything is secure in the van. Get the van warmed up and ready to go. Fitz, see that everything is in order and then come back to help me with the prisoners."

Blake and Nelson nodded, picked up a loaded carton and started towards the exit.

Fitzpatrick slowed and Crowe saw him cast an uneasy glance at the three restrained suspects.

Crowe caught his second-in-command's hesitant look. He gentled his voice and smiled. "We'll be fine, Fitz. Just see to it everything is secure outside and then get back here."

Fitzpatrick hesitated a moment more. "Yes, sir." Fitzpatrick watched Crowe pull a still wheezing Quill out of his chair by the scruff of his collar.

Fitz aborted his own retreat, but waved Blake and Nelson on. Once the door closed on his teammates, he turned back to his commander. "Lieutenant? Colonel Burke doesn't strike me as the type to overlook unofficial things. *Things* like black eyes and lost teeth."

Fitzpatrick threw another quick glance around the room. He settled his worried gaze on Quill's bruised and raw face. "And I'm bloody well sure the cowboy won't either."

Crowe snorted in amusement, the effort forced and unconvincing even to his own ears. "You're probably right Fitz, but you don't need to worry about it." When his second still remained standing there he shouted in annoyance, "You have your orders, Soldier."

"Yes sir." Fitzpatrick nodded in reluctant acceptance, then sprinted out the door, intending to return as soon as possible.

Without a second's hesitation, Crowe shoved Quill down on the floor at Kevin and Liam's feet. "A good soldier always follows orders and I'm nothing if not a good soldier."

Understanding dawned on only one of the young men. Shaking his head in denial, Kevin whimpered, "Oh, Lord. Please, don't."

Drawing his side arm in one smooth, well-practiced motion, Crowe took aim. "Just following orders. Sorry boys." His finger eased down on the trigger and the soft, hollow sound of a bullet fired from a silenced gun signaled the end of a life. A heart beat later, another bullet found a second victim and then the gun went looking for a third.

* * * * *

Corporals Nelson and Blake emerged from the warehouse carrying the last of the evidence cartons. Burke and Burr joined them and helped stack the heavy boxes into the waiting van.

Just as they finished, Burke turned back towards the building. He frowned as Crowe's second-in-command sprinted out of the building, approaching them at a mild jog. The expression on the soldier's face alerted Burke's instincts for trouble.

"Fitz, you're supposed to be with the suspects. What's the problem?" Burke asked. Behind him, the rest of the men stopped what they were doing to listen. Burke's men drew up close behind him. They all recognized the tone of wariness in Burke's voice.

Fitzpatrick licked nervously at his lips averting his gaze. He stared fixedly at some distant point over Burke's left shoulder, his voice tense, clipped and professional. "No problem, Sir. The lieutenant sent me to make sure everything was secure and ready to go before we move the suspects out into the weather."

Fitz brought his gaze back to meet Burke's, a blatant plea for understanding and acceptance clear in his eyes. "But with your permission, Lieutenant, I think it would be prudent for me to rejoin Lt. Crowe as soon as possible, Sir." Then he added, "For safety's sake."

In the background, Nelson and Blake stood very still.

Burke gave into the warning buzz in his head, giving his usual two-fingered hand signal to his team. Burr, Jackson and Weston fanned out behind him, pulling their rifles into position. Burke did the same.

Apprehensive, Fitzpatrick eyed the Americans, then gave Burke a curt, accepting nod.

Burke acknowledged Fitz's nod with a slight tilt of his head. "Why don't we all join the Lieutenant?"

Calling out over his shoulder Burke ordered, "Corporal Blake, radio Inspectors Jameison and Gabriel. Have them meet us here in five minutes to transport the suspects back to headquarters, then stay with the evidence we just collected."

A distant but clear acknowledgment of "Yes, sir," was snapped off. Blake's tone left everyone with the distinct impression that for once, the eager-to-act corporal was relieved to be the one staying behind.

Nelson and Fitzpatrick fell in line with Burke's men and the group entered the warehouse. They were several minutes too late.

* * * * *

The muted plopping effect of the gun's silencer could be heard over the hammering of the rain on the rooftop. Though Quill was staring at the gun as Crowe pulled the trigger, the reality of the shot didn't register with him until a spray of warm liquid splattered his face.

From then on time seemed to move in slow motion for Quill. Soft, small globs of warm wetness slithered down one side of his face, making him shake his head to be rid of it. The sharp turn of his head brought Kevin into focus, his friend's blood-drenched body sliding down towards the floor to hang limp and lifeless from his still shackled wrists secured to the support post.

Beside Kevin's body, a stunned, disbelieving Liam sat slack-jawed and passive, wide uncomprehending eyes staring at his dead brother's mutilated face, making him an easy second target for Crowe.

Sitting closer to Liam's feet than he had been to Kevin's, Quill felt the spray of tissue and blood coat his body. Understanding what was coming next, Quill reached out with his bloody hands, palms outward in the universal appeal for mercy, only to find Crowe lining up his third and final shot.

Quill saw Crowe hesitate, his blank mask of indifference softening for a fraction of an instant before the hard glint in his eyes resurfaced and he lined the gun back up with Quill's head. Spurred on by another spike of fear-fueled adrenaline, Quill used that split second of hesitation, launching himself off the floor and impacting with Crowe's knees.

Thrown off balance by the unexpected assault, the bigger man crumpled, hitting the concrete floor hard with his back. He managed to retain his hold on his weapon, but the impact left him breathless. He shook his head to clear it.

Crowe grunted, startled by Quill's weight as the teenager scrambled up over him, attempting to reach the windows in the back of the room. Lunging forward, Crowe latched on to one of the boy's legs while rolling to one side to avoid getting kicked. He dragged Quill down until his legs were less of a threat and rolled back over to pin him down.

"Leave off, you bastard! Let go!" Quill squirmed and wrestled. Breathing was hard enough without a grown man wrapped in Kevlar sitting on his chest. "Fucking killer!" Quill gathered his strength and blindsided Crowe hard with his bound fists.

Crowe's grip faltered for a moment before he reared back, striking Quill in the face. The first punch blackened the boy's left eye, the second split open his bottom lip. Both blows stunned him, making the room dim and the furniture shimmer.

"Bloody little bastard." Crowe heaved himself up on one knee before coming to a stand over Quill. "Rabbit on me, will ya, ya sodding little bugger. Put a stop to that right off."

Crowe raised his boot and brought it down on Quill's knee, putting all of his weight behind it.

Quill screamed and rolled away from him. Crowe delivered another vicious kick to the back of Quill's knee.

Crowe had no time to waste. The soldiers would be back in a few minutes. Based on what Quill read in the files Crowe had to have all three eliminated before then. He couldn't have one opposing voice survive to challenge his actions and expose what MI5 did to their prisoners. Quill knew too much making him the most dangerous of the three. He heard Crowe let out a controlled breath and knew his life was over.

* * * * *

First through the door, Burke found Crowe standing over the prone figure of Quill, a handgun with a silencer pointed at the teen's head. During the struggle, the two had managed to end up facing the front door.

"Crowe! Drop the gun! Drop it!" Gun drawn, Burke's face was a mix of disbelief and solid determination not to let Crowe pull the trigger.

Both the boy and the soldier were blood-smeared with even the seasoned soldier showing signs of a recent struggle. Burke couldn't see the boy's front, but Quill had his bound arms curled over his face.

Burr, James, Weston, Nelson and Fitz raced in behind Burke, and fanned out over the large room. James and Weston split off and worked their way toward Kevin and Liam.

Burr hung back and kept a watchful eye on Crowe's teammates and his own team's backs.

Standing beside Burke, Fitzpatrick gasped, "What the hell?" then bellowed, "Lieutenant!"

Crowe neither acknowledged Burke's command nor lowered his weapon. Even his second in command's voice didn't jar him from his task. Burke could see the steady pressure increasing on the trigger and he responded in the only way possible to save the boy's life.

He shot Crowe.

His bullet hit the man in the chest, up by the man's collarbone. Blood pooled and saturated his upper body, giving his clothing an eerie, wet sheen.

Crowe jerked at the impact, his body slamming back against a metal support beam and he slid down to land sitting on the concrete floor. Eyes still fixated on his target, the gun slipped from his nerveless fingers in degrees, as shock took over his body. Burke was at his side before he hit the floor, kicking the gun from his hand.

Unrepentant, Crowe looked Burke in the eye. "Son of a bitch. You're a bit early, arsehole. You poxy Yanks are always screwing up things." He gave a dry, mirthless snort. "But not for long."

"Daniel, both McCabe boys are dead, shot through the head." After a pause for a deep breath, James added, "They're both still tied to the post."

Burke's lips formed a grim line at the news, then he signaled Weston to join him. "Ray, stay with him." He jerked his head to indicate Crowe. "I want to check on the other boy." He glanced up to pinpoint Burr's current position and nodded his understanding of the soldier's flank position in the room. "Jack, radio base. Tell 'em we need an emergency medical support team ASAP." His eyes tracked the other two members of Crowe's team.

Fitzpatrick and Nelson drew near to their commanding officer, hovering, restless and uncertain, a few feet away. Nelson could only stare. Fitzpatrick regained his balance faster and dropped to one knee beside Crowe. "What the fuck were you doing? Why the bloody hell did you shoot them? They–"

"I was following orders, soldier." Twisting a bit, Crowe looked at Fitz and grimaced in pain the small movement ignited in his chest. "Do you hear that Burke? Following orders. You won't be able to do anything to me. I was doing my job, my *duty*. What I was sent here to do." His voice was drenched in self-satisfaction.

"Orders? What orders? For murder?" Fitzpatrick gaped at the man. "For Christ's sake, Lieutenant, they were unarmed, tied to a post! Helpless!"

Crowe gave him a disgusted sneer. "Haven't got the stomach for a real soldier's job, Fitz? What...it's okay to wipe out a town full of women and children in Botav looking for one man who bombed a deserted church, but it's not okay to remove three *treasonous* blokes on our own soil? Ones who've threatened our national security and our way of life? What's the problem, Fitz? There were no innocent casualties here, no uninvolved bystanders, no stray bullets to hit an unsuspecting child. It was a clean mission. Two more obstacles to real justice eliminated."

Crowe shot a harsh look in Quill's direction, his voice stony. "I just wish I'd had the opportunity to finish it properly." Settling back against the post, body weight on his handcuffed arms behind his back, Crowe grunted with the increased pain. "No matter really, there's still time to attend to him."

Feeling a sudden flair of anger break through his professional mask, Burke grabbed Crowe by the hair and smacked the man's head back against the metal beam. "Listen to me, Crowe. No one, not you, not your cohorts in this insane plot, not even your government is going to touch that kid. In fact, I'm going to make sure you never even see him again. No one is going to hurt him, not while I'm around."

"Then you bloody well better plan on adopting him, Burke, because the moment he's on his own, he's dead. Just another casualty of war."

Crowe gasped and shifted position again. "He's just a bit of gutter waste, Burke. A little piece of rubbish even his mum tossed away. Not worth the cost of the bullet really."

"Fine, then no one'll object to my keeping him," Burke said.

Both men's eyes fell on the object of Crowe's derogatory remarks. They were greeted with the unfortunate sight of two pairs of brown eyes staring back at them. One pair, belonging to Quill, looked like watery, brown pools, dazed and full of hurt, one eye surrounded by swollen, bruised flesh and dried blood. The other pair, belonging to James, was as close to murderous as Burke had ever seen the gentle man get.

Quill's sobs were quiet and restrained, leaving no doubt in Burke's mind he had overheard Crowe's comments. James lifted the boy's shoulders off the floor and held him.

Burke tightened his grip and jarred Crowe's head hard against the post a second time, unashamed at the twinge of satisfaction it gave him. "Only a twisted fuck like you would come up with such a sanctimonious justification for taking a life. You sicken me, Crowe. There was no glory, no righteous duty performed here. This was murder, pure and simple, no matter how high up the order may have come from–*if* it was a military order and you're not talking through a direct line to God."

He pushed off using Crowe's head as a brace and turned his back on the man. Burke looked at Crowe's men. "If either of you had any knowledge of this, if I find out you're in this with Crowe, I'll make sure you're locked away for so long you'll forget what sunshine and fresh air feels like."

Nelson paled at the accusation and shook his head. "No, sir. No, Sir!"

His eyes traveled over Crowe's crumpled form, then back up to Burke's hard, expectant face. "I-I thought he was the best...I mean, I knew he'd get a little rough sometimes, but...God, I never thought he'd..." Nelson swallowed down the words, uncomfortable with voicing the tragedy. "No sir, I had no idea of his plans, sir."

Satisfied the man was telling the truth, Burke shifted his questioning gaze to Fitzpatrick. "Your commanding officer just used a military operation to commit murder. Why, I can't even guess. Can you?" he asked.

Fitzpatrick straightened up from the floor and assumed a rigid military posture, eyes directed at a point somewhere in the distance, no doubt falling back on his training in times of stress like he had been taught to do.

"No, sir. I can assure you, Lt. Crowe was operating independently. I had no knowledge of his intentions, Sir, prior or otherwise." Fitz paused to steady himself, allowing his gaze to meet Burke's. "If I had, I'd never've left them alone with him, Sir, never. I was only gone a couple of minutes."

His eyes strayed to the lifeless, bloodied bodies twenty feet away. "Just a couple of minutes. And we were right outside the building. I never thought..." Fitzpatrick zeroed in on that reassuring spot in the distance again. "I've no idea why either, sir."

"And Blake?" Burke demanded.

"Trevor's a good man, Commander, he wouldn't have any part in something like this. In fact, he'd be the first one to turn Crowe in if he got wind of it. They can work together, but there's no love between them."

Instinct had already told Burke to trust Fitzpatrick from the first moment they met. This confirmed it for him.

"I'm placing Lt. Crowe under arrest and turning him over to your custody, Officer Fitzpatrick. For the time being, the remaining suspect and the computer evidence will stay in my custody."

"I understand, sir."

"I'm also going to assign Inspectors Jameison and Gabriel to accompany you back to headquarters to be sure all the evidence regarding Lt. Crowe's actions remain above suspicion. I don't want anything to cast doubt on the validity of the case against him when his court-martial comes up."

Fitz flinched at the implication that it would be tampered with. He nodded. Dazed, he watched Burke kneel beside the surviving boy.

Burr moved in closer, trading his role from sentry to medic, forcefully pressing a wad of discarded clothing over Crowe's wound. Without saying a word Burr yanked Nelson down beside him and put the corporal's hand over the makeshift bandage, pressing it hard into the flesh. Then Burr stood and joined Weston in guarding the prisoner. All eyes, including Burr's, turned to the front of the building when the door burst open.

Chapter Eight

Outside of the warehouse, Burke's shot had spurred Blake into taking action. He and both Inspectors busted through the door, weapons drawn. The three of them stopped just inside the doorway.

"What the bloody hell is happening in here?" Blake bellowed.

Burke barked out an order in a tone guaranteed to shake a soldier back to earth. "Corporal Blake! Get back outside and resume your post."

Blake blinked and visibly shook himself at the sound of the Commander's voice. Burke didn't care whether the soldier understood the situation. "I'd hate like hell for the evidence to come up missing while you were watching it."

Confused, but well trained, the corporal obeyed, his hands wavering for only a moment.

In response to Jameison's arched eyebrows, Burke tilted his head at Crowe.

"I'm placing Lt. Crowe in your custody, Inspectors. He's under arrest for two counts of murder, one count of attempted murder and about a dozen military infractions. You'll want to caution him. Make sure he stays in custody long enough to face charges, will you?" He stepped away, then turned back to add, "Oh, and I'm confiscating all the computer files and the remaining suspect until further notice."

Burke shook his head at the twin blank, disbelieving stares, knowing he didn't have time to explain it all. "Talk to Fitzpatrick, he'll fill you in. Gentlemen, you'll have to excuse me, but there's something I need to do."

With that, he left the Inspectors, striding over to where James was still holding a now silent Quill. "How bad is it, Ethan?" Crouching down, Burke positioned himself beside James.

"Well, doesn't have any bullet holes in him. Most of the blood 'n stuff isn't his," James flicked his gaze towards the area where Kevin and Liam lay, "mostly spray. Left knee seemed mighty tender when I patted him down. Can't really tell how bad 'til I can strip 'm down some, take a good look at it."

Burke eased Quill's face back until he could see the extent of the injuries there. "Let's have look at that face, son."

Through smears of blood he could see the boy's left eye was swelling shut. Fresh blood seeped out over the bruising where it had been scraped. His mouth was split in one corner and both his lips and cheek were a blotchy red and purple mess.

Burke shifted Quill's upper body into his own arms so he could examine him better.

James said, "Better take another look at his pupils before that one eye swells shut. He got hit pretty hard, Daniel. Not real sure he's firing both barrels yet."

"Let me see."

Using both hands to tilt the boy's face up to meet his own gaze, Burke examined Quill's brown eyes. He stared into the pupils until he was satisfied they were equal, then stared at Quill's entire face. Quill's expression under the abuse looked as if the boy was old, old and tired. His eyes looked beyond tears.

Burke felt a sharp tightening in his chest, like his heart had faltered in its rhythm, before the sharpness eased to a dull ache under his breastbone. Startled by his reaction, Burke forced himself to set aside his soldier's mindset and see the person in the body he was evaluating.

One wide, unfocused brown eye stared back, its edges rimmed in red and its surface glistening with too much moisture. Patches of pasty white brain tissue offset the crusty rivulets of blood drying over top of the bruised swelling. Quill's light brown curls were matted around his face, a few sticking to his cheek with dried blood. Battered, bleeding and wearing the splattered bits of his friends, the effect was still less unsettling than the lost emotion in the teenager's haunted eyes.

Curled against James' substantial chest, cradled by the big man's massive arms, Quill lay pliant and still, allowing James to support his entire upper body. His backside and legs remained on the floor, tattered jeans and ratty boots made even scruffier by the addition of new rips, stains and scrapes. When his upper torso was repositioned, Quill made no attempt to pull his legs into a more comfortable position or shift them to keep them in alignment with the rest of his body. His arms were straight, lying tucked between himself and James at an awkward angle, his wrists still tied together. Not even his fingers twitched. He could be mistaken for dead if it weren't for the tight rasp of his breathing and the occasional, slow blinking of his one eye.

"He's in shock. Let's get him warmed up and get him the hell out of here. A change of scenery will help." Burke grabbed a blanket off the floor and draped it over Quill.

James shifted up to his knees in one smooth

motion, bringing Quill with him. When he slid an arm under Quill's knees, a sharp gasp of pain stilled his movements. The teen's filthy hands tightened on any flap or edge of fabric on the man's vest they could find to cling to. James altered his hold to support Quill's legs better.

"Ugh!" Snapping out of his dazed trance, Quill jerked his head down and buried his battered face in James' armpit to muffle his shriek of agony.

"Whoa, whoa there, son. Just hold on, hold on." James pulled Quill closer and rose to his feet, unaffected by the additional weight. "Daniel, can you get his legs, keep 'em from swinging too much? We'll put him down on one those mattresses over there. I need to get a better look at that leg before we do anything else."

Burke guided them to the makeshift beds and helped settle Quill down on one. Moving to one side, Burke sat on the edge of the bed and cut the nylon ties from Quill's wrists. Once Quill was free, Burke reached for the abused limbs again only to have the boy shrink away from him. Burke leaned forward, letting his expression soften with a smile that touched his eyes, but keeping his voice firm.

"Hey, it's all right. You're going to be fine, kid. What that other soldier did wasn't right. That's not why we're here. No one's going to hurt you again, I promise."

A disbelieving face stared back up at him. "That's a promise, but you'll have to trust me."

"You're safe, just settle on down, son." James' deep voice was always reassuring, his Texan drawl calm and soothing.

Inching his hand forward, Burke eased his palm over the boy's trembling fingers, never taking his eyes off Quill's uncertain face. The raw, haunted look remained in the boy's eyes.

Burke noticed Quill couldn't keep his eyes from straying over to where his dead companions lay. He shifted until he was between the blood-soaked corner of the room and the teen. The next time Quill glanced over, all he got an eye full of black Kevlar and Burke's face. The boy quickly dropped his gaze.

Burke took each raw wrist in turn, massaging the circulation back into the cold fingers while James worked at splitting the left side of the boy's jeans with his knife. After coaxing a little warmth back into the chilled flesh, Burke wrapped his larger fingers around both of Quill's hands and held on. What was coming wouldn't be pleasant.

"Ethan's going to take a closer look at your leg. He knows what he's doing, but it's still going to hurt a bit."

"You said you wouldn't let anybody hurt me again." Burke could hear the terror in between the tight, shallow breaths. "You promised." Panicked, Quill tried to kick off the bed with his good leg, his arms alternating between shoving and pulling to try to break Burke's grip. "You promised, you *promised*!"

"Stop it."

Burke held onto his wrists and waited for Quill to tire himself out. The effort was costing Quill dearly in the breathing department, each new breath tighter than the last.

When the boy was twisted to his side and faced James. The big man loomed over him, blocking out a large portion of the surrounding room. "If you don't settle down, in about two shakes of a rattler's tail, I'm gonna give you a reason to pitch a fit. Right to the seat of your pants."

Rolling hastily onto his back, Quill turned his disbelieving glare on the giant. "You can't! I'm—I'm n-nineteen."

"Try me, boy."

"You can't do that, you bloody--!"

"And I'd watch that mouth of yours if I were you. Now hold still and let's get this leg tended to." James dug the inhaler out of his pocket and tossed it to Burke who caught it one-handed. "Give him another two puffs on that and see if his breathing eases a mite."

Burke nodded. Unfamiliar with its operation, he studied the inhaler for a moment. Popping the lid open, he shook it before placing it into Quill's unsteady hands. He guided it up to Quill's face and held it steady while Quill clung to it, inhaling as deeply as he was able.

"Pitching a fit hasn't done any good for your lungs or your leg, son." James met Quill's indignant, watery glare with a look that quelled the small spark of rebellion still burning there. "Now lay back, get hold of something and grit your teeth, this is gonna hurt."

James exposed Quill's left leg from the thigh down to the top of his ankle-high boots. A misshapen mass of blue-black bruises and swollen tissue obstructed Quill's knee from view. His lower leg lay slightly displaced to one side, the calf out of alignment with the thigh and his foot rotated to one side at an unnatural angle. A large bruise was forming at the back of the knee, wrapping around both sides toward the front.

James whistled at the sight. "Looks dislocated." Catching Burke's eye, he said, "You wanna wait for the ambulance?"

Burke trailed his gaze over the boy's battered face and mangled knee, then glanced over James' shoulder to where Kevin and Liam's bodies still hung against the post. "No. Do whatever you need to do so he can travel. I want to get him away before MI5's people arrive. We need time to figure out what happened, who ordered this and why. He'll be safest with us."

"You're right, Daniel." James reached for his medical kit to find a compact air splint being handed to him. He looked up and smiled at Jackson Burr's smug face.

Burr said, "Looked like you might need that. Have to get *some* use out of all my years of expensive pre-med."

James unfolded the splint, smoothing out the Velcro straps. "Your momma'll be happy to hear it, Jackson. Give me a hand." He pointed at Quill's calf. "You take a hold here and pull when I tell ya to. I'm going to push the knee back into place."

He lay the splint on the bed and glanced up at Burke. "Hold him down."

"Wait!" Realizing their intent, Quill squirmed and bucked, forcing Burke to rest his hip on Quill's thigh to keep his good leg down.

"You bloody tossers, wait!"

"Do it now," Burke commanded.

Quill's terrified voice had put the tight, painful ache back in Burke's chest again.

All three men moved in unison. Burke pinned Quill's wrists to his chest, shifting a fair amount of his own weight onto the boy's upper body, locking his gaze on the boy's terrified face, trying to relay comfort. Burr wrapped both of his hands around Quill's lower leg and planted his feet apart to give himself a steady base to pull against. James slid his large hands to either side of the dislocated knee.

Burke sucked in a deep breath. "Go."

Quill's scream bounced off the walls and jarred the nerves of the men in the room before it was cut off.

Burke held the unconscious boy pinned to the bed to keep Burr from dragging him off the end of the mattress while he pulled on Quill's lower leg. James worked his skilled hands over the displaced joint, pressing and prodding until enough of a gap was created to allow him to push the bones back into place. Burke heard a pop.

James sighed. "It's in." He tugged the air splint into place, immobilizing the joint. "It'd be best to move him while he's out. That's gonna hurt like the dickens when he wakes up."

James and Burr gathered up their gear. Burr motioned for Weston to leave Crowe to Jameison's care and rejoin the team. With only a parting glance at the men from MI5, Weston moved off to connect with his teammates.

"I'll take him, Daniel." James reached for the boy and Burke hesitated for a moment before allowing the big man to take the boy from his arms.

"Unless you wanta carry him." James had seen his hesitation. "I don't wanta trespass, there hoss."

Surprised by James being able to vocalize what he himself was feeling, Burke gave the giant a rueful smile. He brushed a lock of dirty hair off Quill's pale, still face.

Burke rolled off the bed, pocketing the discarded inhaler. "Let's get him out of here."

James cradled the boy, taking the threadbare blanket with him. He moved into the center of the group, bracketed by an armed teammate on three sides.

"Jackson, Ray, let's go," said Burke. "No one stops us and we give up nothing. They can sort out Crowe and his men. Our job was to get the computer files and the people responsible, what little there is left of both. I think we have that covered."

He couldn't help glancing at the McCabes one last time. The sight of their broken young bodies made his blood pressure soar. "Let's pick up our toys and head home, boys."

* * * * *

Shocked at the story Fitzpatrick told them, Gabriel adjusted to the unexpected turn of events faster than his partner did. He called for MI5's own investigative team and made a cursory examination of the McCabes' bodies and the scene.

"Christ, can you believe this?" Even Jameison's accommodating and always charming demeanor cracked at the sight of the bound and helpless bodies.

The Inspector approached Burke just as the Americans prepared to leave, picking up a black leather jacket from the floor as he walked. "Commander, it's likely that your suspect is also our only witness to what happened here."

"That's a definite possibility, Inspector." Burke made sure he was between Jameison and Ethan. Quill lay unconscious in the huge man's protective arms like a sleeping child. Jameison moved to step around Burke and the soldier cut him off. "But the boy is still going with us."

Jameison took the hint and backed off. "He'll need to be questioned about this if you want Crowe to get what he deserves."

Burke kept his expression neutral, but his eyes and his voice betrayed his anger. "Crowe was the only one in the room with a loaded weapon. All three of the victims were bound and helpless. I saw him standing over this boy. His gun was drawn and aimed at the head of a child he'd already beaten senseless. He refused to drop his weapon when ordered to do so and even confessed to the killings once he was subdued. He stated he was under orders to carry them out. There were seven witnesses to all of that, including three of his own men. If the British government still needs the testimony of a terrified, battered child to convict him, then something's not quite right with your system here."

"I'll still need to know where he'll be." Jameison kept his voice soft and low. He sympathized with the commander, but he had a job to do.

Burke motioned his men to go out the door ahead of him. "He'll be with me. And I'll be wherever it's safest for him to be. You need anything more, contact my commanding officer, Colonel Robert Lansing. I almost always tell him where I am. Goodnight, gentlemen, and thanks for the backup." Burke nodded at Gabriel and passed a wary glance over the other three soldiers before turning away.

"Commander." Jameison tossed the black leather jacket in his hand to Burke. "The kid'll want this, it was a gift."

Burke fingered the new leather and raised a questioning eyebrow at the Inspector.

Jameison only shrugged, not really feeling very proud of having pried the information out of the McCabes' sister under false pretenses earlier. It was a part of the job, but getting their address from her had led to their deaths. He wondered how guilty she would feel when she learned about it.

With a nod, Burke slung the jacket over a shoulder and followed his men out.

Gabriel joined his partner, watching the Americans depart. "Whadaya think?"

Jameison exhaled a long, drawn out breathe. "I think you were right. *SparrowFour* doesn't just fly in and take out a target, they strafe the entire area while they're here. No one's bloody safe. What a fucking mess."

"Wonder what Richmond's going to say about this one?" Gabriel couldn't keep the hint of a smile from his face.

"Who gives a damn what that arsehole thinks? The Commissioner won't be happy, but he'll know how to handle it." Jameison sighed and turned back around to look at Crowe and his ex-teammates. Sirens in the distance announced the impending arrival of the medical team and more backup.

"Right now, I need to know who's the closest in the betting pool. I've got odds on the Americans wreaking havoc in the first four hours of being here. I have to be close."

"You jammy sod. Looks like you might be in for a bit of cash then."

"Hope so. It'll be the only good thing to come out of this mess." Jameison glanced toward the bloodstained post. "That and the kid still being alive."

"Hell, poor little sod. Not much of a nice life ahead of him."

Chapter Nine

Settling onto the middle seat of the van, James rolled the unconscious boy back and forth until he had Quill wrapped in several blankets. Careful to support Quill's splinted knee, Weston joined James on the seat, propping the boy's legs up on his lap. Burr climbed into the driver's side and had the van running by the time Burke slid in next to him. He guided the black vehicle down a narrow alley to avoid the incoming rush of cars as new officers and medical personnel arrived on the scene.

Burke snapped his radio off his vest and dialed the knobs to set its frequency. "I'll radio headquarters and let them know we ran into a bit of a snag." At the sound of a low moan, he paused and twisted around in his seat to nod at Quill. "He alright?"

"Think so, havin' a nightmare maybe," James said.

Burr quipped over his shoulder, "Hell, I wonder why?"

Weston tightened his grip on the shifting legs on his lap. "This one's a survivor. He's fighting to get away, even in his dreams. Probably thinks we're gonna kill him."

Burke watched as Quill's sleep-laden limbs continued to fight off some unknown attacker.

"He might. He's a teenager, a kid," Ray said. "Think about it, Daniel. His friends were just brutally murdered right in front of him, by a member of the British Police Force. He doesn't have any reason to trust us. We were with Crowe."

"He's got a good point, Daniel." Picking up speed, Burr wove their way through the tight alleyways and side streets. "Once he wakes up, he's not gonna want anything to do with us."

James pushed back the blanket to reveal Quill's bruised face, one eyelid fluttered with the effort to open, the other held immobile in swollen flesh. Another moan, deeper and more pain-filled, followed the first. Quill's head rolled from side to side, while his arms struggled against the blankets and some unseen foe, his unconscious mind caught in the grip of a nightmare.

"Slow down, it's okay, son. It's okay, you're gonna be fine, just fine." James pushed the matted hair off Quill's face, letting his fingers worm their way through the filthy strands.

Burke turned back around in his seat and frowned, staring out the window. "That's just too damn bad, because he's not leaving my sight just yet. Until we know what this is all about, and I'm sure he's going to be safe, the boy stays with us."

Burr snorted. "How long do you think we can keep him once we get back to the air base? If the Brits put enough pressure on General Weiss, that useless, old ass-kisser'll fold like a house made of dirty cards." Burr warmed to his subject, one index finger poking the air as he talked. "He'll have that child in an MI5 interrogation room within the hour, emotional trauma and physical injuries be damned."

"Jack, I'm not going to let that happen."

The rain started up again with a vengeance, tapping out a frantic tune on the hood of the van. Burr switched on the wipers and said, "And just how are you going to stop it, Bossman? Last time I checked, a General still out ranks a Colonel, even if you throw in two devilishly handsome sergeants and a so-so weapon's specialist."

Burke cast a look over his shoulder at the youth in James' lap. "We'll think of something. We always do."

Weston leaned forward over Quill's legs. "Who's so-so? Is that another crack about my cologne? I told you, I'm throwing it away." His indignant reply was met with a trio of smirks and Burr barked out a laugh.

Flexing his fingers, James began petting firm strokes through Quill's hair to soothe the restless boy, as he came to. "Hush now, you're safe, you're safe." One hooded, dull eye fluttered open and stared off into the distance. "Hey there."

The gentle Texan drawl held an undercurrent of concern, but Quill refused to show any outward response to it. "Don't think the rascal's ready to be sociable just yet." James shrugged. "Feeling any better, son?"

Quill refused to acknowledge anyone and stared at the falling rain on the window.

Settling Quill more comfortably, James pulled him upright. Burke heard a sharp intake of breath and watched as a grimace of pain from the boy slowed James' movements. "I'll take that as a no. Just try to relax, no one's going to hurt you."

"Alpha Base, this is *SparrowFour*. Come in. Over."

"*Copy, SparrowFour. Alpha Base reads you loud and clear. Over.*"

"Copy, Alpha Base. The mission goal has been accomplished to the best degree possible, but we've run into a bit of a problem here. The situation is sensitive and unusual enough in nature that I'm exercising my rights as ranking officer present and ordering a change of plans.

Security has been breached and I'm not sure at what level. Since there's a life still at stake, I'm taking no chances. You'll be fully informed in person shortly. Over."

There was long period of silence before the radio jumped back to life. "*Copy that, SparrowFour. What is your ETA? Over.*"

Burke glanced at Burr who flashed him the hand signal for twenty minutes. Burke lied into the radio. "ETA approximately forty minutes. Over."

The response was immediate this time. "*Roger that. Forty minutes. See you then, SparrowFour. Alpha Base, over and out.*"

Burr shot his commander a curious grin. "You lied, Daniel. Ray's *Sister* sisters aren't *ever* going to be able to get you through those pearly gates at this rate, Bossman."

Burke snorted and slipped the radio back into his vest. "No, I didn't. It *is* going to take that long to get back to base. I just gave us a little time to think about things. I'm not letting that boy fall back into MI5's hands until I know for sure he's going to be safe and taken care of properly. Right now, I'm not sure that'll happen. We need time to sort this all out." Burke glanced over his shoulder to look at the dazed, battered youth. "I promised."

"You'd better start thinking fast then, Daniel. Twenty extra minutes isn't that much time."

"I know. Drive slower." ☐

Phrases spoken in Burke's voice tumbled in a haphazard pattern through Quill's thoughts, each accompanied by distorted visions of the blonde Commander's intense, protective expression. "I promise", "I won't let them have him" and "He stays with us until he's safe" -- rang in his ears until his conscience forced him to speak out.

"They're going to kill you. The whole lot of you. Soon." Quill's voice was little more than a harsh whisper. Even Ethan had to strain to hear it clearly.

"What?" Burke turned part way around in his seat until he could see Quill. A quick glance at both Weston and James confirmed that the boy had spoken out loud.

Quill swallowed down the dry lump of fear threatening to choke him. Licking at his chapped, cracked lips, he turned his head and lifted it until his good eye could look Burke in the face. Nervous, he glanced up at James and then at Weston before meeting Burke's tight frown.

"In the folder we took. There was a file on you, all of you, *SparrowFour*. The file name, *SparrowHawk*, was so close to our name. Ya know, the one we gave ourselves, *FalconHawk?* I had to check it out."

James tugged the blanket back to reveal more of the boy's face, lifting a knee to bring Quill up closer to his line of vision. "That's what you meant when you first saw me. How you knew my name and what I do."

Quill nodded, careful not to jar his aching head too much. "Ethan James, Sergeant, US Army Special Forces, explosives expert, thirty-nine years old, single. You come from someplace called Texas."

All four men exchanged suspicious looks. Burke said, "Jackson, find a wide spot in the road and pull over."

The van slowed and swerved to the shoulder of the narrow road, swaying with the abrupt stop. Burr twisted his bulky frame around in his seat to stare at Quill. "What's this about someone being killed, child?"

Quill resisted the urge to shift closer to James at the black man's sudden accusatory intensity, but held his ground and tried to move into a less submissive position.

The sudden flare of agony in his left leg stopped him cold, taking away his breath and his train of thought for a moment. Eyes held shut against the pain, he felt a warm touch to the side of his face.

Opening his good eye, Quill was surprised to see the hand belonged to Burke. Even after all his many months of planning and tracking the man, he never thought he'd be this close to him. A flush of nervousness raced through him and he fumbled to get his words out, the hand falling away as he talked.

"In the file, after it gave details about each of you, the last page was an outline, a p-plan, I-I guess. On your next mission, one in a place called Eritrea, you're going to get ambushed and k-killed, murdered." Quill's eye darted from one man's disbelieving face to next. "It's a setup to get rid of you." Quill dropped his gaze and let out a shaky breath. "It said you were all 'obstacles to true justice'." He darted his gaze over each man again before lowering it to study the threadbare blanket. "I guess that means you must be the good guys if that bloody bastard back there was one of the bad guys."

James tapped Quill's forehead with a thick finger. "Watch your tongue." His tone mild and non-condemning, he pushed the boy's head down against his chest, wrapping an arm tighter around the now trembling body.

Burke asked, "How much of this file did you read?"

"All of it."

Quill's mind raced over the possible consequences to him if anyone learned he knew what was in the entire folder of files. He would be killed if he was lucky, tortured for the information if he wasn't so lucky.

"But just that and one other. That's all I had time

for."

He pressed his face deeper into James' clothing. His mother always said he was a terrible liar. She could tell at a glance when he was up to no good. Kevin and Liam had often teased him about his inability to bluff during a card game, poking fun at the nervous, jittery body language that overtook him the moment he tried.

The sudden memory of his murdered friends brought a fresh lump to his throat and he choked back a muffled sob, too tired and too distraught to care if these men thought him weak or immature because of it.

"He's gotta be making this up." Burr said.

"Bollocks! You'll see soon enough. They'll send you to Eritrea and then you'll see, but it'll be too late because you'll be dead." Quill wheezed between sentences, fighting to keep his breathing under control.

"I can't see any reason why he'd make it up, Jackson." Weston rubbed one hand over the denim-clad legs in his lap as he talked. "And if it is true, this goes deeper than a corrupt faction of MI5. It would have to be a sanctioned operation from a higher governmental level to be in an actual dossier within MI5. There might even be a cooperating authority within our own military."

"Do you know what you're saying, Ray?" Burr's voice was incredulous at the suggestion, but a hint of worry had crept into his eyes.

Always calm, Weston nodded, a solemn, grim line set to his mouth. "Yes, I do, Jack. I know exactly what I'm saying. How else would MI5 know we were being sent on a mission to Eritrea next time out if they aren't working with someone from our side? We have to be very careful here."

Burke cast a questioning look at his remaining

teammate. "What about you, Ethan? What do you think?"

James took a deep breath and let it out before looking up from the matted head of hair he had tucked under his chin.

"Well now, Daniel, I think what the boy said goes along way in explaining what happened back there tonight–why Crowe would have orders to kill those boys–eliminate anyone who mighta read those files. Once we gathered up the hardware, all they'd have left to deal with would be three corpses to bury and another successful mission to report. None of us woulda been the wiser about those files."

"Christ on wheels." Burr pounded a heavy fist into the dashboard of the van. "That's premeditated murder." He shot a guilty look at Burke. "It's not like it hasn't been a part of our orders before, but those boys sure didn't deserve to die. Computer hackers and world dictators are *not* on the same criminal scale."

Weston gave his flustered teammate a reassuring grin and clapped him on the shoulder. "No one's saying they are, Jack. I think all of us would agree with you there. Crowe was the only one involved, so there's no one to rat him out. His men were just as shocked as we were."

"We're looking at a peck of trouble, Daniel," James added.

"If this is anywhere near the truth, we're fucked." Burr reached back and flipped a stray corner of the blanket back up over Quill's shoulder in a gruff, awkward display of caring.

"Why'd you decide to tell us about the file, son?" Burke asked.

Quill hesitated a moment before answering. "Y-you stopped him from k-killing me. You're...you protected...you wouldn't let the others take me away." His voice dropped low, every whispered word crackling with emotion. "You kept your promise."

A wry smile twisted Burke's face. "I always keep my promises. Remember that."

He squeezed Quill's thin shoulder, then turned back around in his seat to face the front window.

"What do we do with the boy?" James looked down to see Quill's one bloodshot eye staring up at him. "Don't know 'bout you three, but I'm not too keen on turning him over to anybody until we know who to trust."

"We're not going to, at least not now. Jackson, get us back on the road, our extra twenty minutes are ticking away."

Burke gestured to the left. "Make a left turn at the next crossroads. There's a place we can use for a safe house not far from here. An old friend's place he keeps handy for certain problems he runs into occasionally. We'll split up there. Ray and I can make some calls, set things in motion stateside. There should be a car we can use there too."

"You know some of the oddest people, Daniel. Lucky for us." Burr pulled the van back onto the road and drove off into the morning twilight. "Head back to the base?"

"You and Ethan are." Burke glanced out his side window. "The boy won't be safe if their side gets their hands on him. I don't know if the four of *us* are safe. We need to be on friendlier ground, someplace where we have a little influence and money to help balance out the power."

"You have a plan." Smug admiration rang in Burr's tone.

"Indeed, I do. At least the start of one."

All three of the other men nodded. Burke was the master at the planning and execution of the complex and unattainable.

Weston's boyish face lit up with anticipation. "I'll call my dad. It's early, but no one in Washington sleeps anyway."

Burke looked at him in the mirror hanging over the visor. "And I'll call the biggest political financial backer on the East Coast that approves of military spending. Mother always likes to hear from me, no matter what time it is in New York."

"What do we do with Junior here in the meantime?" Burr gestured to indicate Quill.

"For that, we call the other Washington. I know just the man for the job." Burke relaxed back into the seat.

Chapter Ten

Jackson Burr pulled into the car bay of a deserted garage and parked next to a dark sedan, watching the huge automatic door lumber closed behind the van. The door smacked the floor and Burke got out, entering the dimly light haven that smelled of oil and gasoline.

Burke waited for Ray Weston to ease out from under Quill's legs and pull both of their gear bags from the back of the van. Burke moved forward to intercept James as he slid over on the seat to hand off the injured teenager.

James eased Quill away from his chest, wrapping the thin blanket more securely around him as he started shifting the slight weight into Burke's waiting arms. "Make sure you get a good grip under that splint, Daniel. Don't let that knee take any weight for a good long spell. And keep him sitting up. Breathing's easier that way." James stepped back while Burke helped Quill settle into the back seat of the dark sedan. "Don't forget, you've got his inhaler. Don't let him use it too often, 'bout every four hours, but don't wait too long either. Might hafta take him to a hospital if'n those lungs don't ease up soon."

Patient and obedient, Burke listened to every order his sergeant issued, mentally cataloging all the instructions Ethan reeled off, wondering offhand when he'd lost control of this situation. Quill didn't know how lucky he was to be given a reprieve from James' over-attentive hovering.

Burr stuck his head out the open passenger door

and yelled at James. "For Christ's sake, Ethan, get the hell in here. Daniel and Ray can handle it, you old momma grizzly. Let the man get on with saving our asses."

James tucked one hand behind his back and flipped Burr the finger.

"I think I've got it, Ethan, thanks." Burke bit back a grin, barely managing to keep a straight face.

"Don't pay him no mind, son. He's got a burr under his saddle." James patted Quill's good leg and winked at him before turning away.

James tossed a casual salute at Burke and climbed into the front seat of the van. "Give him something for the pain when you can, Daniel. And make sure he eats something."

Burr punched James hard in the shoulder. "Would you stop already?"

James rolled his eyes and sighed. "How 'bout I show you just how contrary a grizzly really gets when someone keeps poking at it with a pointy stick?"

"Oooh, I love it when you talk dirty."

"Dickhead."

"See what I mean?"

Burke consoled James with a pat on the shoulder. "I'll remember everything, Ethan." He leaned in the open window of the van. "Take your time heading back. That'll give us a few extra minutes headstart. Report in and give our regrets to the commander. Explain the situation. Tell him I decided to make some changes and I'll report in soon. You know the song and dance, Jack."

Burr grinned and nodded. "Cloud the issue, deflect their attention to a minor item, point them in the wrong direction and get the hell out of town."

"You got it. General Weiss will fall all over himself

trying to turn this into a political coupe. Let him, as long as it means he's keeping MI5 busy." Burke raked a hand through his hair. "I don't want anybody to start looking for this kid before we can get him out of the country."

James nodded. "We'll dangle the hardware back there under his nose," he gestured toward the rear of the van. "That'll keep the old buzzard busy for awhile."

"We'll get in contact with you as soon as we get the kid settled with Ellison. You should be back in the States by then. Find out everything you can. We'll make a plan after we know more." Burke thumped the van door with his fist twice. "Now get out of here. Buy us some time. I'll use our usual method of contacting you once we've got things set up."

"You got it, Bossman. We'll see you three stateside." Burr waited for the automatic opener to finish raising the garage door. The van wasn't even in drive before the two big men started their good-natured bickering.

"Nice hand gesture back there, Mr. Manners. Good example to set."

"The boy didn't see it. Unlike that string of cursing you let loose every other breath. It's not like he can't hear."

"Cursing? There ain't no gypsy blood in these here veins, son. That's swearing. This is pure Pennsylvania steel mill worker blood in this magnificent body. No one can swear like a steelman. It's a part of my heritage."

"Well, try. Little pitchers."

"Little pitchers? Little *pitchers*? I can't believe you *actually* said that..."

Shaking his head at the continuing squabble, Burke waited until the van cleared the archway, then lowered the reinforced garage door. He walked back to the open car door in time to help Weston tuck a couple of bed pillows under Quill's leg. There was already one under his head.

Weston glanced up at Burke as he worked. "I borrowed these from the apartment upstairs. Hope no one minds."

"I didn't get you the keys yet."

"Picked the lock." Weston gave him an innocent look and shrugged. "It was faster."

"What about the security system?"

"Bypassed it. It's pretty outdated. Your friend should really look into a new one." Weston's expression changed from wide-eyed innocence to wide-eyed guilt. "Think I should leave him a note with some suggestions on it?"

Burke shook his head in amazement. "Don't worry about it. I'm sure he'll be grateful for the advice, some other time. We've got things to do."

"How long are we going to be here? Do we have time to get him cleaned up?" Wrinkling his nose, Weston added, "He's beginning to smell worse than my after shave and that can't be good."

Taking a whiff of the air, Burke sniffed, grimaced and rubbed a hand under his nose. "I guess we'd better make time. We're never going to get him on a plane looking like this anyway, even a private one."

"Not without being arrested, anyway."

Quill hadn't given them the slightest indication he was listening to them until now. "Try being this close to it, arsehole."

"Hey." Burke yanked the blanket away from the boy's startled face and leaned into the car to hover over him. "You've already been told about that mouth of yours, son. If you want me to scrub out the inside of your mouth after I get done with the outside, you just keep up the attitude. Understand?"

Quill blinked his one usable eye at Burke.

Burke hardened his glare and tilted his head to one side, unhappy with the silence.

Quill finally stammered out a raspy, "Okay."

"Glad we understand each other." Burke retreated a few inches to hand Weston his cell phone. "Ray, you start with the phone calls. I'll go get something to clean him up with and find us something to eat."

"Not willing to risk the wrath of old Momma Bear, huh?"

"I'm not that brave." Burke smacked the younger man on the top of his head. "Or that stupid. You'd tell on me."

"Would not. Not under threat of extreme pain and bodily harm. Wild horses couldn't drag it out of me."

"What if Ethan asked nicely?"

"Well, that's all together different. Then I'd have to tell him, if he asked politely." Ray paused a moment to give it some thought. "Which...Ethan always does...so...I'd have to say...you were right in the first place. I'd tell on you." He nodded to himself. "Yep, pretty much right away."

"I wouldn't stand a chance."

"You'd be bear food."

"Is that right, Corporal?" Burke gave the younger man a fierce glare.

Shuffling away, Weston said, "Maybe I'll just go make those calls now."

Burke grinned. Despite all they had seen and done over the years, Weston still managed to retain the heart and soul of a choirboy. And the manners. Burke made a mental note to talk to Ray's mother about the Sister sisters' undue influence during Ray's formative years.

Just as he was about to head up into the apartment, he heard a faint, but clear proclamation from Quill in the back seat of the car. "Daft as brushes, both of them."

Burke headed up the stairs muttering a proclamation of his own. "Mouthy little shit. Why do I think my life just got a lot more complicated?"

Chapter Eleven

As General passed behind them for the umpteenth time, Burr rolled his eyes and glanced up at James, then straightened into an even more rigid stance than he had been maintaining for the last forty minutes as the General rounded in front of them again. Forty long minutes while General Sherman Weiss vented and fumed, paced and hollered, thumped his desk in outrage and let the entire world within hearing distance know he was unhappy.

Burr took a measure of comfort from the fact all of the General's ire wasn't directed at James and himself. Oh, no, the pompous ass was heaping equal disfavor on the missing Weston and Burke, MI5 in general, Lt. Crowe in particular, as well as a respectable dose for Commander Richmond, the Brixton Police, computer geeks, and the whole of society under the age of forty. The man was florid with rage. A slight tick hammered at the corner of one eye in time to his pounding of the desktop.

It really wasn't too bad, Burr decided. The more time the man spent listening to the sound of his own voice, the less time he had to think about where the other half of his team and their lone suspect/murder witness had disappeared to. Considering the man's random train of thought, it could take hours before the question came up.

The sudden silence brought Burr back from his musings. A quick glance up at James confirmed his suspicions he had been asked a direct question, one he hadn't heard.

James stepped in and fielded the General's remark with his smooth southwestern charm.

"Begging your pardon, General, but I'm sure an officer of your caliber's familiar with the Special Forces code of conduct, sir. Colonel Burke thought it best if the suspect was moved to a more secure location. And I don't have to remind a man with as distinguished a service record as yours, just how important it is for a field team to retain the ability to restructure mission plans as circumstances change."

"More secure than an Allied Air Base?" Weiss's voice was incredulous, but wary.

Back on balance again, Burr jumped back in. "MI5's reach does extend to any person on British soil, sir. The government might be embarrassed enough by their man's actions to insist on the boy being handed over to them."

Weiss's face took on a resigned, hopeful expression, his shoulders dropping. "That might be for the best. After all, he is a British citizen, of age and all of that. Old enough to answer for his criminal deeds."

"That part's debatable, sir. The boy says he's over eighteen, but I'll bet a check on his birth records kicks that fairy tale in the butt." Burr backpedaled at the sudden frown creasing Weiss's heavily jowled face. "Sir."

James glanced at Weiss. Burr waded in again. "Who knows who's involved in this, sir? Lt. Crowe indicted he was acting on orders from higher up. Who's to say the boy won't meet a similar fate as his friends if we release him back into MI5's custody before they investigate Lt. Crowe's claims?"

James let his southern boy righteousness out. "Excuse me for saying so, General, but that'd make us all party to murder, if'n we let that child fall into the wrong hands before we knew he'd be safe."

Weiss paled a little at the suggestion, then blustered. "No one is going to be allowed to harm the boy, suspect or not. He's in the US Army's custody, Sergeant."

Seeing an opening of tremendous leverage Burr moved in for the clincher. "Commander Burke saw it that way too, sir."

Uncertainty overtook Weiss's troubled face, his lips twitching into a grim, hard line.

Burr pushed on. "Knowing the high standard of integrity you hold the men under your command to, General, he knew he could count on you to help him protect an already traumatized young person. Commander Burke was depending on you to use your political savvy and persuasiveness to hold off any forward assault the government interests might make while he did what the Army trained him to do–complete the mission and ensure the best possible outcome."

"He said that? Burke actually said I had political savvy?" Indecision played across Weiss's face.

Burr nodded once and relaxed enough to catch the man's suspicious eye. "I've heard him mention, more than a few times, your role in the Colfer incident a few years ago, sir."

The minor incident had been a small political disaster. Weiss had little actual part in the event, but in an effort to gain recognition, had managed to interfere with and confuse the issue to the point that he actually looked like a hero when the dust cleared. All the parties involved were anxious to forget the incident had ever happened, all except Weiss.

Noting a small, wry smile of amusement tugging

at the older man's mouth, Burr continued. "There's always a note of awe in the Commander's voice when he speaks of it, sir." Burr decided to take a chance the smile on the General face was real. "He also wonders why an officer with your obvious sterling background...makes the change to...agrees to play...that is to say, sir, accepts the role of political liaison between the Allied Forces when you could be servicing in other...more fulfilling, less frivolous, capacities."

Burke never failed to wonder at why the man kept his position. Political appointment or not, it was a high profile assignment, and in the right hands, a pivotal position of power. Burke speculated Weiss was far brighter and savvier than he gave the appearance of being, considering his long and distinguished service record prior to his being appointed to his current position.

But the General now displayed little of the qualities that showed him to be an outstanding officer during his years with the Allies Services. In short, Sherman Weiss was in effect, a put out to pasture buffoon. Burke thought it was an act.

"Is that so, Sergeant?" Weiss' voice had turned very soft.

Burr glanced at the General's face again, and for the first time, caught sight of a twinkle of burning intellect in the man's gray eyes. He suspected Burke had been right.

"Yes sir. The Commander has commented on your varied abilities a number of times. He says his mother remembers when you even played bit roles on the stage for a while when you were in your twenties. " Burr managed to color a bit, even with his dark complexion, adding, "But until now, I thought he was...ah, overestimating the situation, sir."

Burr traded understanding looks with James, who knew where Burr was headed. He, too, had listened to Burke's idle musings on Weiss's past abilities and uncharacteristic current blunders, chalking them up to old age along with Burr. By Weiss' surprised, grudging expression, they should have trusted Burke's instincts on this one.

"What does Burke need done from this end, gentlemen?" Weiss' confused bluster was gone, replaced with a cutting gleam in his appraising gaze.

Both Burr and James squirmed in place, aware they had underestimated this man. Burr mustered the courage to look the General in the eye. "Time, General, just enough time to get the kid out of the country safely."

"And maybe something to keep 'em off the scent of their trail, sir. Sorta like throwing a fox into the hen house, so the coyote can make off with the sheep." James shot a shy, self-conscious smile at Weiss, a look so out of place on a man of his imposing size and stature, that Weiss had to smile back. "If'n ya cipher my meaning, General."

"Indeed, Sergeant James." Weiss sat back into his chair and allowed himself a genuine smile of anticipation. "A distraction it is then, gentlemen." He eyed both men with a narrow, speculative gaze. "Dismissed."

They both saluted and filed towards the office door, relieved and more than a little surprised at the turn of events.

"One more thing, Sergeants."

They stopped cold at Weiss' warning tone, turning around to face a hard, calculating stare. "I hope you both appreciate the seriousness of what you've learned here today and understand it goes no further than this office, and quite likely, will never be spoken of again."

Burr glanced at James, seeking silent permission to answer for both of them. A subtle, familiar flicker of James' eyes was all he needed. "Yes, sir. We understand that. Thank you, sir, for trusting us."

"Yes, well...give my regards to your very astute Commander Burke. I hope he knows what he's doing. Thank him for the tip off. It wouldn't do to overplay my role here. I'll be sure to be more careful in the future." He gave the waiting men one last appraising gaze. "There's a transport leaving for the States in thirty minutes. Be on it. Now get out of here. I have a distraction to set into motion."

Chapter Twelve

Daniel Burke shifted his weight from one foot to the other, and leaned against the thin cushion of the hospital stretcher. Each little movement caused its vinyl covering to squeak and crinkle. The sound was muted and indistinct, but Burke found himself annoyed by it. After all that had happened over the last twelve hours, the young man beside him deserved more comfort than a hard stretcher in a cold, sterile cubicle.

Patting Quill's back to help ease his panic, Burke placed his other hand on the boy's chest and applied a gentle, but firm pressure to persuade Quill to relax back against the raised support of the stretcher.

"Relax, son."

One glazed eye turned to stare up at him, unfocused and wide with increasing panic. Quill's hand was clamped over the clear plastic mask strapped over his nose and mouth, as if clinging to it would increase the amount of oxygen being blown into his face. Burke watched the medicated mist the mask provided seep out from behind its edges and curl up to disappear into the cool air of the room.

Burke brushed Quill's hair away from his face. He had managed to wash most of the blood and gore out of it at the garage back in England, but the curls had become tangled and fly away on the long plane trip to the States, most of which Quill had slept through. It wasn't until they left the private airfield in Seattle that Quill started having difficulty breathing. It was a poor time to find out his inhaler was empty.

"Relax a little bit. I've got you."

Moving in closer, Burke wrapped his arm around Quill's back and forcefully eased him back. After a moment of resistance, he felt some of the tension drain out of the trembling muscles of the boy's back. Despite the fact this was the second breathing treatment Quill had been given since their arrival in the emergency department, an audible wheeze continued to rasp with each rapid breath the teenager took.

A shiver shook the slender frame and Burke released his grip long enough to accept a second blanket from Ray's offering hand, wrapping it around Quill's upper body. The corner of the blanket snagged on the short piece of tubing attached to the IV catheter they had inserted in Quill's left arm and the boy jumped at the unexpected jab of pain.

Burke worked the blanket free and slid his arm back around the hunched shoulders, surprised when Quill's head dropped down to rest on his chest, upper torso pressed tightly against him. He could feel Quill's heart hammering against his rib cage at a startling rate. The small gesture of trust amazed him, and brought that sharp flash of tightness to his chest. This time though it was a pleasant sensation.

A muffled voice from under his chin drew Burke's attention. "Never been...this bad...before." That one glazed eye peered up from under heavy, red-rimmed lids. "Guess the air here...doesn't agree with me." Quill rolled his head to one side and blinked, trying to bring Burke into focus. "It's a bit scary...never been in casualty." Giving up the battle to see straight, Quill rolled his head back down onto its former resting-place. "Don't like strangers...poking at me."

Burke looked up and caught Ray's eye over the jungle of tangled hair. Both men shared a look of mutual guilt, knowing there were going to be a lot more strangers in Quill's immediate future for the boy to deal with.

The brief respite only lasted a few minutes before a nurse pulled back the curtain and entered the cubicle. Quill jumped at the sudden invasion, the jittery restlessness caused by the medications fueling his exhausted efforts to breathe. He lifted his head from Burke's chest to shift position on the narrow stretcher again, one hand still glued to the mask. Burke prepared to release him and back away until Quill's free hand latched onto his sleeve and the boy's forehead pressed back into his shoulder, blocking out the newcomer.

The nurse raised her eyebrows at the obvious dismissal and looked at Burke for an explanation. "My name's Lisa. I'm one of the nurses here. I'm taking over for Kathy, her shift's over. How's he doing?" The question was meant for Quill, but it was clear the distressed teenager wasn't talking now.

"This is his first emergency room visit. He's a little overwhelmed." Burke gave her one of his most charming smiles, dismissing Quill's response as normal. "I'm sure you understand how panicked they get when they can't breathe."

"I'm surprised this is his first ER visit if the inhaler you showed me is the only thing he's been using to help his asthma." The nurse walked over to the opposite side of the stretcher from Burke and put a stethoscope on Quill's back. After listening for a few seconds over each lung, she pulled the earpieces from her ears and swung the stethoscope around her neck. "He's a little better, but not as much as we'd like him to be." She slipped the mask off of Quill's face and turned the oxygen flow meter on the wall off. "This one's done. In about twenty minutes we'll do another treatment and check his peak flow again."

Quill let her remove the mask from his face, but he refused to let her take it out of his hand. He buried himself deeper into Burke's side, one hand still clutching the oxygen tubing and mask, every muscle twitching.

Burke tightened his grip on Quill without realizing it. "What's wrong with his inhaler? I mean, I know medical care in England isn't exactly like ours here, but I'm sure his doctor would have prescribed what's best for him."

"You live in England?"

"No, I don't. But he did, up until today." Burke contemplated all the possible stories he could tell to keep suspicions at bay with the medical staff. Knowing he was dealing with professionals trained to recognize a false story, especially when a young person was concerned, he decided on the tale closest to the truth.

"He and his mother lived there. He's in the States for a bit, spending time with me while we get some issues sorted out." Burke gave her a sheepish smile followed by a 'it's-an-embarrassing-personal-problem' grimace, letting his natural charm do the rest.

"Divorced, huh?" Interest lit up her face, despite her obvious efforts not to run an appraising eye over him. Dressed in a black turtleneck and black dress slacks that accented his fair coloring and blond hair, he knew he cut an attractive figure. "That's...too bad."

The lack of sincerity made it sound congratulatory instead of conciliatory.

"Well, thank you. The sudden changes have been

126

hard for both of us."

"I'm sure. Anyway," she shook herself to shift mental gears back to the subject at hand, "as I was saying, that type of inhaler is meant for someone with emphysema, not asthma. It really wouldn't help him much. I don't think the drug has a different effect in England than it does here." She gave Quill a thoughtful glance. "It's almost like he's been using someone else's meds."

Quill turned away from the nurse, while Burke furrowed his brow.

The nurse smiled at the sight of the comforting, protective huddle Quill sought out with the man she assumed was his father. Shrugging away the mystery, she caught the eye of both Burke and Weston. "I'll be back in about fifteen minutes to set up that next treatment for him." Pulling the curtain closed behind her, the nurse strode out of the room.

The curtain was still swaying when Burke pried the clinging boy off his chest and moved him back enough so he could tilt Quill's face up to meet his eye. "Want to tell me where you got the inhaler?" Burke took Quill by the forearms and braced him upright.

Quill gave a non-committal shrug and forced his good eye to focus on Burke's solemn face, looking for signs that would allow him to anticipate the man's reactions. The slight movement of his shoulders dislodged the blankets and Ray stepped up to his side to tug them back into place. Quill shot Ray a brief, surprised look when he remained standing and began rubbing Quill's back. The boy darted his gaze back to Burke.

"Nicked it."

"You stole it? From whom? What made you think

it would help with asthma?" Burke had to work to keep from gritting his teeth. "Don't you realize how dangerous it is to take medications that aren't prescribed for you? And what about the person you took it from? What did they do the next time they needed it and it wasn't there? Did you even think about that?"

"He had another one. I wouldn't have...nicked it...if he hadn't." Quill's face fell and his words came out in a halting stammer.

"Kev and Liam and me...were in a luncheon. There's an old nob an' his wife...sitting at the next booth. He'd a bad time...with his breathing. Took him a minute...to find his inhaler. The wife found one...in her purse the same time...he got one out of a pocket."

He shot a harsh, accusing glare up at Burke. "He had two of 'em. He's huffing and wheezing...just like I do...and it helped him." He dropped his gaze to study the pattern of the weave in Burke's sweater. "They forgot one...on the table...when they left." He shrugged, trying to lessen the importance of his actions. "So I nicked it."

Keeping his tone mild, Burke asked, "Did they come back for it?"

Quill leaned into Ray's firm massage of his back, soaking up as much of the comfort as he could before it was taken away from him. "Maybe. Don't know. Didn't hang around...long enough to...find out."

Ray said, "That wasn't very nice." Quill just shrugged his shoulders and averted his face away from Ray's.

Inhaling a deep, steadying breath, Burke massaged the back of the boy's neck. "It certainly wasn't the best solution you could have come up with." He felt Quill duck his head lower, "but considering the circumstances, I can see how you'd be tempted. Not being able to breathe must be one of the most frightening things that can happen to a person."

Quill's head popped up, a look of genuine surprise on his battered, young face. He whispered, "It's bloody awful. I'd do anything...to keep it from happening."

Ray stilled his hand, but left it on Quill's back. "Why didn't you just go see a doctor? England's health care is easily available."

"Yeah, if you want...some useless, old bloke...at a crowded clinic. Besides, they make you...fill out all kinds of forms...before they'll see you, and they want...NI numbers and such...to prove you're on your own." Quill's voice grew tight, his words coming in shorter bursts of sharp, clipped phrases. He shifted his weight on the hard stretcher, grimacing when each tiny squirming movement made his injured knee throb.

"So what's the problem?" Ray kept his voice soft and soothing, the tone neutral. "You're over eighteen, right?"

The sudden flush of color to Quill's unbruised cheek told both men Ray had hit a nerve. "Course I am. Nineteen...two weeks ago." His gaze darted around the room avoiding contact with either of the men. "It's just...the paperwork. I-I...I didn't want...any record on me...that's all. Bloody hell! The government...watches those...kinds of places. Don't want them...to know...anything more...about me."

The last was sentence was gasped out between harsh, squeaky breaths. Quill shrugged Ray's hand off his back. Drawing his good leg up, he hunched forward and rested his forehead on his knee, trying to give his chest more room to expand, hands clutching the thin blanket closer around his shoulders.

Ray let his hand drop to his side and met Burke's gaze over the top of Quill's bowed head.

Burke tilted his head towards the chair by the wall and Ray retreated to it. Burke scrubbed one hand over his face, fortifying himself with a deep breath and slipped a firm hand under Quill's chin, forcing his face up. Crouching down a few inches, he stared into the flushed, bruised face to find Quill's eyes closed tight.

"Look at me."

Quill tried to pull his face away and Burke tightened his hand just enough to keep his hold firm. Burke kept his tone calm, but firm, leaving no doubt in anyone's mind he expected to be obeyed. "Must be that hearing problem you had back at the warehouse flaring up again. I said, look at me, son."

A sudden rush of tears cascaded down Quill's face as it crumbled. One hand shot out knocking Burke's fingers away from his face with enough ill-timed force to break open the healing split in the corner of his mouth. Heedless of the fresh damage, he struck out again, trying to push Burke away.

Ray sprung up from his seat and resumed his place at Quill's other side, but refrained from interfering.

"Bastards...why don't...you just...leave me...*alone*." Quill continued to shove at any large, moving object that came close, his voice raising to a shout. "I don't...*need you*...or your *sodding* rules...or your...your *fucking* protection...or your...your...your *damn pity*...I *want*...to be...left the...*bloody...fucking...hell...alone*."

The curtain closing off the cubicle to the rest of the Emergency Department rattled sharply to one side. The nurse and the doctor, whom had first treated Quill, moved to the stretcher, aggressively displacing both Burke and Weston. Both men stepped back and stood against the wall behind the stretcher, out of their way, but near enough to help if needed. The doctor tried to listen to Quill's lungs while the nurse made soothing noises meant to quiet and comfort.

"Quill, it's okay. Just settle down. You're not helping things by getting upset. Slow down." She tried to rub his arm, but he batted off her attempts to touch him.

"Leave...me...alone...just...lea...ah...ah..."

Unable to draw an adequate breath, Quill's anger transformed into panic. His eyes darted about the room, bouncing from nurse to doctor and back again, then flying up to the take in the unfamiliar face of a stranger hovering at the open curtain. Fending off multiple pairs of grabbing hands, Quill tried to launch off the stretcher.

Burke pushed past the stunned doctor and lunged his upper body across the narrow stretcher, managing to hook his arms around the fleeing boy's waist just before Quill's hips left the mattress.

Quill's worn, gray turtleneck sweater rode up during the battle and Burke realized he could feel every rib under the baby-soft, clammy skin. There had definitely been too many missed meals for this kid. With one quick heave, Burke lifted the struggling boy back onto the bed.

Voice harsher than he had intended, Burke barked out, "That's enough," but words weren't getting through to Quill right now. Only small, muffled grunts and gasps escaped the struggling boy.

Burke grabbed both flailing wrists, crossing them over Quill's chest, pinning the squirming body tight against his own. Right on cue, a mask appeared in front of him, spewing a new dose of mist and oxygen. Burke shifted so one hand was free to clamp the mask over Quill's face and hold both it and the boy in place.

Whispering in the ear pinned under his chin, Burke let instinct take over, flashing back to the rare times during his childhood he had needed to be soothed and comforted.

"Ssh, ssh. It's okay, son, it's okay. Relax, take a breath, relax and breathe, relax. I've got you now. I've got you. It's going to be all right. Just settle down and breathe. I'm here."

Quill continued to resist until Burke's soft, continual string of words broke through his terror.

Burke winked at Quill, never breaking the chant of reassuring noises. Quill went limp and curled into Burke. He closed his eyes, bringing one hand up to cling to the man's sleeve while the other covered Burke's hand holding the mask to his face.

The boy's reaction brought a burst of pleasure to Burke. He adjusted his hold to settle Quill into a more comfortable position.

"I was beginning to question the validity of your relationship with this young man, Mr. Burke." The doctor glanced from Burke to the bowed head buried in the folds of the man's sweater. "In light of his obvious, recent injuries, we have to be careful, for his sake." He paused, lingering over the sight of Quill's fingers twisting tighter into the knit fabric. "But I can see he wants you near, despite his behavior to the contrary."

Burke felt Quill's hold spasm at the doctor's accusation, then relax as the anxiety of the moment recessed. He kept his expression relaxed and understanding, even when the uncharacteristic urge to knock out a few of the man's teeth for upsetting Quill again surged through him.

"You'll have to forgive him, Doctor. The last twenty-four hours have been rough. Between leaving his home, the accident I explained he was in just before we left, the unexpected death of his friends and his asthma acting up, he's more than a little off balance."

"Extreme emotional turmoil doesn't help his asthma. Does he always react to stress this way?"

"I couldn't really tell you. I haven't spent much time with him before today." A disapproving look settled on the doctor's face, which Burke felt compelled to wipe off — preferably with his fist. Making a mental note for himself, Burke decided if these aggressive reactions around the boy kept up, he was going to need to add a couple of extra hours to his workout sessions with the punching bag.

"He and his mother lived in England all his life. I'm a Lieutenant Commander with the Army's Special Forces. I don't have much say in where I go or how long I stay there, and no one outside of my team and a few superiors even know where I am at any given time, sometimes for months at a stretch."

Amazed at how easy it was to reveal so many of his own heartfelt worries this way, Burke just let his insecurities have a free voice. At least it should be convincing. It was also a little unnerving how easy it was to adapt the facts of Quill's life to fit into his own. He *could* have been the boy's father, depending on when he was really born, a fact Burke was determined to find out soon.

"It doesn't make it easy to have time for a personal life, no matter how much you may want it." Burke glanced at the man's nametag to be sure he'd remembered it right.

"Just because we're not in an active war, Doctor Litton, doesn't mean all the fighting has ended."

He tightened his hold on Quill just a little. "There's always someone who needs a little extra looking after."

Doctor Litton's olive complexion deepened. He cleared his throat, nodding his head in Quill's general direction. "I can see that. I think you're just the man to do it, too."

Now that Quill was relaxed, the doctor re-examined his breathing, concentrating on each lung field for several long moments. He removed the stethoscope from around his neck and pointed at the mask clamped to Quill's face.

"He's going to need a couple more of those before things clear up enough to let him go home. And that's if he stays calm. I'd like to medicate him with a little something to keep him relaxed." The nurse nodded at the doctor and left the room.

A muffled, low, "no," came out from under the mask. It was followed by a sharp, decisive and more authoritative, "yes" from Burke.

Instead of continuing with the rebellion, Quill only gave an exhausted sigh and dug his fingers deeper into Burke's sweater.

Burke repeated himself for the doctor's benefit. "That was a 'yes'. I think that'd be a good idea. He needs some rest. It's been a rotten day."

Doctor Litton nodded and left the room.

At some point earlier the nurse must have left the room, because she appeared now with a syringe in her hand. Without dislodging Quill's hold, she managed to inject the medication into his IV site, then left the room, promising to check back shortly to see if it was working.

Within minutes, Burke felt Quill relax against him and his breathing ease, as he drifted off into an exhausted, medicated sleep.

Movement at the end of the stretcher drew his attention. He watched Weston lift Quill's legs more fully onto the mattress, then bend over to prop a pillow under the immobilized leg.

Burke suddenly noticed a tall, dark man standing at the opening to the curtained room. He returned the newcomer's highly amused smile with a wry, self-conscious grin. Being caught in such an uncharacteristic, compromising position of playing surrogate father made him blush, but not as much as he thought it would. He was pleased Quill had turned to him, even searched the room for him when he couldn't see Burke standing behind the stretcher earlier.

Weston glanced over at the man and waved. "Hey, Tim. Look what we got on our last European vacation."

The man's smile turned from amusement to genuine pleasure.

"Hey there, Ray." Tim Ellis gestured with an upturned thumb at the two other occupants of the room. "Let me guess. It followed you home and you want to know if you can keep it?"

The confused, guileless expression his teammates were so familiar with descended over Weston's face. "Well, no, actually." Faced with a polite, straightforward question, Weston did what he was taught to do, he answered honestly. "We want to know if *you* can keep it." Weston smiled at Ellis' stunned expression. "At least for a little while."

"What? Is this outrageous request for real?" Ellis looked to Burke for an answer.

Burke chuckled. "Give me a hand, Ray. I think he's considering refusing delivery of our package."

With Weston's help, he eased the boy into a semi-reclining position and worked his sweater out of the lax fingers tangled in the weave. Burke moved away from the bedside, gesturing the man out to the adjoining corridor. Once in the hallway, he stopped and made sure he could see the stretcher from where they stood.

Tim Ellis gave a low whistle of surprise. "You know, Daniel, every time you come to town my world goes a little crazy."

Burke shrugged. "Probably, but what are friends for if you can't come to them with a little problem?"

He decided to ignore the look of doubt and suspicion on Tim's face. "Tell me, my friend. How do you feel about spending the next few days evading probable top-notch military surveillance while harboring a kidnapped murder witness who's wanted for crimes against the British Crown? One who was brought into this country illegally, by me, is very likely an orphaned minor, who's been assaulted by an MI5 officer bent on murdering him after he witnessed the execution of his two best friends, and who is currently suffering the effects of mismanaged, brittle asthma?" He crossed his arms on his chest and leaned back against the wall.

Burke ignored Ellis' raised eyebrows and open mouth to say, "Sounds like a great way to spend a few days, doesn't it?"

Chapter Thirteen

A tall, redheaded nurse walked by, giving them a welcoming smile. Ellis stopped her to ask, "Is there a place we could duck into for more privacy? Someplace close?"

"Sure. Go through the door you're standing beside. It's a supply room. Hardly anyone needs to use it on this shift." She pointed to their left, then gave a little wave goodbye.

Ellis stared after her retreating figure, watching her hips sway under the stretch of her cotton scrubs as she walked down the hall, admiring how the jade color of her uniform brought out the red tones in her hair.

Burke watched the nurse depart, as well. Ellis saw Burke's glance and said, "Forget it. You'll be too busy. Kids and dating don't mix. I tried it once about a year after my wife died. It's more complicated than it looks."

Taken aback, Burke frowned. "There's zero room for a kid in a life like mine. You know that, Tim."

The men entered the deserted supply room. Burke stayed close to the door, peering out the window to be sure he had a good view of Quill's room. He tore his gaze away long enough to meet Ellis' stare. "I missed that boat a long time ago."

Ellis wrapped a long arm around Burke's shoulders. "You need someone in your miserable, self-centered life. He looks perfect for you."

"Judas priest!" Burke gave the man a dark scowl. "I promised I'd take care of him, protect him, but just until better choices become available. And that's where you come in, buddy."

Ellis threw up his hands. "No can do, Daniel. I don't need another teenager."

"Not permanently, you idiot." Burke lowered his voice, forcing Ellis to draw nearer. "I'm not sure who we can trust right now. MI5's involved in the killings in some fashion. I barely managed to stop one of their men from shooting this boy in the head." Burke shuffled his feet and shoved his restless hands into his pockets. "His injuries are from a murder attempt, not an accident. He witnessed two friends being gunned down in cold blood and was standing close enough to be covered in the splatter."

"Christ, no wonder he's a little stressed. Poor kid." Ellis darted an irritated glance toward Quill. "Where the hell are his parents?"

Burke gave a baffled shrug. "Missing father, no siblings. Word is the mother stepped out of the picture about eighteen months ago, for some reason I haven't figured out yet. The two guys killed during the mission were like older brothers to him."

Pity creased the detective's streetwise face. "That's a tough break."

"Yeah, it was. He's had a rough couple of days. I need a secure place to hide him, from both the US Army and the British government, while I check out a few odd things that've cropped up. The kid hacked into some pretty sensitive computer files. It's possible he knows something he shouldn't." Burke rubbed a hand over his jaw, feeling his frustration double.

Ellis asked, "Does he?"

"Maybe, but he's keeping most of it to himself if he does. He hasn't been in any shape to interrogate. He does

admit to reading two of the files, one about my team."
Burke gave a deep sigh and shifted his position, dropping
his voice lower. "I don't know what to believe. But if
what he says is true, my team is scheduled to be
eliminated during our next mission."

"Are you serious?" Ellis' whisper had a harsh,
angry edge to it, his complexion grew dark and deep
furrows creased his forehead.

"Dead serious." Burke nodded and shrugged. "It's
one of the things I need to investigate. I need to be careful
with this. Tip off the wrong people and we're all dead."

"Come on, Daniel. The moment you took him out
of their circle of control, you were all screwed. If this *was* a
sanctioned hit, they'll hunt him down no matter what."

"I know that. At least here, with us, he has a
chance. If we'd left him behind, he'd be dead by now. I
just have to find a place for him."

"You accepted the responsibility the minute you
conspired to keep him away from the authorities and took
him out of the country. Who does the kid have besides
you?" His tone took on a sour, demanding edge. "I'm
guessing the 'here illegally' part you mentioned earlier
means you left England by private means, bypassing the
usual airports, customs, and the need for trivial little
things like passports and visas."

Burke's eyes took on a fire that impressed even
Ellis' hard-nosed attitude.

"We couldn't leave him to be murdered. We had
to get him someplace safe as fast as we could. That didn't
leave official channels as an option."

He began counting off items on his fingers, one by
one. "They don't even have a Bill of Rights in England.
He's completely defenseless. Without a family to fight for

him, they can make him vanish. I stand a better chance at keeping him alive on my own home turf. Here, I have my rank, some solid political backing and a few very powerful friends in the right places to help find a safe place for him."

"Why don't you just consider keeping him yourself?" Ellis held up a hand to hold off the excuses he could already see forming. "Hold on a minute. I saw you with him. He trusts you."

"I can't do that." Burke's tone was firm.

"Why the hell not? Think about this, Daniel. If they really think he knows something they want kept quiet, nothing's going to stop them from coming for him. Not distance and not time." Ellis let the significance of his words settle into Burke. "Who could protect him better over the long term than you and your men?"

Burke sighed, looking older than his years. "You've done a great job with Ben since Debbie passed away. But I'm not you. Our circumstances are different."

Ellis dropped his tough guy veneer. "I understand that, but if the kid knows anything more, you can use the info to protect yourselves. It would be better to keep him with you until you're sure."

Ellis patted Burke on the shoulder. "Besides, you could use another focus in your life. One of these days, you're going to wake up and wonder where all the time went you planned to use on things you told yourself you'd do later. By then you'll have nothing to show for a lifetime of sacrifice and loyal service, except an aging body covered in scars, a tidy bank account and a really nice art collection."

Ellis gave the brooding man a mock punch. "It's not like the Army is the only thing you can do with your life. You have the financial means to do anything you want. Tour the world. Take a bigger interest in your family's banking concerns. Hell, start a business of your own. You're a smart man and, let me be perfectly clear here, a *Goddamn millionaire*. What the hell does the Army still have to offer you?"

Burke shook his head in denial. "I'm career Army, Tim." He waved a hand between himself and Ellis. "Our situations aren't the same." Burke turned away to stare down the busy hallway. "You left the service because your team died. My men still need me."

Ellis moved to stand in front of Burke, invading his personal space, his voice low, giving it a dangerous edge.

"That's right, Daniel. My men died." Ellis' eyes grew cold. "And remember why. They were sent to their deaths by our commanding officer. Sacrificed like expendable pawns in the name of bigger stakes to be won. How is that any different than what the boy says is waiting for your men? What about your obligation to protect them?" Compassion crept back into his voice. "Stay in the game long enough, buddy, and your number's bound to come up. My guess is you've outlived your usefulness, Commander."

Ellis glanced into Quill's room. "I believe the kid. I *know* it happens."

Burke stared through the open curtain at the too-slender figure of Quill Tarquin. Visions of time spent with family in his own home instead of some foreign country being shot at flickered through his thoughts, then moved to his three teammates. The four of them had been brothers-in-arms for so long they had become brothers in life.

Burke glanced back into the cubicle, smiling at the

sight of Weston tucking already-tucked blankets around the sleeping boy. Weston had taken to Quill from the first moment.

Weston was never self-conscious about giving his affection or trust to people he cared about. He never worried about putting his emotions on the line. He was a terrific soldier, one Burke was proud to have at his side and on his team.

"By the way, Ellis," Burke said, "it's a really *tidy* bank account. A really, *really* tidy bank account."

* * * * *

The boy began to stir as the conversation between Burke and Ellis ended. Burke waited while Quill blinked away some of the drug-induced sleepiness and showed an awareness of the other people in the room. Burke gestured towards the two men standing at the end of the stretcher.

"I want you meet a friend of mine, son. This is Tim Ellis. You're going to be staying with Tim for a few days while I figure out a plan of action."

One hand still resting on Quill's shoulder, Burke felt an immediate tensing of the boy's body. A rigid shudder ran through the boy from head to toe, vibrating so hard Burke's hand shook, but Quill remained silent, letting his frightened, angry glare do the talking for him.

Burke read the message loud and clear, shaking his head at the thought that he must be spending too much time with the kid if he could read his mind.

"Settle down. It's just for a few days. I–," Burke shot a dark look at Ellis, "*we* need to clear up a couple of things before we take you back to base. I needed someplace for you to stay where I know you'd be safe."

Quill shrugged Burke's hand off his head and

142

turned his face away to stare at the blank wall next to his bed. Burke took a deep breath and scowled at the amused, knowing look Ellis gave him.

"Okay, I get the message, you're not happy. I can understand that, but it doesn't change anything. Tim's a police detective. He can protect you while I figure out the best plan of action that'll keep you safe."

Quill swiveled his head back around to look at the man. He straightened himself up on the stretcher and looked Ellis in the eye. "Copper?"

Ellis started at the unfamiliar phrase, but nodded.

"Good. Arrest him." Quill turned his face to indicate a flabbergasted Burke. "For kidnapping."

"Why you ungrateful, conniving, little shit." Burke's jaw dropped open. From his seat by the wall, Weston dropped his head down to stare at the floor, struggling to keep from laughing out loud.

Quill ignored his savior's fuming remarks, elaborating with high-speed enthusiasm. "Nicked me, he did. Right out of the bloody country. Forced me to come with him here. Never once asked if I wanted to. And he had a gun. Arrest him."

Quill was breathing better, but his voice was still raw. He had to pause every few words to take a shaky breath, but Burke heard the disappointment and hurt in his soft, accusing voice.

Ellis managed to keep a straight face and he let his voice carry all of the menace and authority he could muster.

"Outside of the fact he saved your undeserving, disrespectful, scrawny ass from being shot, Colonel Burke is an agent of the US government. His actions were done in the performance of his assigned duties and are well within the guidelines of US Army jurisdiction. As such, they're not open to sanctions from criminal laws, young man." He let his intimidating stare hold the boy's glare until Quill averted his gaze.

"And that's 'Detective' to you, boy, but just plain 'sir' will do, too." Ellis waited a beat before demanding, "Understood?"

The word rang out like a shot, making Quill jump. He darted a look at the stranger, worrying the torn corner of his mouth with his teeth. Quill flinched when the detective laid a hand on his lower leg. Embarrassed by his own reaction, he spit out a rash reply. "I understand. Bloody wanker."

This time Burke intervened. He wanted Quill to feel secure, not frightened or rebellious. He took hold of Quill's chin and turned his face to look him in the eye. "Hold it right there, young man. Detective Ellis is a friend of mine and he's doing us, you and me, a favor. So can the attitude. I'm not just handing you off–."

"Dumping me."

Burke was surprised at the amount of bitterness the phrase contained. Clamping down on his building frustration, Burke ignored the interruption. "To just anyone for safekeeping. Ellis can watch out for you, protect you. He knows the military–what to look for and how to deal with it. He's experienced with these kinds of things."

Quill pulled his chin from Burke's grasp and shot Ellis a daring look filled with venom. "Make a hobby out of taking people against their will, too? Oh, I forgot *Detective, sir,* for you it's a bloody career choice."

Burke reacquired his hold on Quill's jaw. The boy winced as callused fingers brushed over bruises and tender, raw skin. One of Quill's hands latched onto Burke's wrist, startling the man with the coldness of the boy's touch.

"Watch your mouth. I'm not going to tell you again."

Quill neither pulled away nor pushed at Burke, but held on as if he was afraid the man would disappear if some type of physical contact didn't exist between them. His one accusing eye stared at Burke. He pulled Burke forward to bury his face in the warmth of the man's now misshapen sweater, his indistinct mumbling swallowed up by the thick, knit weave.

"What?" Burke tried pulling Quill back by his shoulders, but the boy tightened his grip.

Quill pushed his forehead into Burke's chest, freeing his mouth from the folds of the sweater, but only for as long as it took to repeat his plea. "Don't leave."

Burke frowned, rubbing one hand over the hunched back. "You'll be fine. You can trust Tim."

Frantic words came out in a rush between choked sobs and little, wheezy gasps. "Don't leave me. Take me with you. I'll be quiet. I won't get in the way. I'll do whatever you tell me to do. I'll-"

"Wait. Hold up there."

Burke darted a worried glance at Weston, who rose from the chair to stand at the opposite side of the stretcher from Burke, lending quiet support.

"None of that has anything to do with this. I need some time to make arrangements. It's not safe-"

"Please! I'll listen. I won't complain. I'm sorry I asked him to arrest you. I'm sorry!" Quill pulled back enough to make eye contact. "I swear, I won't be any trouble." His voice dropped to a faint whispering plea.

"Just don't go."

Burke held him at arm's length, hunching down until they were face to face. He tried to project as much reassurance as possible into his expression, enunciating each word clearly, wondering if anything he was saying was even getting through to the panicked kid. "*You're* not the problem here, the situation is. I'll be back. I just need to make arrangements — ensure your safety, deal with the charges against you, get your entry into the U.S. official, find you a place to live, somebody to watch out-"

Quill launched himself across the short distance between them again, his head rolling side to side on Burke's shoulder, babbling at top speed. "No! No, no, no, no. She said she'd come back too. But she *didn't*. You won't either. They'll kill you or you'll decide I'm...this's all too much trouble."

Whitened knuckles fisted deeper into his clothing. "Don't leave me behind. You're the only one I know here. Please. Please. I'll be good. You promised, you *promised*. Please, please, *please*."

Most of the soft pleading was in a whispery thin voice that rose and fell with each new gasped breath and ended with a strained sob. The last few words were so weak only Burke could hear them, each one tearing at his heart and battering at his crumbling resolve.

How the hell had this happened? He was a covert ops soldier, a man who had killed scores of men and destroyed entire clutches filled with the enemy. Why was denying this one mouthy, needy brat so hard to do?

The smart thing to do would be to just walk away. The boy would get over it and understand once everything was said and done. And if he didn't, what difference did it make? He wasn't Burke's concern once things got straightened out. In a few days, he'd never see the kid again. Leaving now was the only intelligent, professional thing to do.

Which was why even Burke was surprised when he awkwardly lifted Quill closer.

The curtain was pulled back and the nurse entered. She took one look at the shuddering form huddled against Burke, and listened to the light sobs and the raw gasping wheezes filtered through the thick weave of the man's sweater. She frowned at the group of men hovering around the stretcher. Grabbing the oxygen treatment mask off the wall, she filled it with more medication and turned the flow meter on. Worming her way between broad shouldered bodies, she struggled getting the mask into place on Quill's face, having to force it between them.

"You guys are never going to get out of here at this rate." She sighed and shook her head at the abundance of males. She ran another appraising glance over the men. "Not that I'm saying that's necessarily a *bad* thing, mind you."

Chapter Fourteen

Burke tapped Quill on the forehead with one finger to be sure the boy was paying attention behind the petulant, dark scowl he had plastered on his face.

"We'll be back as soon as we check out a few things, mainly the information you told us about from the stolen data. We'll figure out the best plan of action to keep you out of the wrong hands, until the bigger issue of who's responsible for the events that happened at the warehouse is discovered."

"When Kev and Liam were murdered by a sodding copp–policeman." Quill's nervous gaze flickered up to look at the detective leaning against the far wall. Burke guided his face back until he could look Quill in the eye.

"Lt. Eric Crowe is a British MI5 agent. Hopefully, by now, a soon-to-be ex-agent." Burke looked down for a brief moment to disguise the murderous look he knew was in his eyes. Past responses taught him it was a look that could scare even hardened soldiers, let alone a distraught teenager. He regained control of his anger and looked up. "Not an American police detective. You don't have anything to worry about here, son. You'll be in good hands until we come back."

Though his chin remained immobile in Burke's hand, Quill dropped his gaze, not openly challenging Burke's opinion, but still refusing to acknowledge his reassurances.

Sighing heavily, Burke tapped his 'I-want-your-attention' finger against Quill's cheek. "It'll only be a day or two at the most."

His efforts went unrewarded. He tapped again, but Quill's gaze remained lowered and the silence in the room dragged on. "Do you trust me?"

The muscles in Quill's jaw tightened and Burke felt him swallow several times in rapid succession before a tremor shook his hand, indicating Quill had nodded.

"Okay then. You trust me and I trust him," Burke said.

Quill stayed perfectly still for several long moments, then gave another brief, wordless nod.

"Good." Burke released Quill's jaw. One watery, blood-shot eye looked up at him.

"You really dumping me, then?" Quill's voiced cracked.

Dropping his chin to his chest, Burke leaned over to brace his arms on the stretcher on either side of Quill. He sucked in a frustrated breath and fought to keep from reaching out and shaking the boy.

"What in hell–*blazes* more can I do to convince you? I'm not leaving you behind. I'll be back, I promise. I always keep my promises."

The boy sniffed and rubbed his nose on his sleeve, dragging in a steadying breath. "You buggering off now?"

Quill's tone was less desperate, but an underlying note of hesitancy remained.

Steeling himself against another emotional tirade, Burke nodded. "Yeah, we are. The faster we get things in motion, the faster we can get back here."

Burke started to turn away, but a tug on his sleeve stopped him. He looked down to see Quill's fingers holding onto his coat.

"Wait." Quill's tone was hesitant. "I need to tell you

s-something."

Burke remained silent, waiting.

Quill swallowed and pulled his good leg up, wrapping his arms around it. "Didn't trust you much, you know,...before." Nervous, twitching fingers played with the rings on his fingers.

"But...now's a bit different." He sighed and rested his forehead on his folded arms, hiding his face from view. "It's going to happen soon, sooner than yours is."

All the men moved closer. A confused frown marred Burke's face. "What's going to happen?"

"From the bloody files." The words were whispery soft and strained. "The next...murder."

"What?" The word was a chorus spoken in three different voices, all startled and outraged.

Burke resisted the urge to shake Quill until his teeth rattled and demand a clearer explanation. Taking a deep, steadying breath, he leaned in and rested a hand on the boy's shoulder, ignoring the slight effort to pull away from his touch. He could feel small tremors run through the thin body with each shuddering breath the boy took. Just when he thought Quill had decided not to continue talking, the boy raised his head up and spoke, enunciating each sentence as if he was reading from a report lying in front of him.

"Colonel Brian Wright, codename 'Magpie'. Aged 37. Dark brown hair, gray eyes. Married, wife named Gina. Two children, Gary and Mark. Attached to the Allied Air Base at Hereford. On loan to Anti-terrorist Division, MI6."

He blinked and shifted his gaze until it met Burke's, then dropped it to stare at his lap.

Quill continued, "He's s-scheduled for

term...termination while on family...family holiday in Switzerland." His voice fell to a bare whisper. "They'd prefer the authorities were unable to...unable to retrieve any...physical evidence."

Burke took hold of both of Quill's elbows and gave him a demanding shake. "Are you sure about this? Very sure?"

Quill's face twisted into a miserable grimace and he gave a brief nod. "Aye."

"When?"

Quill drew in a fortifying breath and slowly blew it out. He licked at his dry, cracked lips. "Three days."

Burke closed his eyes for an instant and willed away the building frustration threatening to make him do physical harm to the kid. He opened his eyes to find Quill's guilt-ridden face still staring into his own.

Burke didn't have the heart to add to all the boy's other troubles. This situation wasn't the kid's fault. He was just unlucky enough to have launched himself into the middle of a covert military operation.

"That's quite a memory you have there." Weston cocked his head to one side and studied Quill. "Kind of like when you told us about Ethan's file." He watched twin stars of color bloom in Quill's cheeks, stark against the pallor of the rest of his face.

"Nothing special. Was important to remember it right, is all." Quill's mumble was soft and hesitant.

Ignoring the small audience in the room, Burke wrapped an arm around Quill's shoulders. "Don't worry about it. I'll check into it." He squeezed the back of Quill's neck. "Listen to Tim and behave yourself."

Burke patted Quill's back then released him. "Anything else you should let us know?"

A tense silence filled the room. Burke's voice became stern. "Did you read any of the other files, son?"

Quill lowered his eyes, darting them back and forth, never landing on one spot more than a few seconds at a time.

"No. Didn't have time."

Burke's eyebrows lifted in a silent, imploring gesture.

Quill responded with a choked, "I didn't. R-really." He averted his gaze away from Burke.

"Okay. I'll take your word on that." Burke watched Quill's expression darken. He exchanged dubious, frustrated looks with Weston, who responded with a shrug.

Burke sighed. "But if I find out you've been lying, I promise you're going to be one very unhappy young man."

Quill nodded, trying to hide the tears brimming in his eyes.

Pulling Quill in close for a quick hug, they both jumped when the curtain rattled back. Quill's nurse, Lisa, walked in, a stack of papers in her hand. Waving the papers in the air, she turned a steely look on her patient.

"Oh, no you don't. This is *not* happening again." She let her eye gaze on every person in the room. "Listen up. It's teaching time, gentlemen. I live for these few moments, so pay attention and don't interrupt. What you four know about asthma I could put in a medicine cup and still have room left over."

Lisa upped the intensity of her glare, pinning Burke in place. "I'll start with you, Poppa Man."

Burke snorted, but let it pass when he saw an amused smile touch Quill's lips.

Lisa continued, ignoring Burke's reaction. "I know you're new to the parenting game, let alone the asthma thing, but there's a couple things you're going to have to learn."

"Wait..." Burke was left with his mouth hanging open as, once again, she ignored his attempt to respond.

"One. Stop winding him up. The middle of an asthma attack isn't the time for intense discussions. It's the time for comforting and quiet, *not* a room full of visitors who engage in shouting matches."

She threw Ellis an exasperated glare. "It's always a zoo around you, Detective Ellis, even when you're not the patient." Ellis colored with an embarrassed smirk.

"Two. Treat his symptoms appropriately from now on. These new prescriptions will help and," she pulled a box out of the pocket of her lab coat, "this new inhaler should get you through any flare ups until you get the rest of the scripts filled tomorrow."

She tossed the box to Burke, who caught it one-handed. "Directions are on the box. Read it over, see that he uses it right."

She pointed at the prescription. "Make sure he takes all of his meds the way the prescriptions call for them." She poked one well-manicured finger at the stack. "And that means until they're gone, not until he feels better. Got it?"

Burke nodded, looking vaguely lost.

"And one last thing."

Her tough, no-nonsense tone softened and she reached out to brush a lock of stray curls off Quill's face. "He's still a child, teenager or not."

Quill barked a snort of protest, sounding much like Burke had a minute before.

"Sssh. I'm talking here. Your turn is coming up."

Her gaze had never left Burke's face. "It's your job to make sure he takes his medications, not his. It's your job to monitor his breathing and get help when the home meds aren't doing the job, not his. It's your job, Poppa Man, to be supportive, calming and firm with him when these attacks make him panic. There's nothing like feeling like you're suffocating to unnerve a person."

She thrust the prescriptions at Weston, flashing him a warm smile. "Be a darling and take these for Poppa Man so he can sign the discharge papers."

Weston took the slips of paper and flashed her a sweet smile back, earning him a suggestive wiggle of her eyebrows.

"Sign here, where I put the X." The nurse pushed a clipboard and a pen into Burke's hands, her stare still lingering over Weston.

She retrieved her clipboard and tore off the front copy and handed it to Weston, her hand rubbing against his in the transfer. "You, darlin', can put that with the other papers." She gave him another warm smile before turning back to her patient.

By the time she faced Quill, the warm look was gone replaced with a stern, maternal expression. "And you." She touched Quill's arm to make sure he knew she was talking specifically to him. "You've obviously been left to you own devices for too long. It shows in the lack of proper medical care you've had, your poor understanding of your own illness, and the state of your overall health."

"I eat. Lots." Quill's indignation turned to defensive whining with one disbelieving glance from the woman. "I do."

"Uh-huh."

She looked at Burke for a moment then back to Quill. "You're too thin, probably fifteen pounds underweight for your build. You don't eat regularly or well, and that makes it difficult for your body to cope when a crisis occurs, physically or emotionally, and with asthma you get the limitless joy of experiencing both at the same time."

A smile tugged at Burke's lips.

"I also realize this is a difficult time right now for you and for your father, so I'm taking it easy on you."

A disbelieving glance came from every male in the room, which she ignored. She held up her index finger and waved it under his nose. He tracked her finger's path through the air.

"One. Don't use illness as a manipulation. The last thing you need to do is make it difficult for anyone to tell if you're really in distress or you're just trying to win an argument the easy, underhanded way. You end up risking your life that way."

Grimacing, Quill dropped his face a little lower, but remained silent.

The nurse folded her arms across her chest. "Two. Do what Poppa Man tells you to do. Take your medications when and how you're supposed to. It's not optional."

She reached out and ghosted her fingertips over the bruised swelling on his face and lip. "And finally, you've had a rough twenty-four hours, honey. Your dad and his friend seem like nice men and I can personally vouch for the slouch against the wall. He's a good guy."

Quill gave her an embarrassed look and nodded.

Satisfied, she whirled around and released the catch on the siderail to lower it. "Good. Now that everybody's healthier, happier and better informed, I want you all out of my ER before anything else happens."

She jabbed her thumb in the direction of the exit and pointed to the half-open curtain. "There's a wheelchair outside the curtain." She turned and gestured at Burke. "You lift him off the stretcher and into the chair. Detective, give your friend here a hand supporting that sprained knee."

The nurse stepped back and watched as they all scurried to do her bidding. She positioned herself next to Weston and gave his arm a little nudge with her shoulder. "They take orders pretty well."

He looked down at her and grinned. "You're good at giving them."

"Thanks. How about you? You good at taking orders too?" Although the question was innocent enough, the way she licked at her upper lip wasn't.

Weston stared back, grin slipping a bit, at a loss for words "Ah...well, ah...I-I-I...ah..."

The nurse grinned at his display of shy embarrassment. "You're too adorable." She leaned closer, her voice low and sultry. "If you're ever back in town for longer than a couple of hours, give me a call. There'll be a pair of soft, fluffy wrist restraints waiting with your name on them. Think about it."

"Ah...I don't...that wouldn't...ah, well..."

She slipped a square of paper into his free hand and marched off to take control of the wheelchair. With a backward glance at Weston, she released the chair's brakes, wheeling Quill out of the room. Burke and Ellis followed grins on their faces.

Weston stood alone in the room staring from discharge papers to the phone number on the note, gaping like a fish out of water. After a moment of indecision a single, squeaked word worked its way out of his dry throat.

"Ah...yes?"

Chapter Fifteen

The butler eased the thick, highly polished oak door closed, effectively sealing the room from any sound escaping behind him. Inside, several very important, very worried men sat slumped in deep leather chairs and discussed the politically damaging development of the last two days.

James Davenport sat to the right of the large desk, observing the reactions of the other three men in the room. Even if he hadn't known who the gentlemen were, their tailored suits, university ties, and arrogant attitudes would have told even the most uninformed they were lawyers. They were, in fact, retainers to the Crown from the law firm of Heale, Higgins and Howell.

Ian Farr and Martin Peat, both senior barristers, sat directly in front of the massive desk. The fourth person in the room, Cabinet Minister Lord Justice Alexander Taber, was an understated but powerful presence. A nod or a wave of his finely manicured hand were his only responses so far.

Peat was in favor of telling the truth and letting the chips fall where they may. He thought it would be best if Burke just kept the suspect he apprehended.

Ian Farr fingered the edge of his sharply cut lapel, a grimace of distaste on his face as he said, "If the true facts of this situation reach the public eye, there will be no stopping the press with this one, Minister. Crowe's actions can be presented in a manner that makes the McCabes' deaths look like the unfortunate result of a routine raid. Casualties happen during anti-terrorist assaults. It's a fact of life nowadays."

"Are you advising that Lt. Crowe not be prosecuted for his actions, Mr. Farr?" Davenport asked the question as innocently as he could.

"I'm recommending Lt. Crowe be quietly promoted to ensure his cooperation and silence then quickly transferred to a less high profile assignment for awhile. I'm sure he'll be willing to accept that arrangement over a life sentence in prison." Farr pulled back on the sarcastic tone just far enough for Davenport to let the slight go unchallenged.

Peat shifted uncomfortably in his chair, glancing at the minister's unreadable expression before speaking. "Lord Taber, I'm of the opinion Lt. Crowe should be brought to trial. It will undoubtedly appear like we are sacrificing him as a scapegoat to some, but the man did murder two young men in cold blood."

Farr broke in again, emphatic in his crusade to bury the incident. "Two men caught in the act of treason, Martin. They weren't innocent lambs slaughtered by a big bad wolf in SAS clothing. They were old enough to understand the consequences of their actions."

"They were tied to a post when Crowe shot them, Ian. No resisting arrest, not a potential menace to a heavily-armed, career soldier like Crowe. They were executed. You can't even make a case for self-defense out of it. And the American Commander was witness to the assault and attempted murder of the younger boy."

Peat shook his head and leaned forward to emphasize his point to Taber. "If we cover this up and word ever leaks out, it will be disastrous, sir. Our only hope is to put the surface facts on the table and hope nobody digs too much deeper. The scandal will go on forever if the press gets hold of the truth."

"How do you propose we keep the details of the incident quiet, Mr. Peat?" Taber's tone was neutral, his voice perfectly modulated to be both reasonable and persuasive at the same time. "There is always the threat of scandal these days, no matter which avenue we choose to take. We can't make it our concern."

"Prosecute Crowe and there is no reason for him to keep his silence. Loyalty only goes so far when a man is looking at a lifetime in prison." Farr's tone was smug, having gained the higher ground with the Cabinet Minister.

Peat graciously accepted the obvious, unspoken decision. "So we cover up two deaths and reward a murderer. Are we acknowledging Crowe's claim that his actions were sanctioned as real?"

Farr's gaze briefly touched on Taber for an answer. Taber ignored Peat's inquiring tone, passively confirming the suspicion for everybody in the room. "Don't take it as such a bitter pill, Martin. It's the most practical and necessary path."

Peat asked the more pressing question. "Who is going to handle the American? Burke's record doesn't point to a man who will let this thing slide unchallenged."

"Commander Burke is a soldier. He knows how to take orders. I'm sure a well-placed word with that oaf General Wiess will be enough to dampen Burke's drive. Wiess loves public attention, so shift the focus to him. Play up their role in bringing down a new terrorist threat. Congratulate them on being a driving force for freedom. It will give us time to regroup and form a solid plan."

Up until now, Davenport had been content to just

listen, learning the strengths and weaknesses of the other men. But one important detail was being overlooked. One he knew from experience would be the back breaker of any off the record accord they managed to establish with the Americans.

"What about the boy?"

"The boy?" Farr was feeling too cocky and self-assured since Taber accepted his recommendations. "The brat'll have to be returned, of course. He's a loose end, a potential information leak. We can't control it if he isn't in custody."

Davenport dismissed Farr's rebuttal with a wave of his hand. "Granted, information on him at present is poor, but what we do have, Lord Justice, indicates the boy knows nothing of any importance. The files stolen were vast. No one could have read even a small portion in the time the boy had available. And I'm sure that in exchange for the knowledge, however false it may be, that his friends' murderer is being brought to justice, he can be convinced to remain silent about the incident for his friends' sake. The McCabe brothers' illegal activities wouldn't reflect well on their sister and parents if the facts became public. I'm sure the boy could be made to understand that fact."

Peat jumped into the conversation before Farr could voice a dissenting vote. "He's right, Lord Taber. That and an offer of a lighter penalty for offenses against the Crown, maybe a form of house arrest rather than a prison sentence might sway the decision. He is just a teenager, sir. I doubt the prospect of prison life is an attractive one to him."

Taber paused a moment then closed the folder on his desk, subtly announcing he had made a final decision and the discussion was over.

"Lt. Crowe will be dealt with internally, assuring his silence. Release only the barest of facts to the public and downplay the incident as a routine anti-terrorist mission. They're getting too common these days for many to take much notice of them anyway. Let the Americans have the boy. It will keep them focused on lesser matters."

"As you wish, Minister." Davenport politely accepted the decision, giving no indication about his own thoughts.

Peat slumped in his chair and let a slow breath of pent up anxiety subtly escape. "Thank you, sir. I think it's the wisest course of action with the boy."

Taber leaned back in his chair and smiled at the trio. Suddenly nervous, Peat stood, picking up his briefcase. "Our offices will contact the Americans and arrange for a meeting as soon as possible. You'll be informed every step of the way, Minister." Peat shook hands with Taber and exited the room with a swift, "Good day, sir."

Davenport spared the still seated Farr a thoughtful glance before addressing Taber again. "I'll join the contingent meeting with the Americans, Minister. Commander Burke's mother is an old friend. I believe I can help him see reason in this matter."

"By all means, James. Any advantage will be appreciated. Thank you." Taber's smile turned a little less cold, but the warmth never reached his eyes.

His gaze followed Davenport out the door then landed on Farr. "Do what you can to negotiate the boy back here. Barring that, make sure you know what he knows. Everything. If there is even a hint he knows what was in the files, I want him back or I want him gone, permanently."

Farr took in a deep breath and nodded. "It'll be my pleasure to see to it, my Lord."

* * * * *

Arriving on base, Weston went in search of their teammates. Burke went directly to his commanding officer, Colonel William Lansing. He wondered how much explaining he was going to have to do to justify his decision to bring Quill into the US covertly. The information Quill had given him about the possible assassination of Colonel Brian Wright was too real to be ignored. Burke was still having trouble believing such a widespread conspiracy plot was in place.

As he entered the outer offices of the command headquarters, Burke's cell phone rang. Diverting to a quieter stretch of hallway, he pulled out his phone and checked the incoming number. Ellis' area code and number lit up the display and Burke felt a small rush of panic. Ellis wouldn't call this soon for anything less than a crisis. Either the military was faster than he calculated and had found the boy, or the kid was having more problems with his breathing. Both possibilities chilled him to the bone.

Burke sent a quick glance around to make sure no one was close enough to overhear his conversation then flipped open the phone. "What's wrong?"

A snort of sarcastic laughter from the other end of the line eased his panic down a notch. "Christ, are we over-protective or what?"

Burke kicked himself for letting his wild speculations overwhelm his usual control. His priorities had somehow been rearranged. He never understood how much having a young life depend on you could affect a person before.

"Everything's fine." Ellis' confident voice crackled through the connection. "For now. But you're going to have your hands full in the near future, buddy. This kid's wound tighter than a two dollar watch."

"What happened?"

"He pulled my gun on me."

"HE WHAT?"

"He was having a nightmare at the time, only halfway awake, and confused me with someone else."

"Who the hell did he confuse you with? He'd never met you before yesterday."

"Tell me what the guy who tried to off him looks like."

"Crowe? He's 6-2, about your size and build, dark hair, cut short like yours, blue eyes, talks a little like–" Burke stopped in mid-sentence as the problem became crystal clear. "Oh, for Christ's sake, don't tell me. He thought you were Crowe."

"Got it in one, buddy."

"Poor kid."

"Poor kid, my ass. That tiger nearly shot me with my own gun."

"I'm sorry, Tim."

"I'm not holding it against him. He's been through more than any kid should have to. I'm just calling to let you know he asked for you."

"He asked for me?" Burke couldn't keep the surprise from his tone.

"He feels safe with you, and only you. You need to hurry up your lazy, Army brass ass and get back here."

"I'll be there as soon as I can make sure he's going to be safe."

"Well, hurry it up or you're going to have to make sure he's safe from me too. One more stunt from him and I'm thinking about stuffing him in that old dog crate I've got."

"As long as it's clean and you feed and water him, I'm not objecting. I shouldn't be that long, but I'll send someone else out if things get lengthy here."

"Deal with it, he wants *you*, Daniel."

"I hear you, I hear you." Burke sighed, confused about what the kid expected from him and even more confused about what he wanted to give. "I just don't know what to do about it."

"Give it some time. It'll work out."

This was getting more complicated than he had ever imagined. This kid had turned his life upside down in less time than it normally took Burke to be fitted for a new suit.

"Commander Burke?"

A nervous, young voice made Burke snap around. A fresh-faced corporal stood several yards away, ridge and pale, his expression tense. Burke nodded at him.

"Colonel Lansing requests your presence in his office, sir."

Burke returned the young man's salute with a nod. "I'll be right there, Corporal."

The soldier hurried away and Burke turned back to the phone. "Listen, I have to go. Tell the kid...hell, I don't know. Tell him I'm working on things." His voice became softer. "Then remind him I'm coming back for him. Soon."

"We'll both be staring at the front door, buddy. See you *soon*."

"Asshole."

Burke pocketed the phone and headed to the colonel's office. How was he going to keep his deadly and unpredictable professional life from destroying Quill?

Chapter Sixteen

His sixty-two years more evident than usual, Colonel William Lansing appeared sleep deprived and worn. The past thirty-six hours had taked a toll on everyone. Burke squared his shoulders and waited for Lansing's next question.

It had already been a long and detailed meeting with his commanding officer. In the end, he was confident Lansing understood and grudgingly supported his unorthodox move to take the boy out of the country. However, Lansing wasn't so supportive of Burke's decision to spirit the boy away and hide him from the very forces that were supposed to be protecting him.

"Daniel, you need to bring the boy in. It's not going to set well with the brass if you don't. It looks like you don't think your own people can be trusted."

"Honestly, Colonel, I'm not sure they can. From what the boy told us, if these plots are true, there's an American faction of the assassins too."

"That's preposterous. The Army wouldn't allow it. It couldn't stay hidden for long if it did. You've lost faith in an institution you've served all your life, Daniel."

Burke gathered his thoughts. He'd been happy in the Army. Content in covert ops, and proud of his career and the military branch he served under. But things were changing for him. Mid-life and a lifetime of compromises for his country's sake were catching up to him.

If the institution that had been his whole life might be involved in the kinds of acts Quill had told them about...it shook the foundations of his faith. He had a moral responsibility to find out the truth for those who were targeted for execution.

Burke dropped all pretense of formality. "It's not just one particular thing, Bill. It's like, like a wave of unease has been building up inside of me lately. And all of a sudden, this poor kid gets thrown in my path, ripped away from everything he knows and shoved into a world where no kid should ever be. I find myself questioning my motives for doing things. I wonder about the missions I've taken my men on. Were they done for the reasons we were told? How many of the men we've taken out on orders, just like Crowe was supposedly doing, were innocents? Removed just so the path would be a little less bumpy for the next politically-correct, sanctioned power to take over? How many secrets did we unknowingly help the Army keep?"

"That's not how we work, Daniel. Sure there were missions you didn't have the full story on. You didn't need it. People higher up than you or I made the decisions to green light those missions and sanctioned the end results. It's not important or healthy for us to know everything about them. We're soldiers. We have a job to do and we do it, with a minimum of questions asked. That's who we are, Daniel. And you're one of the best at it."

"I'm not so sure anymore."

"Listen to me. It's not unusual for a man who's done the things you and I have done for our country to have a few moments where we feel the need to question our lives. That's what makes us the good guys, the ones with a conscience. It's when you start letting indecision affect your performance that there's a need for concern.

Your government is still the foundation of freedom you've always been proud to serve, Daniel. I think you've just been blindsided by this whole thing because of the boy."

"Fine. Then prove it to me. Prove the kid's wrong, that this is all just some crazy conspiracy the kid made up to keep his terrified, underage butt out of prison."

"How?"

"Quill told me he read one other file besides ours. One concerning the assassination of an Army colonel attached to MI6's anti-terrorist division out of Hereford. He's scheduled for termination while he and his family are vacationing in Switzerland. Check with the man and see if he's planning a trip there anytime soon."

Lansing's face clouded over with doubt. "All right. What's his name?"

"Colonel Brian Wright, codename 'Magpie', aged forty-seven. Brown hair, gray eyes. Wife's name is Gina. They've got a couple of boys, Mark and Gary."

Lansing raised an eyebrow. "That's a lot of detail for someone to have remembered from a one time read of a file that couldn't mean anything to him." He crossed over to his phone and buzzed for his aide.

"Yeah, well, the kid seems to have an eye for details."

Further conversation was interrupted by the aide's response. Lansing assigned him the task of locating Wright ASAP. Pulling open a drawer, he produced a bottle of brandy.

"Drink?" Lansing offered.

"Thanks, I think I will, Sir," Burke accepted the glass.

They spent the next fifteen minutes chatting, consciously avoiding the subject at hand. As the moments wore on, a feeling of dread settled in Burke's stomach.

The buzz of the loudspeaker jolted both men and they exchanged a sheepish grin while Lansing activated the intercom on his desk.

"Yes, Corporal?"

"Sorry for the delay, Colonel. I was informed there's been an accident involving Colonel Wright, sir, as well as a bit of a problem locating him."

"What kind of accident, Corporal? What happened to him?" Lansing's voice held a note of shocked disbelief.

"They don't actually know just yet. He's missing, vacationing in Switzerland somewhere. That's all I could find out on the phone, sir."

Lansing paused a moment, finger posed over the intercom buttons, ready to end the call. "Thank you, Corporal. I'll handle it from here." He finally looked up from the speaker to meet Burke's eyes.

Burke said, "Quill's right. He's been right all along. Three people have died needlessly in the last thirty-six hours. God only knows what else was in those files. "

Burke and his team were next. Instinct told him to play his cards very, very close to his chest from now on, even around trusted friends. There were too many lives at risk to take any chances. The threat level against Quill just took a giant leap upward. He needed to get to him.

"This could all be a coincidence." Lansing didn't even sound like he believed his own words.

"Not likely." Burke rose from his chair and placed his empty brandy glass on the corner of the colonel's desk.

"If we're done here, sir, I'd like to hook up with the rest of my team. I haven't had a chance to touch base with them since I got back."

"The British Crown is sending over a negotiating

team to meet with General Sands. They should arrive later this afternoon. They want to extradite the boy back to his own country. You're going to have to produce the boy soon, Daniel. I should order you to do it now. He *is* a suspect in a treasonous act."

"He's also a victim, a kid who was nearly murdered by a British officer of the Crown. I'm an eyewitness. They'll have to prove their bureaucratic needs are more important than the boy's physical and emotional ones before I turn him over."

"You're sounding pretty possessive there, Commander. Make sure you know what you're letting yourself in for. It could become quite a fight."

"I've got a few aces up my sleeve, sir."

"I don't want to know anything about them. I'm giving you a measure of leeway here because of your record for getting the job done using unorthodox methods, but I may be forced to have you turn the boy over, if this isn't concluded in a satisfactory manner for everyone involved soon, Daniel."

Burke only nodded.

Lansing tipped his head and gave Burke a small twisted smile of acknowledgment. "I'll have you notified when the Brits arrive. Make sure my office knows how to reach you. The sooner this is sorted out the better."

"Yes, sir. I'll be available. And thank you Colonel, I appreciate your confidence in me."

"Don't prove me wrong, Commander."

"I'll try not to, sir." Burke left the room and went in search of his team.

* * * * *

The image of Burr and James huddled together in Weston's company released a small ball of tension in

171

Burke he didn't realize was there as he caught the flow of the conversation.

"She gave you her number? A nurse who looked like a babe gave *you* her number?" Burr's dark face went slack with disbelief.

"Well...It has an area code for that part of the state and seven more digits after it, so I'm fairly certain it's a phone number, yes, Jackson." Weston's innocent choirboy persona was in place. "But I must admit, I'm not completely at ease with her last comment before she walked away."

"What comment would that be, Lover Boy? Let's play doctor next time you're in town?" Burr chuckled at his own joke, wiggling his brows at the blushing younger man. A small snicker escaped James, although the big man tried to contain it. Weston's blush deepened.

"I don't remember her exact words, I was somewhat taken off guard at the time, but it was something about a pair of wrist restraints with my name on them." Weston cleared his throat and bobbed his head in his familiar gesture of reassuring himself of his facts. "On the heels of the complimentary, but highly suggestive 'taking orders well' comment, I was left a bit...confused...about her...expectations."

The chuckles burst into outright laughter. James and Burr doubled over, leaving an embarrassed, fidgeting Weston the only one standing. Burr wiped tears from his eyes and dropped onto a nearby chair, while James easily lowered his bulk to the floor and leaned against the side of Burr's chair. All three men noticed Burke at the same time, but Weston greeted him for all of them.

"Hi, Daniel. That took less time than we thought it would. These two hyenas," he gestured at Burr and James, "were sure the Colonel'd be grilling you for hours." A fresh round of chuckles broke out. Weston shot both men a grimace, producing a louder burst of laughter.

"I wondered if a pack of jackals had made it onto the base." Burke's smile widened.

He had seen the nurse giving Weston the eye and slipping him the paper, but he hadn't asked any questions about it. Weston was very open about his feelings with the three of them. If he wanted to discuss it, he would. And apparently he had, a fact most other people would be regretting right now, but not Weston. He took the teasing and the jibes from his teammates in stride.

Weston shook his head and sat down onto a chair near his tormentors. Burr reached out and slapped his knee, while a playful James encircled Weston's wrist with the fingers of one hand, mocking the act of cuffing him. Weston knocked away both of their hands.

Burke moved into the center of the fray and got comfortable on a chair. "Okay, guys, leave him alone. Save it for when he actually calls her and we have to pry the details out of him after he comes back three days late from their date."

Weston blushed scarlet and broke into a shy bout of laughter, tossing Burke a thankful expression.

"We've got something more pressing than Ray's love life to discuss," Burke said.

"Twisted as it is," Burr threw in one last barb. "Ethan and I had an interesting discussion with General Weiss before we left, Daniel."

"Real interesting. We danced the two-step for awhile at first, but in the end he took to the job of distracting the Brits like a rattler to a sun-baked rock." James tapped the side of his nose with one finger.

"Understood exactly what we needed and why, no bluster involved. Even agreed with it."

Burr nodded.

"Heard the man called an emergency meeting with all the head honchos involved, and bitched and hollered for so long they never even thought to ask him where the kid was until it was too late to do anything about it. Even implied Crowe, and whoever supported him, conspired to implicate the US Army in a plan to commit premeditated murder." Burr's tone held a fair measure of awe in it. "I'll bet they tripped all over each other backing away from that one."

"Pretty gutsy decision for the old man," Weston agreed.

Burke picked up on the subtle looks Burr and James were giving him. He'd hoped the General would show his true colors when the chips were down. The stakes in this game were too high to let political niceties and power plays get the upper hand over a boy's life.

"I'm glad to hear it. He's what probably saved our butts." Burke was pleased to know his assessment of the General's character had paid off. "We'll have to remember him in the future when we need a friend in high places."

"Just how much are we going to be needing 'friends in high places', Daniel?" For a change, Burr's teasing, sarcastic attitude was nowhere to be seen.

"Unfortunately, a whole lot. And soon."

Running a hand through his hair, Burke looked at each of his men in turn. He'd realized his own military career was coming to a close months ago. But he wondered if he had the right to ask the same thing of them.

Disbanding the team would probably protect them

after he left, at least for a little while. Eventually though, the problem would catch up with them. Whatever the reason they were to be eliminated, it was all of them, not just him, and the other men would still remain targets.

At least his plan would keep them together in civilian life. He just hoped they would be interested. They were going to need to stay together if they were going to survive this mess.

Burke had decided to lay his cards on the table. "If we stay–"

"If we stay? Where would we go?" Burr's expression turned darker than his complexion.

"Back to civilian life."

"Why? What happened, Daniel?" James asked.

"It's about the other file Quill told us about in the hospital, isn't it?" Weston understood everything immediately. "I told Jack and Ethan about it." The former choirboy had a way of getting through subterfuge to the true heart of a matter.

Burke nodded.

"Quill was right, the guy's real and going on vacation to Switzerland," Weston said.

"Worse. He's real, he went to Switzerland and now he's missing. Just like the file said he would be, eliminated without a trace."

Silence filled the room, each man tensing in their seats. James voiced it for all of them. "Then we're next. Our next mission is supposed to be our last."

Burr stared off into a corner of the room. "And we won't know what direction it's coming from, friend or foe."

"Kinda narrows down the options, doesn't it?" James toyed with a strap on the sleeve of his vest before raising his gaze to meet Burke's head on. "My momma'll be happy to see me home. Lately I've been hankering for a few lazy days down at the old fishing pond. Guess I'll be getting the chance a lot sooner than I thought."

Burke was surprised to hear the acceptance in the big man's words. More startling was the unmasked pleasure in his tone.

Before he could speak, Burr echoed the sentiment. "About time, really. The age factor in the unit has gone way beyond most covert ops teams. Old bodies can't take the strain and stress the way those youngsters can."

Burke smiled at the burly, physically fit man's attempt to provide an external excuse for his decision. "I'm appalled, Jackson. Are you actually admitting to slowing down?"

Burr scowled at Burke. "Of course not. I was talking about you. I hate to be the one to tell you, but there's a lot of silver threads mixed in with that blond hair, Bossman." He ran a palm lovingly over his own head. "I, on the other hand, have none."

Weston rested a consoling hand on Burr's shoulder and whispered, "That's because you're bald, Jack." He patted the shoulder again. "It's all right though, it's expected in men of your advanced age."

Burr shrugged his hefty shoulder with a jerk. "Some of us don't need it to attract the ladies, boy."

Weston's smile was generous and playful, but he turned serious. "We could stay and fight this. We know vaguely where and when to expect the attacks."

"This time." Burke shook his head. "No, Ray, if they fail this time, there'll be another attempt. And if they suspect we were forewarned, they'll assume Quill read the files and told us."

"Or that we reconstructed the files from the hardware?" Ray said, "Maybe we could deflect the suspicion from the boy."

James shook his head. "That's a no go there. The Army already pronounced the bits and pieces we gave them back at the base in England as non-retrievable trash. They'll know that by now."

"How much Quill really knows won't matter. These people won't take the risk, they'll just kill him." Burr turned to Burke. "You don't mind if I bunk at your place for awhile, do you? All of my stuff is at the estate anyway."

Burke chuckled. "I hadn't planned on you going any other place, Jack, not until you want to."

The black man nodded. With no living relatives of his own, these three men were the closest he had to family. Burke was his best friend. Burr had grownup in Pittsburgh, but had no ties there. He always made camp wherever Burke was. It was a relief to Burke to see that wasn't going to be changing any time soon.

Weston squirmed in his seat, catching the three questioning stares as he settled.

"Oh. Well, I was just thinking. My mother's been badgering me, not really *badgering*...well, maybe badgering is the right word...anyway, she's been hoping I'd start thinking about leaving the service soon. She really thinks I should start working on establishing my career as an artist, with more solid pieces and some art shows and such while I'm still young.

"I mean, she's right, and she's my mother and she's a brilliant artist and an accomplished business woman, but...but, I *really* don't think I want to go back to California. At least not yet." His smooth, young face wrinkled up in a confused grimace. "Am I making myself clear at all?"

Burr winked at Burke before answering. "You're saying you're not ready jump from the adventure of black ops into the sedate life of a West Coast painter?"

"Well, yes...something like that, Jack." Weston flinched and grimaced again. "But more like, I'm not sure I want to settle that close to my mother. I mean I want to continue with my art, I'm just not sure California is where I want to live."

Burke decided to take a chance and throw out the idea he had come up with. "How would you like to explore it, part-time, in upstate New York? The estate is close to the galleries and art houses of Greenwich and the Big Apple, Toronto's an hour's flight away and Ramona is the best cook in New England."

"I'd need a studio, Daniel. A large, airy, room filled with natural light." Weston was hopeful, but cautious.

"The terrace room is perfect for it. It's yours, if you want it, Spencer."

Weston's eyebrows rose at the sound of his given name. "You're serious." He paused and blew a stream of air out pursed lips before continuing. "I know we've all thought about leaving the service at one time or the other." He looked at Burke directly. "I guess I'd rather do it on our own terms instead of being forced out. Thank you, Daniel. I think I will. On one condition.""Thank you, Daniel. I think I will. On one condition."

"What's that, Ray?"

"You tell my mother."

Chuckling, Burke agreed. "Done. I'll even let her redecorate the estate."

"You said part-time, Bossman." Burr leaned

178

forward and propped his elbows on his knees, his total focus on the man before him. "What will we be doing the rest of the time?"

Burke nodded. "I've been thinking about this a lot lately. This situation just pushed it all to a head."

"I want us to stick together. I want to keep doing the type of work we've been doing — evening out the balance of power, helping people, fixing things. Like protecting an abandoned kid who's been thrown to the wolves."

"How?" Burr's tone held a reassuring tone of interest.

"By using the training and skills we've been honing for the last decade or more. I thought the four of us could form a consulting firm, one to evaluate and upgrade security for businesses and private concerns. We could establish ourselves a home base at my place, I have the capital to fund the start-up, and we have all the resources we need between the four of us to do the job."

Burke leaned forward, running a hand through his hair. "We've all made a number of good contacts and important friendships over the years. We could do this, make a good living at it and still feel good about ourselves at the end of the day. I've been missing that feeling."

Burke turned his attention to James, who had been quiet up to now. "How about you Ethan? Can I interest you in a new line of work?"

A wry smile pulled at James' face. "I've been wanting to leave for awhile now, Daniel. Just been waiting for the right time."

Burke paused, then shook his head in disbelief. "I'm beginning to wonder how many of our missions were actually like Crowe's. How many 'obstacles to justice' did we remove based solely on someone's need to change the balance of power for their own personal goals?"

His tone reflected both embarrassment and uncertainty. "I just can't be sure any more."

"None of us could've suspected any of this, Daniel. But now that we've got a clue, there is something we can do about it." Burr jerked his head toward Weston and James. "That's if everyone's agreeable?"

"I've just been biding my time until you three got tired of playing." James rocked up off the floor and towered over the others, stretching his massive frame. "My family was looking forward to seeing me home for a piece, but they'll sure be pleased to find out I'm a civilian again."

"I take it that means you're in?" Burke asked.

"I'm in, Daniel. On one condition."

"Whatever it is, you've got it, Ethan." Burke smiled at the mock scowl James threw his way.

"If Ray gets the terrace, I get a place for my hobby too."

"I'll build on a room if I have to."

"Don't need to. I want the run of the stables. I got me a fine little filly back at my daddy's ranch I've been aching to spend time with. Her daddy's a wild mustang from down in the southern mesa and she's got more spirit and sense than most people I know, you three included."

The big man ignored the outraged expressions on Burr's and Weston's faces.

Burke stood up and extended his hand to James. "It's a deal. The stables are yours. Fill them up with whatever you want, Ethan."

James shook Burke's hand in a hearty grip, exuberant over the turn of events. Burr and Weston joined in and soon all four men were planning their new future as civilian consultants. The biggest stumbling block would be arranging their immediate, honorable discharges to coincide with Daniel's resignation. Ray had a few ideas on that score.

They spent the next three hours planning the birth of their new company, tentatively named Sparrow Four Consulting. They were interrupted once by a corporal alerting them to the arrival of Ray's father, Patrick Weston. Two hours later, the British arrived.

Chapter Seventeen

Daniel Burke took in each of the serious faces surrounding the conference table. Patrick Weston, Ray's father, sat on his left, lending moral support and a huge amount of political muscle to Burke's case. Major Adrian Woods, an attorney from the U.S. Army's legal staff, sat on his right. Beside Woods was General Philip Sands, ranking officer at the base. Colonel William Lansing, Burke's immediate commanding officer, sat to Sands' right, with Mr. Ian Farr, a lawyer from MI5's top-level legal advisory board next to him. Director General James Davenport rounded out the group of important people hastily assembled to decide the sentencing, management and displacement of one orphaned, teenage boy. To Burke, it was a little bit of overkill.

Patrick Weston's smooth, persuasive voice interrupted yet another pointless argument between the legal representatives of both sides. "Gentlemen. Don't you think you're being a bit presumptuous here, talking jail terms and treasonous acts? The boy hasn't even been charged yet, let alone found guilty."

Both lawyers looked at Weston, their expressions reflecting the blank stare of the misinformed.

He smiled a gracious, forgiving smile and took the floor. "I have it on the best of authority, someone who was actually present during the entire assault on the boy's home and on his person, I might add, that one Quillan Tarquin was never cautioned by any agent of the British Crown, MI5 or SAS agents. Nor was he Miranda'd once he reached American soil. In short, gentlemen, the boy has never been arrested."

He watched the faces at the table. "Assaulted, injured, accused, forcefully relocated for his safety, traumatized and victimized, but never arrested."

There was a strangled grunt directly across the table from Burke, as Ian Farr stirred back to life. "There can be no doubt the boy was involved, Mr. Weston. He was present at the siege on the hackers' stronghold, he was caught destroying evidence, and collaborative statements by people who know him state he is a genius with computers."

Ian Farr twisted his long, gaunt face into a grimace of distaste. "Some even imply the arrogant little bastard is the brains behind this whole, distasteful, treasonous act."

Burke leaned forward, turning the full intensity of his annoyance on the man. "That 'arrogant little bastard' as you put it, Mr. Farr, is a teenage boy. One who has been beaten, crippled, and nearly murdered. He witnesses his two best friends brutally executed. Murdered by an officer of your Crown, one sworn to defend your people. 'Little', yeah, he's way too thin. 'Bastard', maybe, but 'arrogant'? He's too damned terrified to come anywhere close to that. Having a black ops assault soldier beat the crap out of you, then try to splatter your brains all over a room will do that to a kid."

Burke's tone got softer as he continued, his temper raising to an unhealthy level.

"Daniel." Weston's voice has a warning tone to it. After a tense moment, Burke leaned back into the chair, sending one final glare to Farr.

Davenport's soft, calm voice broke through.

"I'm sure the point Mr. Farr was attempting to

make, Commander, is that there is a high level of suspicion this boy was party to the entire hacking incident. Based on his close association with the known perpetrators, it is highly likely he was involved."

Farr regained his confidence. "Exactly. Cautioned or not, a measure of the guilt for these illegal acts rests on Tarquin's shoulders."

Weston sighed and opened a folder in front of him, casually running a finger down the top page. "Quillan Tarquin, born August 23, 1987. I believe that makes him *sixteen*, not nineteen."

With the exception of Burke, every man at the table reacted silently to the news. Farr wrinkled his nose. Peat bit at his lower lip. The military officers merely took in a deeper breath than usual. Weston had already warned Burke about the boy's tender years.

"A minor, one that was never actually seen destroying evidence. The boy never admitted to having or destroying evidence at anytime. All the facts so far are circumstantial, I must remind you. Kevin McCabe made a point of *denying* Tarquin's involvement in the hacking and the selling of the stolen information. And since he's dead, there's no refuting his claim. The boy merely lived with the brothers. According to your own Child Services department records, let's see..."

Weston ran his forefinger over the report as if he was trying to find a detail, though Burke knew the man knew the file by heart. "The boy has no criminal record. No living relatives to look after him. Maybe if CS had done their job two years ago, we wouldn't be sitting here discussing his future at all."

Farr couldn't keep the sarcasm out of his voice. "If I may ask, exactly why are you here, Mr. Weston? The

Army has its own capable representation in Major Woods."

Farr gestured to the quiet, middle-aged officer. Woods seemed content to sit back and let Weston lead the way, a calm, amused look on his lined face.

"Major Woods is most capable," Weston nodded to the man, "and he represents the Army's interests quite well, but I'm here to ensure Commander Burke's private interests."

"His private interests?" Davenport quirked a bushy, white eyebrow at the son of his longtime friend.

"Yes. Since he's going to be a private citizen by the end of this conversation," he ignored the stunned faces around the room, "and the decisions made here today concern him and his future plans, as well as his entire team's."

Weston fixed a hard stare on Farr. "Rest assured gentlemen, whatever measures and safeguards it takes to ensure Quillan Tarquin is well taken care of and protected from any future assaults or charges from this day forth, *will* be hashed out here today."

Weston pulled another file from under the folder on Tarquin and presented copies to both General Sands and Lord Davenport. "These papers state I legally represent the personal interests of Colonel Daniel Burke, Sergeants Jackson Burr and Ethan James, and Specialist Spencer Weston in this meeting. I'm here to help negotiate the future welfare of both the Tarquin boy and the Army unit known as *SparrowFour*."

This wasn't news to Burke and his men had informed them of their decision before the meeting. The corners of Lansing's mouth were drawn down into a tight frown. Satisfied his point had been made Weston continued. "Shall we begin, gentlemen?"

* * * * *

Returning to his room on the army base, Burke dropped onto a chair and sank into the cushioned backrest. Burr, James and Weston took the three remaining chairs at the dinette set.

Now Burke just had to explain everything that happened at the meeting to his men. Looking at the expectant faces around him, he couldn't keep from breaking out into a smile.

"Well, guys, you're looking at something I haven't been in so long I've forgotten how it feels–a civilian."

"They went for it." Burr's voice held a satisfied tone then shifted to a more cautious attitude. "All of it?"

Burke's smile turning into a grin. "Believe it or not, yes, they did. Ray's father is a very persuasive man." He slapped Ray's shoulder, triumph and gratitude all rolled into one brisk gesture.

"General Sands made some vague reference to a call he'd received from Washington just before the meeting." A small frown creased Burke's forehead. "I think we have a friend in unknown places to thank for that."

"Maybe it was your momma's influence, Daniel. She's a right powerful woman," Ethan said.

"Maybe, but I think Sands would have mentioned her if it had been." He shook his head.

Burke scrubbed a hand along his growing five o'clock shadow. "My resignation's effective immediately. I just have a few days of debriefing and the final paperwork to sign. You three will have a bit more official time in the ranks yet, but that's just on paper. Your honorable discharges with full benefits will take a couple of weeks to get through the paper mill, but General Sands has granted a leave of absence for you three until it's official."

Burke felt a burst of warmth flashed through his chest at the sight of their familiar, weathered faces. Each of the men exchanged high fives and Burr raised his fists in celebration.

They'd had no time to get used to the idea of being civilians again. It was daunting to Burke, who had contemplated it these last few months. Even Ethan was a little unsettled and he had wanted this for sometime now, as well.

"We didn't get away scot-free though."

Ray sat forward in his chair and tapped his fingers on the tabletop. "Quill?"

"What are we going to do with the boy, Daniel? I can't say as I'm looking kindly on the idea of sending him back home." Ethan had been spinning a pencil through his fingers and the thin wood suddenly snapped in two.

Ray nodded and joined in. "That's right. It's not safe. How are we going to make sure he has someone to protect his interests there? A good lawyer isn't enough."

"Damn right. Whoever's behind this whole Goddamn mess will have their hands on him the minute he's in custody. You know the kid doesn't stand a snowball's chance in hell on his own."

"Too bad he doesn't have a family." Ray's gentle insistence hit the heart of the matter.

"Hell, he needs an armed division of Marines." Burr tapped the table's surface, though he pounded with his coiled fist, beating out a frustrated rhythm on the cheap, wooden surface.

Burke couldn't have asked for a better opening.

"Maybe he just needs us."

Three surprised faces snapped up. Ethan was the

first to dissolve into a knowing, almost smug look.

"You're keeping him."

"You're keeping him?" Burr and Weston's voices blended into one.

Burke keep his face straight and answered, "Technically, yes, but I prefer to think of it as *we're* keeping him."

Ethan just smiled and nodded. Ray sat open-mouthed.

Burke braced himself for a verbal blast from Burr. From the color of the big man's face, Burke wouldn't be disappointed.

"Well, for Christ's sakes!" Burr punched one of his coiled fists into Burke's shoulder, delighting in the rocking motion he created. "Welcome to parenthood, Bossman."

Stunned, Burke had to hold back the urge to laugh. "I can't believe you, Jack. You're the one person I expected to have to convince about this."

"I want the kid to be safe and that means more than in a clean, dry cell away from the general population in a prison. He may have had a hand in the hacking, but he sure didn't deserve Crowe. Any debt to society he needs to pay was covered in that little murder attempt of the Brits." Burr leaned back in his chair and let the deep scowl on his face ease away.

This time Burke did laugh out loud. "Good to hear you say that, Jackson, because the kid's going to be around for a long time. A long time."

Ray laughed. "My dad worked his magic on the lawyers didn't he?"

Burke nodded. "That he did, Ray. He got them to drop the threat of prosecution for the hacking and the treason charge, in exchange for seven years of house arrest, counseling by an independent child psychiatrist, and the boy has to be available for questioning as their investigation continues. I made sure it didn't have to be in person. We don't want anyone to have free access to him until this whole conspiracy is uncovered."

Burr stood up and rubbed his hands together, shaking out the kinks and aches his muscles got from long periods of inactivity. "Looks like the only thing left to do is go get the kid." His round face beamed. "I have the sudden urge for a cigar."

Weston said, "I always wondered what it would be like to have a younger brother." His faraway look vanished and he turned to grin at Burke. "I'll have to break my sisters to him gently, over time. I think I'm beginning to see all kinds of possibilities in this."

Burr clapped Burke on the back, turning serious again. "I'll make arrangements to get the kid. You give Ellis a call and bring down his anxiety level."

Burke nodded. "He'll probably kiss you for that." Burr only chuckled and walked over to the phone.

James had been unusually quiet. "Did they give you any hint about what's really going on here, Daniel? I don't think they'd give up so easily on the boy, especially if everything he says is true."

"I know, Ethan, but I don't have a clue. I did learn one thing, though."

"What?"

"Our next assignment was going to be in Eritrea, just like the kid said it would be."

* * * * *

Taking in a deep breath to steady himself, Ian Farr dabbed a handkerchief at the sweat beading on his forehead. "I realize we've lost the best opportunity to put an end to the leak, but there was nothing more I could do about it, sir. Colonel Burke made an extreme bid on the brat's behalf."

Farr listened to the man at the other end of the line a few more moments, his eyes closed and mind racing.

"That won't be possible, Lord Taber. Getting to Tarquin now is going to be a great deal of work. The American has agreed to accept responsibility for the boy. Making a move on a sixteen-year-old is one thing, but a black ops colonel is different. I'm not prepared to handle that on my own."

Farr pressed his lips into a thin line. "I understand, sir. I'll see if my contacts here know where the boy will be."

He straightened his impeccable suit.

"Thank you, your Grace. It is an honor to serve you in all things. I'll be returning to London on the evening flight with a full report."

Chapter Eighteen

Quill tried to count the number of towering trees lining the roadside. He'd never seen so many colors in so dense an area before. The London Park was the biggest wooded area he had ever been in. This view, with its dazzling array of gold, orange, red and mahogany hues, was breathtaking.

He burrowed down deeper in the blanket wrapped around his body as he shifted his weight to ease the stiffness in his injured leg. He appreciated the roominess of full-sized vans. He just wished he hadn't had to strap on that stupid seatbelt the giant had insisted he put on.

Quill twisted sideways on the seat, trying to keep the belt from digging into his side. "Why do I have to wear this thing? I'm not a baby! I don't need a pram."

One stern look from Burke stopped his complaints. He was still burning from the shame he felt over the whole gun thing. Burke had been understanding and supportive over the incident, making Quill feel all the guiltier. The quick hug Burke had given him had undone his carefully-crafted control. Unwanted tears filled his eyes, his nose became congested and he grabbed his inhaler before the wheezing started. Now he could add humiliation to his guilt. He felt his face flame and hoped the men thought it was asthma-induced.

Sighing, Quill darted a quick glance up to the next seat to check on his newly acquired benefactor. He still didn't believe Burke was going to be his guardian for the next seven years. What was life going to be like with this man? Would he still want him after he found out Quill's secret?

He was startled to find Burke returning his gaze. "It's a fairly short ride from the airport. We'll be home in just a few minutes."

Caught off guard, Quill resorted to surliness to hide his anxiety. "Home's a long way from here, if I had one, which I don't."

"Then this will have to do until you find one." Burke kept his voice neutral, trying to smooth over the situation. "You'll like the estate. It's got a lot of wooded grounds to explore when you're able. You'll have your own room, and there's a computer room jam-packed with equipment you can investigate. And you'll love Ramona, my housekeeper. If it's edible, she can make it into a masterpiece."

Burke smiled and pointed out the van window at a large, white stone building in the distance peeking out between groves of trees.

"There it is. My home. I haven't been there myself in over six months. It's good to be back, especially knowing I won't have to leave unless I want to from now on."

"Some of us can't leave even then." The sound of Quill's complaint was half-hearted and lacking in any real bitterness.

Quill strained to get a better look out of the window as they came closer to the building. The van turned and the partially concealed estate emerged.

The mansion's white stone surface glistened in the subdued afternoon sunlight. Its immense square dimensions dwarfed the nearby trees and made the vehicle parked in the front drive look like a toy. Massive pillars of polished granite stood on either side of the double entryway, like guardian soldiers. All the large, multi-paned windows were accented and bracketed by decorative ironwork. The landscaping was neat and trimmed, lush and green in contrast to the changing colors of the surrounding woods. All traffic sounds from the main highway had long since faded as they had moved into the secluded estate's grounds. It was peaceful, serene, immaculate and imposing.

Quill gave a low whistle of surprise. "Fucking hell, it's a tomb. I'm going to be living in bleeding *tomb* for the next *seven years!*"

Burke landed a sharp rap to the side of Quill's head. "Watch the language, scout." Quill glared but Burke ignored him and settled back for the remainder of the drive to the front door.

Quill limped through the foyer, angry with himself for insisting on walking all the way up the stairs and into the house. He was exhausted. He hobbled past a smiling dark-skinned woman, who acted like she was barely restraining her hands from reaching out and pinching his cheeks. A stoic, older man in a severe black suit wore an expression of mild disapproval as easily as he wore the suit.

Just as Quill's steps began to falter, he was lifted off the ground. Carrying Quill like a small child, Burke made short work of the remaining distance into the living room. Quill was deposited on a deep leather couch.

Quill blushed and squirmed away from Burke's hold. "Leave off." He scowled. "I'd have managed, you berk."

Before Burke could react to the sass, an immaculate, manicured hand shot out and whacked the teen on the back of the head.

"There'll be no such language used here, young man."

Stunned anyone knew what he had just said, Quill swiveled his head around to find himself hovered over by the black-suited man who had just spoken with a crisp, British accent.

"No need to clump me, guv. Didn't mean nothing." Quill rubbed at the sore spot on the back of his head and studied the gray-haired man before turning to Burke. "You just startled me, is all. Not used to being hauled around."

He hoped Burke would hear the apology in his words. Kevin and Liam had understood his need for distance and physical space. Quill suddenly pictured his two friends, lifeless and tied to a pole and felt overwhelmed and terribly sad. A quick, sharp intake of breath helped steady his wavering control, but he shivered involuntarily nonetheless.

Burke wrapped a blanket around his shoulders.

"Sorry. I'm a bit knackered after all this traveling. Seems like I've been on an aeroplane for the last three days."

"Don't worry about it." Burke smiled at him and Quill felt himself relax a bit. The older man shot a glance sideways at the gray-haired man still standing behind the couch. "Don't mind him either. His bark is worse than his bite."

An indignant snort interrupted his next sentence and Burke sent another sideways glance to the other man, this time with an amused twinkle in his eye. "Besides, you're both going to have to get along, if for no other reason then I don't have time to play referee."

The man moved in front of the sofa, unruffled, the

picture of formal bearing and tasteful aplomb. Burke gestured at first the man then at Quill.

"Marcus Plant, meet Quillan Tarquin. Quill, Marcus."

Burke turned to Quill and tapped his cheek. "Marcus runs my estate, the household staff, the grounds, the security. If you need to know something, ask Marcus. He'll know. You two will become the best of friends."

Quill sullenly massaged the back of his head.

Plant brushed off his own spotless lapel, his face pinched and hard. "In time. No doubt." Plant's tone matched Quill's disbelieving expression.

Quill snorted and directed his next comment to Burke. "Only going to be here seven years, mate. Don't think it's enough time."

Quill gave Burke a half-hearted smile to take some of the smart-ass sting from his words. A light pinch to his earlobe caused him to jump, unsettling his injured leg. One hand flew to the offended ear and one to the complaining knee. He glared up at Plant.

"What you want to go and do that for, you daft bugger?"

"I'm well aware of what common street slang passes for in London as language these days, young man. I have a niece living in the East End of the city. We chat frequently. Don't think any of your cockney foolishness will be left unchallenged. Each slur or insult will garner you a well-earned punishment."

A cool, steely glare accompanied the sermon. "I hope your earlobes aren't extremely sensitive."

"Bloody he–, I mean, come on now." Quill's indignant words bounced off Burke with little effect. "Do I have to put up with this?"

Sliding a pillow under Quill's braced leg, Burke grinned down at the cringing boy. "Yes. If I survived it growing up, you can too." He patted Quill's shoulder and moved off toward the sounds of commotion coming from the front foyer. "My advice to you, kid, is deal with it."

Burke exited the room knowing that once Quill figured out that Plant was a big softie under all the brusqueness he'd have the run of the place.

Throwing an uncertain scowl at Plant, Quill met the man's unforgiving expression head on for a few heartbeats then lowered his gaze to study the fine pyramid print in the blankets weave. He had to bite the inside of his cheek Burke was so fond of tapping to keep the flurry of unappreciative words forming on his tongue from jumping out and earning him another painful thump.

A sudden, loud spattering of excited Spanish broke the tense silence. Plant followed Burke back out into the main hall.

The over-sized doorway between living area and hall allowed Quill to watch. James, Burr, and Weston, all lugging various duffel bags and satchels, joined Plant and Burke. The animated woman Quill assumed to be Ramona fluttered amongst the big soldiers. Her speech was fast-paced and filled with words he didn't recognize. This didn't appear to be a problem for any of the others. They nodded and answered the woman at what seemed to be the appropriate times, causing another burst of excited chatter to break free.

Quill grew tired just listening, trying to grasp some small bit of information.

He sank down further into the warmth of the heavy blanket and let the conversation flow over him, catching a phrase or a sentence from one of the men that made sense to him. He listened until his eyes grew heavy and even the men's words became as garbled and meaningless as the woman's. The last thing he remembered was thinking he wasn't going to have any earlobes left after living here for the next seven years.

He never noticed when the group of people from the foyer moved into the room with him, nor did he register the feminine, dark hand that petted the hair back from his bruised face. The murmured blessing escaped his notice as well. The Spanish-accented words, spoken with the gentleness of a mother for a sleeping child, were heard only by the few surrounding him.

* * * * *

Ethan James set the phone back into its cradle. The smile on his rugged face generating a similar expression from his three companions.

"Well, that about does it. I'm all set to leave tomorrow 'round noon. I haven't been home to my daddy's ranch in more than a year. Momma's got one devil of a barbecue planned. You're all welcome to tag along."

The four men sat at the south end of the large living room in front of the massive stone fireplace. Two more matching couches, like the one Quill was sleeping on, bracketed the hearth. Burr and Weston sat on one and Burke and James faced them on the other.

Burke appreciated James keeping his tone low so as to not to wake the sleeping boy on the couch at the far end of the room. His voice had a note of hope in it, but his raised, questioning eyebrows showed he knew an affirmative answer was farfetched.

The sleeping figure on the couch snored and Burke

grinned. "Thanks, Ethan. Another time. The kid's going to have enough to adjust to. When I think he's ready to be smothered in loving kindness, chatter, and Texas barbecue sauce, I'll let you know."

Looking up from the manual in his hands, Weston seconded the idea. "I'm good with Daniel's plan, Ethan. You enjoy this time alone with your folks and I'll be there for the next one. My parents both decided they needed to come to me this time. Which means I have no idea when they'll show. They're both unpredictable, but reliable, if that makes any sense."

"Makes about as much sense as anything else you say, Ray." Burr reached across from his seat beside the younger man and ruffled Weston's hair. "But we're used to it."

Burr had long ago moved his few meaningful possessions to the estate. "I'm going to pass this time around, too, buddy. You go enjoy the folks, give them my best and tell them to start cooking now for when we do get a chance to visit. I could eat a whole mountain of those enchiladas your momma makes. The ones with all those little red peppers in them."

James chuckled. "You just use them as an excuse to gulp down all that tequila, Jack."

"True, but I'm not sure which one burns more, the peppers or the Gold."

"I'll make sure Daddy stocks up the liquor cabinet before then. Just remember, he's looking forward to a rematch with you at the totem."

Burr groaned and flexed the muscles of his bulky arms and shoulders. "For a man his age, your daddy is one strong S.O.B., Ethan. He damn near killed me last time."

The last time Burr had visited James' parents, the

elder James, a man of massive statue and girth like his son, had challenged the athletic, broad-muscled Burr to an Indian test of strength. Both men took turns climbing a thirty-foot totem pole with their bare hands with a fifty-pound stone tied to their backs. They had to retrieve a small cup of water off the top of the pole and return the cup to the ground intact in the shortest amount of time. The elder James had beaten the much younger Burr four times.

"You tell that sadistic devil to practice up. I'm going to whoop his butt next time. This year I'm practicing with Ramona tied to my back."

A burst of laughter from the group caused the jumble of blankets on the far couch to stir, but the boy settled back down within seconds. The men exchanged guilty looks then broke out in a new round of subdued snickers.

Burr turned serious again. "I'm going to start checking around for some dogs. This place needs canine patrols. The grounds are too widespread and dense. Besides, I've wanted to try my hand at breeding. Now's a good a time as any to get started."

"Good idea, Jack. I've put off getting dogs thinking they needed to have their owner around more often then I could be here. Now's a good time to get some." Burke flipped through a notebook resting on the coffee table in front of him.

"I've got dinner with my mother planned for this evening. She has a few ideas about marketing our company. We want to get the word out about us. We're military trained, black ops, able to develop new and test existing security systems. I think word-of-mouth will do us more good than direct advertising. The woman has the ear of every major businessman on the East Coast, even the ones who are afraid of her."

Again the other men smiled and nodded, but there were no chuckles of amusement. They knew Norris Burke was a formidable woman. Since her husband's death, she had taken charge of the family's investment firm and managed to increase the family fortune many times over. She suffered fools for only a brief instant before cutting them loose.

As hard as she was in the boardroom, she doted on both her sons. She lavished both time and attention on them in equal amounts. Her eldest, Patrick and his wife Gwen as well as their twins Mercy and Kent were frequent visitors in her home.

Whenever possible she over-indulged herself with Daniel and his three closest friends as if the men were all her own offspring, offering advice, criticism and affection in large quantities on the sparse, irregular visits the Army had allowed them over the years.

Norris Burke was delighted beyond words her son had resigned from the military to start civilian life.

Another restless, frantic movement drew their attention to Quill. The boy grunted sharply in his sleep, struggling with the blankets then burrowed back down into the nest surrounding him and all but disappearing in the mound.

The four men shared a concerned look, which Burke acknowledged with a small tilt of his head.

"I'll ask Ramona to sit with him until he wakes up. Ethan, you need to pack. Ray, let Marcus know which room your mother would like to stay in. He'll make sure there's fresh flowers brought in for her."

"She likes orchids." Weston flipped James a nearby

manual on weapons registration in the state of New York.

"Tell Marcus. He loves it when women swoon over his attention to those little details."

Burke turned to his best friend. "And Jack, maybe you can find some time to look over the grounds and the blueprints of the estate. Marcus has the place pretty well covered for normal circumstances, but you and he have to sit down and discuss what needs beefing up. I'm not expecting any warning before the next murder attempt is made."

Burr stood up and wandered over to the bank of French glass panels that opened to the south.

"You got it, Daniel. I'll walk the perimeter to the house and take a look around. Figure out where the best sniper spots are. We need to trim back the plant life a bit. Some of those trees are too close to the house."

Burke joined him and followed where Burr pointed. He clapped the big man on the shoulder.

"I'll leave it to you, Jackson. I'd join you, but I have to get ready for a dinner date with a very lovely older woman who will skin me alive if I'm late."

Chapter Nineteen

The crystal on the table was very old, a pattern Burke first remembered from his days as a toddler, when Marcus would run interference between the priceless stemware and his curious little fingers. Now his fingers tapped restlessly against one of the wine goblets as he waited for his mother's reaction to the news about Quill. Heaven knows what she'd say about her son taking the responsibility for a British teenage ward for the next seven years.

The sharp, brown eyes appraising his face dropped to his nervous fidgeting, stilling his hand. Burke cleared his throat and shifted in his seat, silently admonishing himself for falling automatically into the role of adolescent teenager in his mother's presence.

It had been years since she had wielded any authority over him beyond his genuine desire to please her and return her love and affection, but her sharp wit and steely stare had been known to bring seasoned, corporate executives to heel.

Burke chuckled out loud, the sound bringing a smile to his mother's cream-colored, beautiful face and softening her expression.

"You've managed to shock me. I didn't expect you to make me a grandmother quite so soon after your retirement."

He could feel the blush go all the way to the roots of his hair. Burke laughed again and held her hand across the small table. The delicate feel of her small bones brought back memories of the times these very same hands had held him and soothed his fears as a child. Her hands were deceptively fragile.

"I haven't adopted him, mother. He's a ward of the state. I've been appointed his guardian."

Norris studied her son's face. "Doesn't he mean more to you than that? It's going to be a long seven years if he doesn't."

He was taken aback by the icy words. "I've barely had time to get to know him. I've been spending all my time just trying to keep him alive so far."

She stopped eating and put her fork down on the table with exaggerated care. "So you're really just his keeper, a jailer while the child does his time under house arrest."

"No! That's not the case at all."

Norris carved a few more thin slices of meat from her steak. "Good. Otherwise you'd better get busy finding someone else who can do the job right. A boy needs more than a bodyguard, Daniel, and if you can't provide it, find someone who can."

"Mother!"

She hadn't even met the kid yet and she was defending him over Burke. The sharp end of a sterling silver steak knife was pointed at the tip of his nose.

"Listen to me, young man. Children need to know there's someone who cares about them. This boy's going to need all that and more." She gave him one of the appraising looks she normally saved for prospective employees. "You may not be the best one to give it to him."

"Thanks for the vote of confidence. We'll do fine. He's a tough kid, a real survivor. He fought off an

203

experienced black ops assassin, witnessed things no kid should ever have to and suffered through a painful injury without one word of complaint since."

Burke realized he had a desperate need to protect and care for the boy. "I've kidnapped him, fought for him, given up my career for him and opened my house and the rest of my life for him. And if anyone is going to be there for him, whether it's for the next seven years or the rest of his life, it's damn well going to be me."

His shouts reverberated in the room. He sucked in a ragged breath and sat back in his chair, trying to get comfortable and not succeeding. "I'm sorry. I didn't mean to raise my voice. I just...He makes me...I don't know what I'm trying to say."

A smug, self-satisfied smile tugged at the corners of Norris' perfect, ruby tinted lips. "Well, finally, a bit of emotion about all this. I was wondering how this young man managed to creep into your life, make you turn your back on a career that defined your whole life and had you drag your entire unit along with you. That's one powerful child. Especially since you've been talking about him as if he was a stray puppy you found on the side of the road. One you'll keep warm and dry and feed until his real owner shows up for him."

"That's not true." After the impact of the statement settled in, he raised one thoughtful eyebrow. "I don't act like that, do I?"

"If you have to ask..." Norris returned her attention to her meal, leaving her son to figure out things for himself.

"Dear Lord." Burke leaned back into the deep upholstered chair and raised his wineglass, studying the glistening pattern while he mentally reviewed the last few days.

Norris cleared her throat and touched the corner of her mouth with her spotless white napkin. "Am I ever going to hear you say his name? In all the conversations we've had about this, I've never heard you even mention it."

"What? Really?" He set his glass back on the table, shaking his head. He looked off into the distance and tried to reconcile his present thoughts with the feelings of protectiveness churning through him.

"Not once."

Burke became silent for a moment, then turned to his mother, determined to understand himself, for everyone's sake. "When I joined the Army, it was all I ever wanted. I had a job I was good at, one that helped people. I had recognition, respect, rank and good friends. The best possible friends, brothers. Jackson has been a part of my life since college, but if I hadn't joined up I would never have met Ethan and Ray. I can't imagine my life without them being there."

Norris reached out and laid a comforting hand on her son's. Burke grasped her fingers and plunged ahead. "But the last few years, something's been missing. When Beth disappeared out of my life, all thought of a family disappeared with her. It's been sixteen years and I still get that empty feeling in the pit of my stomach whenever I think of her."

Her long, thin fingers laced through his, giving him the courage to finish. "I look at this kid, at Quill, and I think about how much his eyes look like hers and how much his hair is the same shade of brown. And I start to think, actually believe, God's decided to reward me for my sacrifices. That he's giving me back a little piece of her."

"That's a beautiful thought, Daniel. He does mean something to you."

"More than I would have ever believed possible. But I keep wondering 'why now'?"

"Life is made up of little coincidences. Fate has more of a hand in our lives than any of us would like to believe. If it hadn't been for Freddy March jilting me at Sarah Harper's birthday party and leaving me alone on the dance floor, I would never have met your father."

The memory of the familiar bedtime story brought a small twist of a smile to Burke's lips.

Norris squeezed her son's hand. "Don't waste time worrying over it, enjoy it. This boy has awakened your parental instincts. Not just because he needs to be protected either. Any police agency is equipped to do that." She pointed a finger at Burke, tapping the air in front of him every time she said the word 'you'. "It's you he's bonded with. You he looks to for comfort and has from the start of things."

"And you would know all this because?" Burke had his suspicions.

"I talked to James Davenport just before you arrived." Her tone was much like an old-time schoolmarm forced to explain her actions to a foolish pupil. "He told me everything, within reason." She crossed her arms over her chest and gave a small, satisfied nod.

Norris sniffed, a slight edge of disdain emerging. "I know more about young Mr. Quillan Tarquin than you do, I'll wager." She gave Burke a look down her thin regal nose. "*I* know his name and I'm not afraid to use it."

Burke laughed and brought her hand to his lips for a quick kiss. "I see that. What else did Lord Davenport tell you about Quill? See, I *can* say his name."

Norris smiled then became serious. Even her eyes became wary. Davenport was one of her oldest and closest friends. She respected his opinion and listened to his advice. He gave her information about the happenings in London even her son wasn't privy to.

"James told me that Quillan's life is still at great risk. He personally feels that returning the boy to England at the moment is a bad idea, but he has to represent the Crown's interests."

Norris gave her son a direct, pointed stare. "At least, it had to appear MI5 wanted him back."

Taking another sip of wine, Burke contemplated the thinly veiled inference. Norris Burke wasn't known for beating around the bush. This had to be a delicate subject; one Davenport wanted her to discuss with him.

Burke offered the most obvious question. "That opens the question as to why MI5 supports a position different than the Crown's?"

"Sometimes it's best if one hand doesn't know what the other hand is doing in order for justice to be serviced. You should be familiar with that, Daniel."

"Someone in the upper levels of the British government is involved in the conspiracy or the cover-up? And Davenport knows this because he's been investigating it? Or is he the cover-up?"

His mother gave him a feigned look of surprised and took a bite of her dinner. "Hmm. This is excellent. I'll have to remember to compliment Cook."

Burke ignored her. "That would mean he's been working on this for some time. He knew about the file before Quill accessed it."

Burke felt a spurge of anger rush through him.

"They knew about it and left it in there so the responsible party wouldn't be wise to the fact MI5 was on to them. It's all part of a set-up. The McCabe brothers stumbled across the file and tripped up both sides by putting it out into the open. Neither side wants any witnesses left."

All of this could have been avoided, the loss of the McCabe brothers' lives, Quill's injuries, the attempt on his life–everything leading up to this point could have been avoided.

"Christ, I should have known something was up. My unit being called in to help wasn't a coincidence, was it? Davenport needed someone to put a leash on Crowe and he thought involving my team would be enough to curb his homicidal tenancies."

"James said he knew you weren't the kind of man to stand by and let a man like Crowe commit murder, even if it was on the order of a higher authority. He said you'd have a vested interest in this mission for some reason."

She swallowed another bite. "I'm sure he was doing what was best for everyone concerned. It's unfortunate those two boys died, yes, but it's my understanding there's a lot more at stake, Daniel, many more lives than just these. You did save a child. Don't forget that."

"Barely. He suffered a trauma that will probably haunt him the rest of his life." Burke pushed his plate away and stood up.

"I need to check on things at the estate. We need to get things in order faster than I expected." Kissing her offered cheek, Burke indulged her with an affectionate hug. He stepped back and framed her face between both hands.

"Mother, I know James has been a friend of the family for years and he cares deeply for you, but when he was speaking about the lives that had to be sacrificed for the greater good, did he mention that my team was next on the hit list? Are we as expendable as those boys were?"

A small gasp told him she hadn't known.

"He expected you to be better able to defend yourselves, I imagine." Her normally confident voice quavered.

His hands slid from her face. "And anyone who comes after the boy is going to see just how goddamn well I can do that." He dropped a quick kiss on her finely lined forehead. "No matter which side of this conspiracy they happen to be working on."

"I'll tell James."

"It's safest if you stay out of this. I'll tell him myself."

Burke glanced at the remnants of the meal. He reached out and ran a finger over the edge of the wine goblet. "Come over in the morning. I'll introduce you to your new grandson."

Her smiled changed from tentative to brilliant. The tension evaporated from the room.

"I'll do that."

He bestowed another kiss on her cheek and left the room.

At the table Norris Burke picked up her fork to finish her meal, hesitating just a moment to contemplate the new developments.

"A grandmother again. I'll have to get my new grandson a present. What does one buy a teenage felon?"

* * * * *

Entering the main hall, Burke was greeted by the

muffled sound of laughter. Following the thread of merriment, he walked through the partially open doors leading to the living area. He stopped just over the threshold.

Quill was awake and propped up with his back against one of the overstuffed couch arms. His injured leg was supported by a throw pillow and draped with a blanket. He looked tired, pale and tousled with sleep. A faint, shy smile creased his face every now and again in response to some comment or move made on the playing board laid out on the coffee table in front of him.

Weston, James, Burr, and Ramona surrounded him, avidly engaged in the game. Each appeared to be interested in drawing the young man into the midst of the conversations and jesting.

Ramona had a natural ease with people. Her casual, colorful dress reflected her Guatemalan heritage and accented her high cheeks and dark complexion. Her long black hair was held in a knot at the nape of her neck, streaks of silver-gray adding depth and a touch of aristocratic style to her appearance. Her dark eyes were bright with laughter, but showed a shadow of concern each time they landed on the flustered, thin boy beside her.

Burke watched, silent and still, taking in the sights and sounds of his new life with this motley crew of a family. The people in this house made up the core of his life now. This was his future and he was damn well going to see to it that no one took it away from him, any part of it. Not now, not ever.

Moving into the room, Burke felt a jolt of pleasure at the shy grin that jumped to Quill's face. In that moment, with that smile on his face, Burke caught a glimpse of Beth in the boy's features. It rocked him, hard. That was a smile he thought he'd never see again.

The bruises on Quill's face stood out in shades of dark blue and purple blending into a nauseating yellowish green. Fine lines from pain creased the corners of his eyes. The kid was worn out.

"I see just about the whole clan has assembled. Plotting to overthrow the entire government or just me?"

A round of chuckles mingled with several cheerful calls greeted him. Burr scooted to one side making a space for him on the couch facing Quill.

Burke shook his head no, and crouched down in front of Quill. The boy gave him a questioning look and drew back.

"It's late and you've had a hard couple of days. I've dragged you from one end of the country to the other and over two continents. How about we get you settled into your room."

"I'm good to go, guv. Not that tired." His tired, Cockney-accented words were barely understandable.

"Yeah, well, I am." Burke stood up and slipped his arms under Quill, urging him to stand. "And you're going to need your rest for tomorrow."

Taking most of the boy's weight on himself, Burke eased him across the room. "Because at ten o'clock my mother is coming over to meet you and boy, you had better have all your wits about you for that."

At the doorway, tired of the limp and drag progress they were making, Burke bent down and lifted Quill into his arms.

Quill pushed against Burke's chest and sputtered. Too drained to fight, he gave up and relaxed into his grip.

Chapter Twenty

Burke settled into the comfortable, old armchair at his desk. His private study was off his bedroom, affording him a secluded sanctuary from the rest of the house. The walls were adorned with every imaginable type of artwork from cartoon illustrations to oil paintings. Burke had eclectic tastes in art and his private collection reflected it.

On the wall to the left of his desk, where he could glance at it without difficulty hung a pen and ink caricature of a familiar MI5 officer. The drawing reminded him that having power and authority didn't make a person immune to acting like an ass.

Keeping that in mind, Burke picked up his private extension and dialed a number from memory. A series of subdued clicks and dead air pauses interspersed with a dial tone and then the low melody of the electronic dialing filled the span of thirty seconds before the phone was answered on the other end. Burke never even heard it ring.

"Expecting to hear from me?" Burke couldn't keep a small measure of the irritation he felt from showing.

"I wouldn't be worth what the Crown pays me if I hadn't been. You're too wise and too wily not to have figured out most of this already, Daniel. I won't insult you by implying otherwise." Davenport's crisp accent and elegant voice telegraphed a subtle rebuke at Burke's impertinence.

"And I'm supposed to be all right with this? Just

accept the fact my men and I were set-up?" He didn't give Davenport a chance to answer. "You do remember two young men died, don't you, Sir?"

"I remember one young man lived as well, and only because you were there. A young man who is turning out to be more important than you may think."

"I don't need riddles at this stage of the game, sir. I need answers." On a higher level Burke understood the need for secrecy and double talk, but this had gotten personal and he'd had it with any more subterfuge.

"Daniel, you have as many answers as I do and it's taken me an entire year to gain what you've unmasked in three days."

"More riddles. Excuse me if that's not enough. I have other lives depending on me to figure this out."

"Surely you understand your involvement was a necessity? This assassination conspiracy your boy stumbled onto has been under investigation for over a year. We couldn't jeopardize the progress we've made by letting them become aware of the fact we were onto them. We needed a unit that could be trusted, one skilled enough and with a reputation large enough Crowe would think twice about doing anything out of line."

"You seemed to have slipped up on that one."

"Yes, we failed. No one could have predicted how much of an egomaniacal murderer the man was." Davenport's voice was matter of fact. "It was unfortunate, but sometimes sacrifices have to be made for the greater good."

"I'll remind Quill of that when he starts grief counseling. I'm sure he'll get a lot of comfort from it." Burke dearly wanted to ruffle someone's composure right now.

"You might want to keep in mind you managed to unearth the fact you and your team were in danger, too. If General Weiss hadn't assigned you to the mission, you would all probably be dead at this moment."

"Weiss is part of this?" Burke couldn't resist giving a dry, mirthless chuckle. "No wonder he was so eager to help. And here Jack thought it was his impressive powers of persuasion. He'll be crushed."

"It was an added bonus we didn't know about at the time. We were aware of the file's existence, but had no clue it was being kept in an MI5 data system. Tampering with it would undoubtedly alert the people responsible. The exact content, the agents marked for assassination, remain unknown." Davenport let guilt work on Burke's conscious before adding, "We were hoping you might know a way to correct that."

A small, insistent voice saying Davenport knew more than he claimed began to nag at Burke. "I don't. The boy swears he didn't read anything more than the files he already told us about."

"And you believe him?" Davenport paused. "I see."

Burke was surprised how defensive those two little words made him feel. "He's a kid. His life's been turned upside down and inside out. He needs time. Don't you think finding out his mother is dead is enough for him to deal with right now? Enough for all of us to deal with?"

"He knows?"

"It was in the last group of files he read."

"That's unfortunate he had to learn about it that way."

"Yes, it was." Burke's voice sounded bitter even to his own ears. "For all of us."

"The agents in that file don't have time, Daniel."

"As someone in the know once told me–sometimes sacrifices have to be made for the greater good."

"I believe it when I say it. You, on the other hand, don't. This isn't some ridiculous group of conservative, altruistic fanatics weeding out the morally strong to give free rein to their vigilante methods. The roots are deep in the Middle East. There is much more at stake here than just the removal of what one group sees as obstacles to true justice, my boy."

That phrase was beginning to annoy Burke.

"Whoever they are, Sir, they had better know this– if they make a move on my kid or my men, I won't rest until they're eliminated, wiped from existence. I won't even feel the need to leave enough behind for DNA testing to identify the bodies."

"I'd expect nothing less."

Burke's voice held a warning note. "No matter which side of the line they're working for, Lord Davenport."

"I'll be sure to pass that along."

Burke could almost see the older man's bemused smile. Preparing to hang up, he was startled when the Brit spoke again. His tone had taken on a coaxing, conspiratorial element that had been missing in their conversation up until now.

"Daniel, if you should decide that you might want to lend an active hand in this matter at some point, check your e-mail within the next sixty seconds. It will give you the means to do so. Goodbye, my boy. A pleasure speaking with you, as always. My best to your mother."

The line went silent and another series of nearly inaudible snaps and clicks told Burke the multiple connections were closing one by one.

Irritated by the cloak-and-dagger game, he activated his desktop computer, opening the e-mail program. A flashing red exclamation mark drew his eye. He clicked it open and printed out the text before even attempting to read it. His sixty seconds were almost up. He managed to save a copy to a miscellaneous file just as the message blinked out of existence.

Moving at a more leisurely pace, Burke transferred it to a password-protected file then sat back to really take a look at what it told him. It was a group of nine digits that looked like account or access codes, along with a jumble of both lower and upper case letters. At the end was an e-mail address with a domain name few people would recognize. Burke, unfortunately, was very familiar with it, however.

Burke sat back in his chair, whistling softly under his breath. Unless he was mistaken, he had just been given access to Britain's most secret files.

* * * * *

Burke really didn't know what woke him. A feeling, a nudge from his finely honed instincts, demanded he come back to consciousness like the insistent tugging of a toddler. He lay listening to the sounds of the house, trying to pinpoint what was different. In the hall the ancient grandfather clock was ticking a familiar, soothing sound. Beyond that, the house was silent.

Knowing from long experience silence didn't mean safety, Burke removed a handgun from his bedside stand and loaded a clip into it. He slipped from the covers and moved barefoot, soundless and sure, to his bedroom doorway. There he listened, his hand on the brass doorknob, then eased the well-oiled door open. Gliding into the dimly lit hallway, he stayed close to the walls, crouched and ready for any assault that might come from the thin, gray shadows.

Burke's bedroom, bath, and personal study took up the entire west wing of the second floor. The east wing housed Plant's private quarters which could be accessed by a separate stairway from the back of the house. Next to Plant's room was the computer room and one remaining guest room where Quill slept.

A quick glance into the open, unoccupied computer room let Burke rule it out as a source of his unease. He eliminated Plant's room too. It was isolated to provide Plant with privacy. Burke couldn't have heard anything from there. That left only one place as the possible source of the problem.

His hand inched open the doorknob to Quill's room. Just as it released the catch, a muffled moan followed by a sharp, gasping sob broke the silence.

Burke shoved open the door, rolled across the floor into the room, crouched low, gun raised and ready. He found himself facing a sleeping boy struggling to free himself from a confining sheet.

Both bedside lamps had been switched on sometime during the night, bathing the room and its occupant in a washed-out, hazy, white light.

Placing the gun out of sight on the bureau, Burke closed the bedroom door, taking no pains to keep silent. He didn't want a repeat of what had happened with Ellis.

Still asleep, Quill was struggling against the twisted sheets, a slight sheen of sweat covering his face. Though the room was a perfect sixty-eight degrees, a shudder ran through the slight frame and gooseflesh covered Quill's arms.

Quill's fine-boned features reminded Burke of his former sweetheart. The boy's hair, unfettered by dried blood, sweat or nervous hands, had the same natural curl and part in the front like his had, a Burke family trait.

Quill shifted restlessly again. The boy began to whimper and cry out, jolting Burke.

"Please! Don't...don't, please don't! No!"

The last plea was desperate, blood-chilling even for a man as hardened as Burke. The last word cut through him like a knife, forcing him into action.

Sitting down on the edge of the full-sized bed, Burke took a firm grip on the tangled sheet and began working it away from Quill. The boy responded with an increase in his struggles and the whimpering became a constant buzz. Leaning close, Burke let a soft litany of soothing words flow as he worked.

Still caught in the blanket of deep sleep, Quill turned his head toward Burke's voice and slowed his frantic movement. Burke began rubbing his thumb over the center of Quill's forehead, each measured stroke calming the boy.

Never breaking contact, Burke freed the covers and settled them over the shivering figure. It took ten minutes, but the whimpering quieted and Quill relaxed into a more restful state. Only then did Burke ease his hand away, dropping it to tug the blankets under the boy's chin.

The role of comforter and parent was new to him, but each time Burke found it easier. By the third night of soothing away nightmares, it was starting to feel natural, maybe even right.

Chapter Twenty-one

The dark paneling and deep cordovan leather furniture in Burke's study gave it a rich, lived-in feel. Quill could sense the man's confident, easy presence even though the room was unoccupied. Slipping through the half-open door separating the master bedroom from the study, he seated himself behind the carved mahogany desk and rested his crutches against its edge. He began turning over objects and looking under folders and tablets, searching for a hint to the estate's network password.

Quill had overheard Burke telling Burr, James, and Weston to be prepared for something called a 'black bag job'. Quill understood enough of the conversation to realize it had to do with the assassination plot he had stumbled onto.

As Quill listened to Burke's conversation, Plant had entered the hallway. Quill had to continue into the room to cover the fact he'd been eavesdropping. Burke ended the conversation and Quill had missed hearing any more.

The lives and deaths of so many people lay in that one file. The guilt from keeping silent ate at Quill. He wanted to tell Burke the truth. Even if the man looked at him with nothing but disgust for the next seven years, at least he'd have done the right thing. Every day that passed deepened his responsibility. The burden was suffocating Quill, but nightmares of being murdered like his friends were enough to keep his mouth shut.

Quill moved the desk mat and looked under a

small brass desk clock. Picking up a silver frame, he flipped open the embossed cover and stared into a face he recognized from his dreams and pictures his aunt had shown him. Tears welled and Quill batted them back, determined to keep control.

"She was beautiful, wasn't she?"

Burke's low, almost reverent voice made Quill jump. He fumbled at the frame as it slipped from his hand. It clattered to the padded desktop. Quill was unprepared for any conversation dealing with his long missing mother.

"You have her smile. Her eyes, too."

Self-conscious, Quill dropped his gaze back to the photo. He fidgeted in the chair, the well-oiled mechanism making a mere whisper of sound as he twisted and turned in place. His first instinct was to run, but he couldn't avoid this any longer.

"But that curl...in the front of your hair? That's from me."

Quill sucked in a reedy breath and chanced a glance at his father. Burke stood just inside the frame of the door, a serious, but gentle expression on his face. Quill felt the tears he had been holding back threaten to break through again.

"And you have her intelligence-my brazen guts, but definitely her brains."

Quill shook with the force of sudden rage flooding through his body. Who the bloody hell did this guy think he was? Had Burke known all along? Was this all a game to the man? Just because he'd gotten his mum preggers, then skipped town, did he think it gave him the right to torture Quill like this?

A massive lump formed in Quill's throat. He felt

like he'd swallowed one of Ethan's size nineteen boots, making it impossible for him to answer. Another glance at his mother's picture and the rage drained away to be replaced by a feeling of loneliness so fierce his chest ached.

Wasn't this what he had been hoping for since the day his aunt had told him who his father was? Wasn't this why he had turned his perfect memory and outstanding talent with computers to hacking...to find this man? Over the last year he had thought of a thousand things he wanted to say when this day came and now he couldn't even choke out a word.

Burke walked further into the room and leaned against the side of his desk. He picked up the silver frame, turning it to gaze at the dark-haired woman, longing and pain apparent in his eyes. He brushed the fingertips of one hand over the glass, tracing the outline of the woman's lips.

"We were very much in love."

A derisive snort from Quill followed the declaration. "Not enough to stay around."

Burke tried not to react to his son's bitter words.

"*She* left *me*."

"Riiight."

Burke straightened up and put the frame back down on the desk. "You have to understand, son. It was a different time. We were on different career paths. Young, just starting out, determined to make a difference in the world, ambitious."

"Then you should have kept your nob in your pants, you smarmy bastard."

Counting silently to ten, Burke held his temper in check, but just barely. "I didn't know about you. I wanted to marry her. I was undergoing a training program with British forces. I was...out of communication for over a year. When I got back, she was gone. Your Aunt Sheila told me Elizabeth had moved away. Beth was focusing on her career and had moved on with her life." Burke eyes glistened with unshed tears and his voice had a tremor to it. "Sheila was holding you in her arms when I came by. She told me you were *her* son."

Burke shook his head at the memory. "I spent the next decade or so regretting losing my chance to have a son like that beautiful baby with the woman I loved."

He reached out and touched Quill's shoulder then let his hand drop when Quill shrugged away. "And now, fifteen years later, I find out you *are* my son."

"How long have you known?"

"About two months. An old family friend highly placed in the British government let me in on it. A man named James Davenport. He's the director of MI5 now."

"He's a part of this?"

"I don't know. I don't think so." Burke glanced away. "I hope not."

Quill sneered. "You don't pick your mates very well do you?"

"I think I do just fine."

Quill's emotions were all over the place–bouncing from resentment to anger to longing. Resent took the lead. "Fucking bastard!"

"Sometimes, yes."

Burke loomed at Quill's side, his presence oddly reassuring. Solid, real, there. Not some phantom father in a half-remembered dream.

"What-what do you want from me?" Quill sounded both was hopeful and frightened.

"I should be asking you that. You're the one that's been dogging my steps for months."

Quill frowned. "How'd they know?"

"You're very clever, son, a genius with the computer." There was a definite note of pride in Burke's voice. "But Army intelligence is more so. There are a lot more of them and they've been at it longer. But it *did* take them a while to figure it out. No matter what files were broken into, from minor mission assignments to confidential reports, I was always involved. When they saw the pattern, I was informed."

Quill ducked his head.

Burke swiveled Quill's chair around and crouched down in front of the boy. "Do you really think it was a coincidence Lord Davenport called my team in?"

The teen glanced up for a split second then dropped his gaze. His voice was a strained whisper. "Thought it was more of my bad luck."

The corner of Burke's mouth twisted up in a half smile. "Not a chance. But I was expecting an enemy from my past, not the mess we found."

Quill's embarrassment flashed to anger. "Excuse me for messing up your fucking perfect life."

He tried to bolt from the chair. Burke pushed him back down with one hand and held him there. "I was talking about Crowe."

"No, you're not! The minute this is over, you'll send me off! You don't care about me! I'm just a fucking *mistake* you made years ago."

Quill's tone turned bitter and he choked back a sob. "Guess that's the story of my life! Mistake from the first fuck!"

He struggled out of Burke's stunned grip and

223

bolted to the other side of the desk. "I never asked to be born and I never asked for you to fuck up my life now."

Burke shook his head. "Really? Then why were you tracking me?"

"I-I don't know! I wanted...I needed...I don't fucking *know*, damn it! I don't know! Maybe I just wanted to pretend I had a father!" A visible tremor ran him and he wrapped his arms around his own body to stop it. "I don't have anything else left now, do I?"

Quill let the tears run down his face to drip from his jaw. He grabbed the frame from the desktop. "I guess we both got a surprise. You got a criminal for a bastard son and I got a cold-hearted arse with a hero complex for a father!"

He pitched the silver frame, forcing Burke to scrabble to catch it. Quill turned and raced from the room in a tear-blinded stumble.

Burke let him go. He closed his eyes for a moment. "Well, that went all to hell in no time."

Burke sat down at his desk and fingered the picture frame. Elizabeth's beautiful face looked back at him, pulling all the wistful memories of her into his thoughts. Quill definitely had her eyes and her smile. Burke ran a light touch over her face, whispering to the empty room.

"This fatherhood thing is all new to me. You could have given me a hint, you know. Sixteen years later and you're still surprising me. So where do I go from here, Beth?"

* * * * *

Once he made it to his bedroom, Quill sat down on the bed, shaking. He wasn't ready for this. He needed more time to adjust, to get to know his father. The man expected him to fit right in and join in his little collected family.

But it wasn't that easy.

He'd been on his own for two years. Everything was different here. He couldn't talk the way he talked, he couldn't go where he wanted to go, and people demanded to know where he was twenty-four hours a day. They made rules for meals and bed and even rationed the amount of time he was allowed to use a computer! Goddamn wankers! He was nearly twenty! All right, nearly seventeen, but they didn't know that! Of course, Burke would figure that out pretty quickly.

That would be another nail in his coffin, another example of what a liar he was, how much he didn't deserve to be Burke's son. He really shouldn't blame Burke. What kind of a hero wanted a lying criminal for a son?

But if he could do something to show Burke he wasn't a total fuck-up maybe, just maybe, he could buy himself a little time, to work his way in, maybe grow on Burke. The man *was* his father.

Maybe, over time, some biological instinct would make Burke want him to stay around. Maybe he could help it all along. If he could just get back into the computer system where the files were housed, he could find a clue about those people. Burke said it himself, he was a genius. He could do this. He had to do this. Because if he couldn't win Burke over, he didn't have anyone left.

Quill brushed the tears from his face, sniffed and pushed up off the bed. If Burke hadn't followed him after that scene, he was obviously going to leave him alone for awhile. This was his best opportunity.

He eased open the bedroom door and glanced

down the hall. The door to Burke's own private suite was across the open landing, partially blocked by a huge wooden cabinet. The hallway was silent.

The room housing the estate's computers was beside Quill's, joined by a common alcove. It only took him a few seconds and he had plunked down in front of the main console. He began running through password after password to gain access. Then inspiration hit and he was into the system.

The new password was 'fatherhood'.

* * * * *

In the quiet, richly-appointed, private home office of Lord Alexander Taber, an insistent, rather annoying little red icon on the computer monitor began to flash, over and over and over again.

Chapter Twenty-two

He knew it. There was absolutely no question about it. Only three days had passed since his arrival and he was positive he wasn't going to have any earlobes left by the time seven years were up.

Quill rubbed at the aching kernel of flesh that used to be his left earlobe and scowled. The pout earned him an unrepentant glare from his tormentor, Burke's personal attendant, Marcus Plant.

It just wasn't fair. All he had said was that he wasn't hungry. Maybe he had called the man old. Well, maybe he'd said old, pinched-faced git, but the man didn't have to try and remove his entire ear. It was just an expression, a way of venting some of his mounting frustration.

Quill shifted his weight on the kitchen chair, grimacing at the renewed ache in his knee. Three days had helped the healing process, but the knee was still tender.

A visit from Burke's private physician had netted Quill a pair of crutches, an order for a x-ray and a pending appointment with a psychologist specializing in traumatic events. Quill didn't plan on keeping that last appointment. Kev and Liam's deaths were two things he wanted to tuck away, not talk about.

The large, airy kitchen was filled with oak cabinets and marble countertops were topped with bright copper canisters and pots of herbs. Pungent strands of garlic and peppers hung in ropes near the stovetop and the main counter. The room always smelled of warm bread and honey. Quill was drawn to it like a magnet to iron filings in the sketching toy he'd had as a small child.

The round, scarred wooden table held room for six. The first time he had made it to the table with the rest of the men, Burke had insisted on adding a leaf to it, saying his family had grown so much that the table needed to expand as well. The warm smile the man had given Quill almost made him cry. The evening meal had been full of laughter, good food, and a surreal feeling of belonging.

This morning, Quill and Burr were the only people sitting at it. The rest of the household was up and involved in their day already. Quill hadn't seen Burke since he had come home last evening.

Jackson was digging into his breakfast like a starving man, leaving no room for idle conversation.

Quill had spent the night tossing and turning, trying to fight off shadowy, faceless attackers and erase Kev and Liam's last moments alive. His relentless memory played the murders over and over again in his sleep, reinforcing his guilt over surviving. It spilled over into his waking hours, torturing him.

He needed some space to think. He'd been taking care of himself for two years. He didn't need muscle-bound, armed babysitters and sharp-tongued, ear-pinching disciplinarians or even cheek-patting, sweet-natured mothering. And he sure as bloody hell didn't need an overbearing, over-protective, but distant father.

Looking for Burke had been a mistake. Not fighting harder to escape Burke's hold once Quill was safe had been the biggest mistake of all. Quill was sure Burke couldn't really want *him*; he'd want to find out about the people in the file and then his interest in him would be over. When that happened, Quill knew he would be forced to stay in a place completely foreign to him. All of it gave him nightmares.

And nobody here in the 'tomb' seemed to understand. The only solution was for Quill to stay aloof and not get close to any of them.

A soft caress to Quill's hair startled him. He glanced up to catch Ramona's bright smile, her fingers lingering, smoothing down the ends of his hair. She placed a plate of toast, eggs, and something he didn't recognize in front of him.

His stomach growled and his mouth watered, but the sudden memory of the taste of copper in his mouth soured his appetite. He didn't think the sensation of warm blood and tissue slapping his face would ever leave him. Quill brushed one hand over his lips then pushed the plate away.

"Thanks, not very hungry."

He gave the woman a smile he hoped softened his refusal.

"Can't be true. I heard your stomach complaining all the way over here, boy." Burr forked another mouthful of fried potatoes into his mouth and chewed, gesturing toward Quill's waiting plate. "Eat up if you want to go into town with Ray and me. The doc wants you to get an x-ray of that gimpy leg of yours and I'm going to call on the local vet and get some leads from him about dog breeders. No reason we can't do both at the same time."

Burr pushed the plate back in front of Quill.

"But not unless you eat. I don't want to be listening to your empty stomach growling the whole ride."

Cautious, Quill picked up a piece of toast, tore a chunk out of it, chewed then swallowed. His stomach growled its approval. He stuffed the remainder of the wedge in his mouth.

"Could we stop by a market? To buy software? Grand – Mrs. Burke, gave me a gift card. She said it was just like cash. I'd like to look at a program I've been reading up on."

Quill smiled at the memory of the older woman. She had insisted he call her "Grand" instead of Mrs. Burke. She claimed all her grandchildren did, but he thought she secretly just liked the name.

Burr paused then grunted. "Okay, but you've only got fifteen minutes to look. Any more is too long in one place and we're leaving whether you've got what you wanted or not."

"Deal." Quill managed to get the word out around another mouthful of food. He was rewarded with a mild tap to the back of his head.

"Swallow first."

The distinct, clipped tones of a well-bred, upper class British aristocrat renewed the ache in Quill's earlobe. Plant didn't glance at him, expecting immediate compliance.

Quill satisfied his need for revenge by gulping the rest of his food and washing it down with the entire glass of milk in a series of hurried, loud swallows. He caught Plant rolling his eyes. Quill smiled.

Burr pushed back from the table, grabbed both his own and Quill's plates and deposited them in the sink. Ramona paused in her luncheon preparations to take the remainder of the dishes from Burr's hands, tsking at him the entire time. Burr grinned and said something in Spanish that made the older woman blush and smile like a schoolgirl. A faint sigh of irritation came from Plant.

The entire scene made Quill's chest ache and he fought to choke down a sob that came up from nowhere. He brushed a hand over his eyes. The urge to break out in tears for no reason at all was becoming harder and harder to suppress. This confused and irritated him. He hoped the more time that passed, the easier it would be to deal with the events of the last few days, but it didn't.

He wanted desperately to confide everything to Burke-the file content, the extent of his knowledge about the plot and the fact he had been tracking Burke for the last eighteen months. He had come close, but each time he tried, his insecurities popped up to silence him. He consoled himself with the thought that Burke seemed to be growing more at comfortable around him, easing some of Quill's reservations. One day Burke might be willing to accept him for who he was.

The soothing, familiar voice broke into his thoughts. He glanced up to see Burke enter the room, coat on and Quill's leather jacket in hand. "If you two have stopped feeding your faces, I'd like to get a move on. I have a conference call coming in later this afternoon."

Burke threw Quill his jacket then grabbed the crutches leaning against the nearby countertop and held them so the boy could stand. Quill complied with the unspoken command.

"It'll be good to get out for a bit."

Burke tapped his cheek in the now expected gesture that was coming to mean so much. "Glad you feel that way. You haven't been on your feet for any great length of time. I don't want you getting too tired."

"I'm good. Don't worry about me." Quill eased himself to a stand with a small grimace of pain.

Burke said nothing, but patted his cheek again,

letting his palm linger over Quill's face as if checking for a fever. The small show of affection, this tiny, brief piece of physical contact was the only time Quill had allowed anyone to touch him in recent days. He found himself shrugging off helping hands, steadying touches, and even light pats from Ramona with equal irritation. The gestures didn't stop and his response was never questioned or rebuked, each shrug met with an understanding look or smile.

"Let's hit the road, men. Ramona is whipping up her famous, irresistible chili rellenos and I want to be home in time for lunch."

Burr snagged a piece of red pepper from the pile Ramona was working on, making off with a second piece from the opposite side as she turned to swat his thieving hand.

Burke teased, "You just finished breakfast, Jack."

The antics continued as Burr made off with a few more choice pieces of food. "I'm just a growing boy, Daniel. I need sustenance or I'll waste away. End up looking like a lamp post."

"Like the one's in the older section of Pittsburgh with the big, round, shiny, bald globes on top?" Burke placed a hand on Quill's shoulder, guiding him toward the back door.

Burr ran a hand over his polished head. "Don't be dissing the dome, Daniel. It's my babe magnet."

Something close to a small laugh escaped Quill. "Babe magnet? A bald head? What kind of women like that?" He grunted in between the jarring thud of the crutches as he walked.

"Ones with taste, son, ones with taste. Did you know caressing the surface of a bald man's head is similar–."

Burke cut off the rest of Burr's sentence. "I think we've learned enough about sex appeal and the wonders of baldness for one day, Jack."

"Just trying to be helpful."

"Well, stop." Burke insisted playfully.

Burr winked at Quill, returning the teen's smile. Using a loud stage whisper he said, "Talk to me later, son."

Quill snickered again and lowered his head to watch his feet.

Chapter Twenty-three

Burke, Burr, and Quill were in and out of the outpatient services of the small local hospital within an hour. They arrived during a slow period for the radiology tech. The x-ray process went quickly, but it left the still healing Quill with a sense of deep-fatigue. His steps back to the van were careful and measured. By the time he'd pulled himself onto the seat in the back of the van, a fine sheen of sweat covered his face and body.

Burke helped him lift his injured leg up onto the seat. "How are you holding out there? Want to cut it short and go home?"

Quill blinked at the word 'home' but recovered fast enough to shake his head before Burke made the choice for him. "No, no, I'm top of the line. Just not used to working so hard to walk. The sticks help a lot, but they're awkward."

"You're sure?"

Burke's sharp gaze felt like a laser beam scanning him for imperfections. He knew the man hadn't missed the sweat on his face or the drag in his step. "I'm sure. Want to go look at that software package you told me about. The one for the Linux box. Like to have a peek at that, I would."

Burke looked Quill over a second time then nodded. "Okay, but we'll go to see Jackson's vet first. That way you can sit and rest before trying to browse through a store."

Not wanting the man to hear him wheezing, Quill

settled for returning Burke's nod.

"Good boy," said Burke. He gave Quill a quick pat to his leg and slid the door shut, blocking out the damp, chill autumn air. The cool breeze had felt good, but the increased pollen in the air from the dead leaves was getting to Quill. He fumbled in his jeans pocket and wrapped a hand around the inhaler Burke had let him carry. The solid weight of the cylinder calmed his rising anxiety letting him concentrate on slow, even breathing.

Scenery flashed by at a leisurely pace. The second time he saw the same hardware store go by he leaned forward so he could see Burr's face in the rearview mirror.

"We're going in circles. Why?" His soft London accent held a note of fear.

He watched Burr exchange a quick glance with Burke. The blond man flashed him a reassuring smile and wink before returning to scan the surrounding scenery. "Just a little evasive maneuvering, son. It's what we do."

Burr drummed his fingers on the steering wheel and studied something in the rearview mirror. "You can take the man out of the military, but you can't take the military out of the man."

Quill had been through too much lately to have their casual attitude do more than reaffirm his unease. "Is there trouble? Are we being followed?"

The two men exchanged another look before Burke turned again to face him, his eyes gazing out the back window more than at Quill. "There was an out-of-state car trailing us for a while but it's gone and nothing unusual has taken its place. It's just safest if we work like there is a problem. That way if one develops, we're always more prepared to handle it. It's a way a life for men who do the kind of jobs we're involved in."

Burke studied Quill a moment. "We're good at it. Don't worry." He turned back around, cocked his head to examine the view out of his side window. "And you might want to use your inhaler."

A guilty blush crept up Quill's cheeks. Glancing back over his shoulder, Burke ignored it. "The animal hair at the vet's might be too much."

Quill was grateful to get some relief before the wheezing got too bad. Let them think he was weak.

They made several more passes by things Quill thought he remembered seeing before, then Burr stopped outside of a two-story Victorian. The house was painted in multiple shades of blue and green and trimmed with miles of sand-colored gingerbread. A large picture window, edged in blue and green stained glass, showcased the front room. It reminded Quill of a small ocean in the middle of a tree-lined, landlocked street.

A matching wooden sign was planted in the tidy front yard. It announced this was the residence and office of Dr. Dima J. Ivanov, D.V.M. in bold, boxy, gold lettering. Between the rough-sounding name and the Spartan choice in printing, the image of a large Russian bear came to Quill's mind.

Great, he thought, another massive, pushy man to add to the group already dominating his life.

Once through the main entrance door, faints sounds of barking dogs and the odor of disinfectant and soap met him.

A petite woman in a well-worn lab coat and jeans came from an open doorway to greet them. Her black hair was worn pinned up at the nape of her slender neck. The orchid sweater she wore brought a violet cast to her almond-shaped eyes. A smile graced her face, but confusion tugged wrinkles into the center of her forehead.

She gestured at Quill's crutches; his knee still encased in the bulky immobilizer. "Good afternoon, gentlemen. Are you sure you're in the right place?" Her voice was light, but confident, a faint accent laced through some of her words.

The question was meant for all of them, but it was easy to see her interest centered on Burr. He returned her smile full force, stepping closer.

"Even if I'm lost, this is definitely the right place." He extended his hand, rested her offered palm between both of his, lingering over the touch. "Jackson Burr, at your service. Day or night, just call."

The woman laughed and slipped her hand away.

Burke picked up her hand as she withdrew it and beamed one of his own charming smiles. "Daniel Burke. We live on an estate just north of town." Burke turned to include Quill, drawing the boy closer as he talked. "This is Quill."

Quill was grateful for the steadying hand the gesture afforded him. He really wanted to sit down.

"We're looking to add several guard dogs to the grounds, but Quill and I are just along for the ride." He tipped his head toward Burr. "He's the one who needs to speak to Dr. Ivanov."

It took an obvious effort, but Burr managed to tear his gaze away from the woman's features. He craned his neck to see past her for evidence of where the man might be. "Oh, yeah, the doctor. Is he in?"

The woman hid a chuckle behind her hand. "Yes, the doctor is in."

"Is he busy? Do I have to make an appointment? I just need some advice on where I can find a reliable dog breeder locally. It should only take a couple of minutes of his time." Burr eyed her slender form again appreciating her curves. "Unless you can help me. Maybe over dinner?"

"I thought this would just need a 'moment' of the doctor's time?"

Burr responded to the teasing note in her soft voice.

"I was wrong. Happens every twenty years or so."

"Just every twenty years? Wow, that must be tough for your friends."

"They've learned to adjust."

The woman's laughing eyes darted to Burke in time to see him hang his head to hide a smile.

Burr and the woman wandered toward the doorway she had just come out of. Quill turned away, limping towards the empty row of visitors' chairs on the far side of the room, Burke at his elbow. It was plain to see this was going to take a lot longer than he had thought.

Quill made it to the beckoning comfort of the first chair. Burke silently insisted he move down one chair so he would be between the door and Quill.

Quill watched Burke do a quick scan of the front yard and street. The blond man pulled at his coat as he sat and Quill's gaze dropped to Burke's waist. His mind automatically registered the outline of an object and realized Burke was armed. The fact the man felt he needed to be armed when he left his home sent a fresh surge of fear through Quill.

A sudden shout from Burke froze the panic buzzing in his head. "Jack, incoming!"

Quill was on the floor before he understood what was happening, Burke's weight pinning him to the hardwood floor. A blur of activity across the room told him the other man understood the cryptic message. Quill watched as Burr hustled the petite woman off her feet and behind a thick, old wooden desk. It was amazing to see the speed he managed while being oh so very careful, like he was handling an antique porcelain doll. Quill wondered how she managed to keep from screaming. He wanted to.

The front window in the room exploded in a waterfall of shattered glass and wood. The bits and pieces rained down on them, a spray of bullets hitting the far wall, puncturing the beautiful wood paneling at a chest height.

Quill's world slid and twisted again. Burke latched onto his collar and began scrabbling crab-like across the room, dragging Quill with him. They reached the relative safety of the desk and Burke slid Quill in beside the woman. Burr clamped a possessive arm around the boy and drew him in closer. A shower of bullets riddled the air above them.

The two men lay face-to-face, handguns drawn and faces grim. Burr tried to look over the top of the desk, but another volley of fire forced him back down.

"Did you see how many?"

"Two. At 1 and 10. I don't think they can change angle, but 1 o'clock is moving closer. Expect him in about three. I'll take 10 o'clock."

Burke patted Quill on the cheek, shoving him closer to the floor at the same time. He gave the doctor a reassuring smile.

"Stay down and do what Jack tells you, okay?"

His mouth suddenly as dry as the day-old bread Liam used to buy, Quill nodded. Burke patted Quill's cheek again then started to scurry away towards the back of the house. On impulse, Quill reached out and grabbed his sleeve before it disappeared from his reach.

"You're coming back, right?"

"Damn straight I am. You can't shake me this easy, kiddo."

Burke slipped his sleeve loose and took Quill's cold fingers into his own for a brief moment before continuing his crab-like journey.

Consumed with a growing terror of being abandoned once again, Quill gulped several times to keep from throwing up when Burke disappeared from sight. A light touch to his back startled him. He jerked back and stared into a pair of almond-shaped, concerned eyes.

This woman didn't even know what or why this was happening and she stood a good chance of being shot, but here she was, offering comfort to him. A wave of guilt washed through him. Quill swallowed down the bile rising to the back of his throat.

Quill whispered, "He'll stop them. He's done it before. We'll be okay."

Her expression changed from concern to alarm then anger. She reached out and touched a drop of black liquid on the floor. She traced the trail with her hand until it rested against Burr's body.

"My God, you've been shot."

Burr ignored the trickle of blood running from his left shoulder, creating a black sticky puddle on the floor. He glanced at the widening stain and grunted a low, dismissive sound.

"Scratch. Maybe the doc can look at it later. Does he have enough sense to keep low back there?"

Burr jerked his head in the direction of the back offices, never taking his eyes off the front door and missing window.

"There isn't anyone back there except a few dogs in the cages."

"Where the hell is the doc?"

"She's laying right next to you, you big, dumb–."

"Ah-ah-ah. Little pitchers." Burr shook a finger in the air at the woman.

"What the hell does that mean?" Ivanov asked.

The woman ducked and pressed closer to Burr as a fresh round of shots filled the air. Nothing broke or splintered in the room. The gunfire was taking place outside.

"Just an expression a buddy of mine uses when there's kids in the room. He comes from a big, old-fashioned family. You'll like him."

"I don't even know him." She ducked lower, frowning at Burr.

"You will. I'll introduce you when we have dinner. So you're Dima Ivanov? Nice name. Unusual, but nice."

Ivanov raised her head to reply. Several single shots hit the wall behind them and Burr knocked her to the floor again.

"Who said we're having dinner? You're a gun-toting maniac. People are trying to kill you!" Her words were a little breathless from either the impact or the nearness of Burr's body. From the look on her face, Quill couldn't be sure which was the cause.

"Excitement is my middle name, darling," said Burr.

"It's Doctor, not darling."

"Dima. I'll take that as a yes."

Burr shoved her closer to Quill. He swiftly rose to his knees, braced his outstretched arms on the splintered desktop, keeping his body shielded.

The front door kicked open and bounced hard off the jam guard. A man dressed in dark blue clothing and a ski mask crouched in the opening, a semi-automatic rifle cradled in his arms. He had to pause a moment to avoid the door's return.

Burr didn't hesitate. He fired and kept firing until the man crumbled to the ground then rose and crossed to the body, kicking away the rifle. Quill watched him reach down and feel for a pulse. Satisfied the man was dead, Burr flattened himself against one wall and scanned the outside perimeter.

Two shots close together echoed in the street, then an anguished cry. An eerie silence taut with apprehension hung in the air.

Quill felt a sickening thud in his chest, like a brick had been smacked against his rib cage. Air froze in his lungs. Bright lights sparkled at the edges of his vision. The room seemed to constrict around him.

A heavy hand landed on his good leg, jolting him. He drew in a ragged gulp of air, darting his gaze away from the bloody body by the front door to meet Burr's intent, questioning stare.

"You okay, boy?"

Burr's sudden touch had been alarming, but the deep, rough tones of the black man's voice flowed over Quill's raw nerves, reassuring and calming him. The boy nodded, afraid to trust his voice just yet.

Burr crouched in a tight huddle at the end of the receptionist's battered desk, gun still trained on the waiting room entrance. He systematically scanned the room looking for trouble. A sound at the back of the house made Burr bring the gun around to point at the doorway

Burke had used to leave.

Quill buried his head in the folds of his coat sleeve for a moment, bracing for another round of gunfire and death. He and the doctor were stretched out beside Burr, hugging the floorboards like a life raft. Quill could feel the woman next to him shaking. He realized he was shaking, too.

Lifting his head, Quill focused on the same doorway as Burr. The shuffle of feet from down the hallway made his chest tighten. Just when he thought his head would explode from the paralyzing effects of holding his breath, he saw Burr lower his gun.

"'Bout time. I was beginning to think you're getting old." Burr grinned at Burke as he walked into the room. "Get him?"

Burke shook his head. "I tagged him, but he got clear. I couldn't do much about it considering where we are." He reached down and helped Dr. Ivanov to her feet.

"Who *are* you people? What just happened here? Why is there a *dead man* in my reception area?" The doctor brushed off Burke's helping hand. She looked from one man to the other.

Burke shrugged and gently pushed past her to kneel beside Quill. "You okay?"

The boy nodded, the gesture too quick and too jerky to be believable, but Burke accepted it. He held out a hand and Quill grabbed it, using the man's strength to pull up off the floor. Once on his feet, he was slow to let go of the support.

Dr. Ivanov huffed at being ignored by Burke and stalked over to Burr's side. Her anger drained away when she reached the fallen man. She crouched down beside Burr and checked the hooded stranger for a pulse herself.

Not finding any she stood back up, glancing around her office.

"You sure know how to make a first impression on a girl, Mr. Burr." Her voice made it clear this wasn't a good thing.

"How about you call me, Jackson."

"How about I call the police?"

"You really think gunshots went unnoticed in this neighborhood?" Burr said. "I think we'll have lots of company, real soon, but if it'll make you feel better, go ahead."

"An explanation would make me feel better."

"Anything for you, just not right now."

Burr called to Burke. "Do I need to check the perimeter again?" Burr grabbed a wad of gauge off a nearby shelf and shoved it under his shirt, stopping the trickle of blood from the wound.

The sound of multiple sirens filled the air. Flashing red and blue lights filled the streets. "Guess not." Burr tilted his head at the growing chaos and shrugged. "This is going to take a bit of explaining, Daniel."

Burke settled Quill onto the one chair that had survived the assault, draping his own leather coat over the boy's shoulders. "I know. Let's hope the Chief of Police is an open-minded man."

Dr. Ivanov moved away from the dead man and crouched down beside Quill, checking the young man over. "He's pale, sweaty and he's not talking."

Quill leaned away from her and tried to smile reassuringly. "I'm okay. Just a bit of a fright with all the gunfire and what not. I'm fine, really."

She stood and crossed to a nearby closet, returning with a soft, well-worn blanket. Wrapping it around Quill, she turned to Burke. "Forget about the police. I'll handle them. I know most of them. Cops are great dog lovers." She tugged the blanket closer around Quill and tipped his head back to check his pupils. "He's on the verge of shock here."

"He's had a rough couple of days." Burke patted Quill's shoulder and the boy flashed him a smile. "My son's tough. He'll be all right."

In the process of closing his eyes, Quill jerked back awake. He nodded at the man. "I'm good." He paused a moment, then added, "Da'."

Burke's face lit up at hearing the Cockney slang for father. Quill ducked his head. The sounds outside the house drew his attention as a number of police officers advanced cautiously on the house.

Burke peered over his shoulder at them then back at Quill. "I know you're fine, son." He jerked his head at the approaching officers. "Now I just need to convince those officers of that."

Chapter Twenty-four

Sitting on the leather sofa in Burke's study, Quill took in the circle of tense men seated around him. He ducked his head and began to pick at the straps holding his knee brace in place.

After two hours of explanations and phone calls, the authorities had reluctantly released Burke, Burr, and Quill from questioning. However, there were loud, clipped promises of future inquiries by the unsatisfied and skeptical detectives.

The policemen had been relentless in their questioning of Quill until Burke had made them stop. Dr. Ivanov had also intervened on his behalf, which put a surprised, pleased expression on Burr's dark face.

By the time he made it through the front door, all Quill wanted to do was rest. Unfortunately, Burke wanted to talk. Plant, Weston, and James met them at the door and accompanied them into Daniel's study.

Ramona fluttered around them for a few moments, satisfying herself they were all in one piece then bustled off to fix a late meal.

In the study, Burr, Weston, and James seated themselves in various chairs surrounding Burke's desk. Burke remained standing, arms crossed, leaning against the front of his desk. Plant moved to the bar and poured brandies. Burr nodded his thanks. James and Weston refused. Burke answered with a polite, "Thank you, Marcus."

Plant poured a drink of his own, then turned to Burke. "As soon as Jackson called and informed us of the incident, Ethan and Ray helped tighten down the estate's security." Plant walked as he talked, ending up at the end of the sofa Quill sat propped up on.

Plant continued. "The secondary outer perimeter sensors are on, the wall electrified to its highest legal voltage, the cameras are doing continuous sweeps. The interior windows, doors and access panels were all sealed with the exception of the front entry." He took a small sip from his glass then added, "Now that everyone is inside, that's been secured as well."

Burke nodded several times as Plant ticked off the checklist on his fingertips.

"Computer network?"

"All new passwords installed." Plant flicked a narrow-eyed glance Quill's way. "That is all except the computer the urchin's been allowed to use." Twin spots of color spread across his cheeks and he became completely entranced by the straps to his brace, giving them his undivided attention.

"For some reason, that machine won't respond to the system commands." Plant turned back to Burke, his tone packed with easy authority. "I took the liberty of unplugging it."

"Bloody hell, you did!" Quill's head shot up and he tried to leap from his seat. Unbalanced by his inability to bend his knee, he fell back down onto the cushion with a pained grunt, hands balled at his sides.

"Stay put, boy." Plant looked down his nose, lips pinched together in a severe line.

The color in the boy's cheeks intensified and his eyes grew wide. "You didn't, you bastard!"

"Language, boy."

Plant stared for several seconds letting Quill feel the full effects of his glare.

His words were clipped and accusing. "Why shouldn't I have?"

Before Quill could answer, Burke sat down on the stout coffee table in front of the boy. Quill jumped and pressed back into the cushions.

Burke narrowed his eyes as he studied Quill, making fine wrinkles crease the weathered skin at the corners of his eyelids. "Yes, why shouldn't he?"

"N-no real reason, I-I've–I *had* a program running." Quill's frown pulled his eyebrows together to make a deep furrow in his normally smooth forehead. "If it gets shut off, I lose the connection."

"What kind of program?" Burke took a sip from his glass.

"Just a little something I wrote." Quill uncurled his white-knuckled hands and shrugged.

"What's it *do*?" Burke took another sip then set his glass down on the table. Quill flinched at the heavy thud of the glass against the thick wood.

Quill swallowed hard and began picking at the brace again, avoiding Burke's face. "Gathers information."

Burke's blunt-fingered hand settled over his, stilling the nervous fidgeting. "From where, son?" Burke removed his hand, but stayed in Quill's personal space.

Quill's expression turned from uncertain into growing panic. He bit at his lower lip and his jaw moved as if he wanted to speak, but he remained silent.

"The men who ordered today's little activities wouldn't have done it without a damn good reason to launch an assault in public."

Burr's deep baritone joined in adding, "Too many witnesses and too much explaining to have to do. It was a big risk." Burr pointed a finger at Quill. "One that didn't pay off."

Quill's face tensed. "What? You sorry about it didn't?"

Weston stood up. "No, Quill. He's saying this doesn't make sense. They wouldn't risk public exposure just to tie up a loose end."

Quill's face twisted into a confused grimace. "A what?"

"A loose end, a piece of unfinished business, a detail that got missed." Tilting his head at Quill he added, "You."

A shudder ran down Quill's back. He slid lower on the couch.

Burke wiped his thumb across his lower lip, nibbling on the thumb pad. "I knew it wouldn't take them long to find you, and start shadowing us, but they didn't have any solid reason for a public hit."

James leaned forward to prop his elbows on his long, lanky legs. "Could be someone acting on their own, but not likely. Shooting up the main street in broad daylight is an act of suicide."

"Or desperation," Burr said. "Something's changed."

"Now they have a reason," Weston added.

Quill squirmed as everyone in the room turned their attention to him.

Burke dropped his tone to a low, soothing register and asked, "Did you give them a reason, son?"

"I...I..." Quill shrugged his shoulders.

"What's the computer doing, boy?" A harder note crept into Burke's voice now.

A single tear broke loose and ran down the boy's cheek. He swiped viciously at it. "Quill! My name is

Quill!" He pounded one balled fist against his uninjured leg. "Is it too hard to pronounce for you? Too foreign? Too nerdy? *What*? Why don't you ever use it?"

Quill glanced at the stunned men around him, his voice quivering. "I feel like the family pet! 'Come here, boy. Sit. Stay. Roll the bloody hell over!' I'm a real person!"

Quill wrapped his arms protectively around his middle, hunched forward, chin jutting out in defiance, and waited. His shoulders heaved under the rapid, furious breaths as he blew off his long pent-up frustration and rage.

Slightly stunned, Burke tried remembering the last time that he'd used the boy's given name. Tracing back over the last few, hectic days, he realized he couldn't remember ever using it, at least not when talking directly with his son. "You're right. I'm sorry. I didn't mean it to sound like that. I do know your name, Quill."

As sudden as the emotional outburst overtook the teen, it faded away. Quill sighed with his whole body, slumping against the couch. "Wasn't sure you could say it."

"I can and I will. A lot more often. I promise. And–"

Sniffling, Quill wiped at his nose with a shirtsleeve and interrupted. His voice sounded tired, with just a touch of sarcasm in it. "I know, I know. 'You always keep your promises'."

Burke suppressed a chuckle.

Plant took advantage of the sudden, brief silence. He leaned down and spoke directly into Quill's ear. "What was the computer upstairs doing and why?"

Quill jerked and shied away a few inches. He gave the Brit a glare then licked his lips, biting at the lower one before speaking.

"It's monitoring someone's e-mail account."

Burke raised both hands in the air, palms out. "And?"

Quill pulled a huge breath and began a rapid explanation, an endless sentence full of technical jargon and computer slang. "The program files I pinched showed they were all sent to a number of addresses. I did a little...exploring online and one turned out to be a personal account." He hesitated a moment and got an encouraging nod from Burke.

"So...I sent the account a Trojan e-mail, a legitimate looking message with an embedded application." Quill could tell he was losing a part of his audience already by the blank expressions James and Weston gave him. "Some browsers will automatically run these, like when the search toolbar program hooks itself into your main browser program."

Several of the men nodded and Burke gently prompted him on with wave of his hand. "Go on, we get the idea."

"Okay." As Quill warmed to his subject, his shoulders straightened and he became more animated, forgetting for the time being he was admitting to an illegal act and revealing more than he wanted.

"The Trojan is a monitoring application that loads itself as a browser extension, like a toolbar. It keeps track of all the Internet activity from this personal address and passes the information back to the computer upstairs."

Burke dropped his face into his hands and rubbed the rough palms over his face.

Quill frowned at Burke's gesture. "Don't you get it? It'll tell us who knows about this whole thing. Names, accounts, contacts. Everything!" He slouched back down against the cushions. "Or would have, if it hadn't been shut down!"

Burke walked to the desk and unlocked a drawer as he talked. "Is it still running, Marcus?"

"Yes, I put a firewall around it as soon as I realized it wouldn't respond to the system, but it's still receiving data."

Plant moved to retrieve the empty glasses and returned them to the bar. "But apparently, I didn't do it soon enough."

Burke took a box of ammunition from the drawer. "They caught on pretty quickly. They must have been expecting it."

Pulling his handgun from his shoulder holster, Burke began reloading it. He noticed, but didn't comment on, Quill's sudden tensing at the sight of the weapon.

Quill's voice squeaked and he scanned each of the faces in the room. "It can't be seen, it's got no visible interface. They couldn't have detected it."

Burr, James, and Weston began a similar check of their handguns. Plant left the room with a terse, "I'll check the system."

Quill watched the activity around him. He stood up, holding onto the arm of the couch, swaying in place. He gave a guilty start at the sound of a sharp, metallic snap as Burr rammed a clip home in his nine-millimeter gun.

"I'd have had it connect to a zombie site instead of directly here, but I didn't have time to set one up."

Burke walked back over to stand in front of his son. He patted the boy on the shoulder, leaving his hand resting there.

"I didn't know this would happen, Da'. Honestly. I-I thought I was helping." Quill dropped his chin to his chest for a moment then straightened up. "I wanted to clean up the mess." He waved a hand limply in the air at nothing tangible. "Do the 'right thing'."

"I understand that, Quill. But you should've come to an adult first. You don't know what you're dealing with here, son. We're not talking computer viruses and hidden e-mail attachments. These men are using guns and explosives."

Quill swayed under Burke's steady hand. "Thought it was safe. Didn't think they'd try anything here. Not with you." He shrugged, the movement tipping his precarious balance off. He plopped down on the couch, his arms braced for the fall. He stretched out his injured leg. "One of the addresses must have been someone pretty high up to have gotten their attention so fast. Wonder which one it was."

Burke sat back down on the coffee table to bring himself back to eye level with his son. "How many were there?"

Quill's attention remained focused on a point somewhere across the room. Distracted, his head tilted to one side and he gnawed at his lower lip several times before saying, "Thirty-two. But half of those were in-house accounts and a couple were just routine security. There were only about six that looked promising."

"Where'd you get them, Quill?" Burke's tone was conversational.

"Found them in the extension files of the folder. Easy pickings if you know where to look." Quill continued. "Might be the one with the South African server base. Didn't think that one was real."

"You memorized thirty-two account addresses from a file you never read?" Burke's quiet voice brought instant stillness to the entire room.

Quill jerked around to face Burke, taking in the stares of the three remaining men as well. Realizing what had just happened, he paled, silently moving his mouth without making a sound before blurting, "No...I-I mean...nobody could...I just...um."

"You read all the files in the folder, didn't you, son?" He touched the top of Quill's bowed head and his son nodded. "And somehow, you memorized them all."

Quill nodded again, turning scared eyes up to face his father. "Couldn't tell you. Couldn't tell anyone! You don't understand what was in them. Files of dozens and dozens of people, agents, soldiers, whatever. Pictures of them and little stories of their lives and the names of their kids."

Tears welled up in his eyes. He wiped at them with the back of his hand and sniffed, clearing his throat to continue while the men listened to his quivering words. "And then," sniff "it listed the best ways to surprise them and sometimes it'd mention the things they're the most afraid of...the things–the things that'd make it easier to murder them."

Panic set in and Quill openly sobbed. He flexed his hands again and again, clenching and releasing his fists a few inches above his lap.

Burke stilled the motion with one of his own hands then softly said, "You have a photographic memory, don't you?"

In answer, Quill focused on that far away point across the room again.

"Christ-in-a-hand-basket." Burr's sudden expletive

broke the tense moment.

James stepped closer to the boy and said, "You've been carrying this around by yourself, son? All this time?"

Burke raised a hand in the air to halt the interruptions. Burr shrugged an apology. James sat on the arm of the couch opposite Quill.

"That's how you knew so much about Ethan when we first met. And the details about Wright." Burke looked off to that same non-existent point across the room. "You read the whole file while Jamieson and his partner were picking up the McCabe brothers."

He pulled his attention back to Quill, his face alight with new insight. "That's why you were destroying everything. Not because you knew the authorities were on to you. But because you'd read the files and were scared out of your mind. Scared the people you stole them from would find you. You've got every word of it in that confused, teenage head of yours, don't you?"

Taking a deep breath to clear his sinuses and throat so he could talk, Quill briefly glanced at each man, then settled on Burke. "Eidetic. It's called eidetic memory. There's no such thing as a photographic memory. That's just on the telly."

Quill wiped at the tears dripping off his chin. "I couldn't tell you at first. I didn't know what to say. I was scared and I didn't know you." He swallowed audibly and darted a guilty glance up at Burke through dark eyelashes. "I mean, not really 'know you, know you' and then I just kept thinking about how much trouble I'd be in if you knew."

Quill's voice became heated and his body took on the animated gestures of frustration. His arms jerked, legs jiggling and his speech grew louder with each sentence.

"Bloody hell! They killed Kev and Liam and they didn't even know what was in it! I got beat up and sentenced to seven years for just taking them! They'd hang me for treason if they knew I'd read them!"

Burke laid a hand on Quill's jittering knee. "No one's going to hang you, son. It wasn't going to happen before and it's not going to happen now." He patted the knee in reassurance. "You're not in this alone now, Quill."

"'Kay, Da'." Quill managed to squeeze the two words out before tears returned full force. His shoulders heaved in time to the quiet sobs and he hung his head. "I just wanted my father. A home. Not all...this...this..." His sobs grew stronger.

Burke only hesitated a moment before moving to sit beside his son on the couch. Wrapping both arms around Quill, Burke pulled him to his side, allowing the teen to bury his face against his shirt. It took several minutes before his sobs faded to small irregular sniffs interlaced with occasional weary huffs.

Burke exchanged silent looks with Burr over Quill's bowed head, one finger tapping twice at the face of his watch, indicting he needed two more minutes with the boy.

Two minutes came and went, then five. When Burr stroked his chin with one hand, the fine bristle of new beard made a rasping sound in the still room and snagged Burke's attention as well as that of James.

With a wave of Burr's hand the big Texan stood up. Burr pulled four compact walkie-talkies out of a small duffel bag and tossed one each to James and Weston, leaving the fourth on the desk for Burke.

"Ethan and I are going to make a visual of the outside perimeter of the house before it gets dark." Burr jerked his head toward Weston. "Ray'll do the room to room check from the inside. Maybe Marcus can give him a hand when he's done with the computer check."

Burke nodded. "Sounds good. Quill and I were just on our way to check on Marcus. Be careful."

Quill straightened up, but didn't move from under Burke's arm. James winked at Quill as he Texan rose from the couch. Burr punched Quill lightly on the arm before leaving the room with James.

Weston took the long way around to the exit, passing by the back of the couch. He didn't pause or speak, but he patted Quill's back on the way out.

Burke stood, pulling Quill to his feet with him as he rose. He grabbed the discarded crutches off the floor and handed them to his son. "We've got a lot more to talk about, Quill, but first we've a few other priorities in the way."

"Aye, I understand. I'm good for now." Taking the offered crutches, Quill nodded and followed his father out of the room.

At the doorway Burke turned to Quill and said, "And, just so you know, I can remember your name just fine, Quill." He patted the teen's shoulder. "I should, it was my father's name."

* * * * *

Plant sat rigid and still at the computer Quill had taken over as his own, his focus intent on the information on the screen. He flashed through a series of short e-mail messages as Burke and Quill came in the room.

"Glad you're here. I think you'll find this all very interesting." Plant kept his attention on the monitor while he talked. "It seems our young *urchin*," there was a hint of disapproval in the man's voice, "has tapped into a wealth of personal information about a number of interesting activities."

"Such as?" Burke walked over to Plant's side and leaned over the retainer's shoulder. Quill eased into the chair next to Plant, close enough to see the computer screen, but out of Plant's reach. "And by the way, the *urchin* is my son."

Plant gave an impolite snort. "I know."

Burke straightened and his jaw snapped shut in surprise. "How? I just found out myself a few days ago."

"Good God, man! Look at him! Elizabeth's eyes, your hair and jaw line. Your reckless attitude, too, I might add. His age is right. And the *name*, for bloody hell's sake. Quillan? How many Quillans are there in the world?" Plant's tone was smug as his fingers continued to fly over the keyboard.

"He's a cocky brat." A sharp intake of breath from either side of him put a smirk on Plant's lips. "Just like you were at his age. Who else's would he be, my boy?"

"You could have said something," Burke huffed.

Plant's eyebrows arched and he gave an indelicate snort again. "And spoil this moment? Not a chance. I've been waiting for years to see justice done for all the stunts and schemes I endured while you were growing up." Plant grinned at Burke. "I think this lad is just the ticket."

"You have an evil streak," Burke proclaimed. "You know that, don't you?"

"Yes. And I know who gave it to me. Now be still and look at this one." Plant pointed to the monitor, slowly scrolling through the newest message so Burke and Quill could read it. "The date on it is from before our brilliant child here did his criminal deed. The account is out of the country, South African, oddly enough."

Burke scanned the message, taking in enough to realize the person sending it was involved in the assassination plot. He moved from the body of the message to the top of the page to memorize the sender's name. He whistled softly, stood up, and folded his arms across his chest.

Both Plant and Quill looked up at him, speaking in unison, "What?"

Plant glared at Quill and the boy returned it.

Burke ignored the tension between them. "I know that addy. I don't who it is, 'desireme2' covers a whole range of possible subjects I'm not going to get into now, but I've seen this one."

Burke glanced at the open door and down the hall to where his own bedroom suite and private study was. "I got a present from a friend the other night. And this," Burke pointed at the address, "was in that package. I'll have to look it up to see who it was connected to."

He gave Quill a wry smile. "You didn't get the eidetic memory from me, son." His voice turned wistful. "Must have been your mother."

Quill kicked at the leg of his chair and shyly informed his father, "It's not genetic, just a random happening. Luck of the draw." He frowned. "Or maybe it's the short end of the stick."

"I think the people in that file will think differently when we're able to alert them to their situation, Quill. Think about that."

Quill shrugged, becoming subdued and distant. Burke studied the hunched boy, wondering if he should let him have some time to deal with the day's events so far or push for more. Plant interrupted, drawing him back to the screen.

"You should probably be aware of something else, Daniel." Plant brought up a second message from another file. "There appears to be a senior level MI5 man taking bribes." Plant dropped his voice, making his next words a warning. "A *very* top level man."

He held Burke's gaze for a moment, and then turned to Quill. "Can you track down where a particular message is being sent to and to whom?"

Startled, Quill blinked a few times before answering. "One of these messages?"

"Of course, one of these, you twit." Plant's tone was as sharp as one of Ramona's favorite paring knives.

Burke smothered a grin. Plant slid out of the chair and Burke held it in place until his son had settled onto it, Quill's injured leg held out at an awkward angle from under the desk.

Quill shifted to get comfortable in the chair then moved the mouse pad closer. Once he was satisfied with the set up, he turned to the keyboard. The boy's fingers raced across the keys almost faster than Burke could follow the movements. Screens changed at a rapid rate, some coming up in machine language code and others in English. They were all Greek to Burke.

Five minutes into the search, Quill bent one leg and tucked it up close to his chest, working the keys around his folded limb. Burke thought the boy resembled a teenaged praying mantis, all lanky limbs and hands hooked over the board.

Ten minutes a later, Quill sat back and pointed at the screen. "The message from 'desireme2' went to a blind server in the Cayman Islands. Then it was routed up to a server in New York and then on to Washington, D.C. The final account is listed to a Mr. Michael Jeffrey Gerund, the third. Know him?"

Burke nodded in a dazed fashion. "Oh, we know him." He patted Quill's back. "Us and half of the civilized world."

Chapter Twenty-five

Burke, Burr, and Weston had been in the living room discussing strategy when the assault team arrived that same evening. Burke thought the flame-thrower was a bit over the top. Weston took down the soldier using it five seconds after he came through the front door. It always pays to have a good sniper on your side.

The first assault used plastic explosives to destroy the front portico and the heavy oak entry door. The resulting fires were short-lived. There was impressive damage to the stonework.

James had been upstairs packing for his pending trip home to Texas and he was able to eliminate a number of the attacking opposition from the second story landing as the black-cloaked men entered the house.

Knowing the entire strike force wouldn't be in one place, Burke worked his way toward the rear of the house where he had left his son.

Quill was in the kitchen helping Ramona prepare a quick meal of sandwiches and fruit when the first explosion rocked the front of the house. Startled by the unfamiliar shock wave of thunder rumbling through the foundation of the stone fortress, he looked to the older woman for an explanation. "What's that?"

Ramona paused in the chopping of onions and wiped her hands off on the colorful towel tucked into her apron's waistband. Living in the war-torn countries of Central America most of her life had exposed the middle-aged woman to many things North American housekeepers never dreamed of. Ramona knew the noise of explosives quite well.

Keeping the sharp kitchen knife in her hand, she grabbed Quill's arm with the other. "Come! ¡Ahora!" She tugged the confused teenager toward the far end of the kitchen.

"Why?" Quill resisted, then gave into the persistent pulling. "What's happening?"

"They have come!" Ramona's voice was hushed, each word tinged with urgency. She pushed at Quill, hastening him across the large room. "Hurry, child, hurry!"

Just as they reached a small alcove at the back of the kitchen, the lights went out. Ramona opened a door and shoved Quill into a small room. Following him into the large, windowless pantry, Ramona snapped closed the door and locked it with a key from her dress pocket. A dim glow from two low wattage emergency power lights snapped on as the estate's back up generator came to life.

Glass shattered nearby as the lock fell into place, followed by distant gunfire. "What do we do? What happens if–?" Quill's voice shook.

Ramona placed a hand over his mouth. She maneuvered him to the back of the room, out of direct line with the door, and angled them both into a corner between metal shelves packed with canned goods and canisters of dried foods.

The harshness of Quill's rapid breaths filled the air and echoed in the close confines of the crowded space. Gripping the kitchen knife with one hand, Ramona wrapped her arm around Quill's trembling shoulders.

The handle to the door rattled. Nearby gunfire split the air, the impact shaking the door. Quill pushed at

Ramona and tried to break free of her hold. "Bloody hell! Not again!"

Ramona pushed the boy back, placing a finger over his lips to silence him again, one hand briefly caressing his face to comfort him. She pressed Quill's shoulder until he crouched awkwardly on the floor, his braced leg unable to bend. She moved several boxes to hide him from easy view. Standing protectively in front of him, Ramona slid the large kitchen knife into the numerous folds of her gathered skirt.

A blast of rapid gunfire hit the door again, shattering the lock and one hinge. Ramona flinched and threw an arm up to shield her face, ducking to one side to avoid the spray of bullets bouncing off the metal in the room. The door burst open, still attached by the top hinge.

Terrified of the unknown, Quill peered out from a crack between the boxes. He watched the battered door swing closed again at an awkward angle, partially blocking the doorway. It was then forced back against the wall with a solid kick from a black-clad leg and boot. In the open doorway stood the figure that fueled Quill's nightmares and invaded most of his waking thoughts.

Even with the dim lighting, Eric Crowe was bigger and uglier in real life than Quill had remembered him. The man's broad, weapon-clad frame filled the smoking doorway.

A whimper escaped the teen before he even knew it was forming. Pressing hard against the cold wall behind him, Quill shrank back, as if he could merge his very molecules with the house to avoid detection by his greatest horror.

Crowe moved cautiously, automatic gun held ready, his eyes scanning every inch of the dimly lit, well-stocked pantry. Crowe paused to search the shadows, then headed straight toward Quill's position.

"I know you're here, you wee bastard. Can hear you breathing." A soft muffled whimper broke the stillness and Crowe moved deeper into the room, targeting Quill's hiding place with ease.

"Scared, are we?" Crowe chuckled, a hard mirthless grunt, and pulled his gun in tighter, preparing to fire into the stack of boxes protecting Quill. "You should be, lad. You're really going to die this time. I don't fail at the same assignment twice."

Crowe widened his stance and took aim. He curled his fingers around the trigger and applied slow pressure, a pleased smirk on his thin lips.

A sudden scrape of a shoe on the bare flooring broke his focus. He spun, arm and gun instinctively raised to the new danger. A flashing swirl of bright color swept over him and the sharp, biting pain of a knife dug into his right arm.

"Son of a bitch!"

The hoarse, pained cry from Crowe pulled Quill out of his paralysis. The boy peered out over the boxes again.

Crowe's gun fell from his useless right hand to clatter to the floor. Immediately his left fist lashed out, catching his assailant in the face. Crowe stumbled back against a row of shelving. Casting a wary glance in Quill's direction, Crowe crouched over the fallen body.

"Goddamn wetback housekeeper. Should have guessed she'd favor a blade. Their kind always do."

Crowe bent lower and took the knife from Ramona's hand. The blade glinted, catching the few rays of muted light in its gleaming steel, outlining the dark trickles of blood on the edges. Crowe pulled out his side arm with his left hand, aiming it at Ramona's head.

Crowe's intention caused a sudden spasm of cold fear to grip Quill's stomach. A burst of adrenaline hit him hard, taking away his breath. He bolted from his hiding place, shoving the boxes in Crowe's direction, knocking the man to the floor. The gun spun away into the room's shadows.

Quill sprinted towards the gaping hole of a doorway, jumping the unconscious housekeeper's legs and stumbling over the splintered debris of the door.

Just as he crossed the threshold into the kitchen, Quill felt his feet pulled out from under him. A heavy weight scrambled up his body and settled on his back, pressing him cruelly onto the cold tile floor. Pain from his injured knee forced a grunt from him. The side of his face was ground against a thin line of rough grout, his curls used as a handle to guide the assault.

"Kind of feels like old times, doesn't it boy?" Crowe's cigarette-drenched breath came in rapid, sour puffs across Quill's bruised cheek. "But this time we'll get the ending right."

Crowe twisted his left hand deeper into Quill's hair and pulled hard, forcing the boy to come to his feet.

The bloodied kitchen knife burned a line of sharp pain under Quill's jaw, the edge scoring the top layer of his skin. Crowe pulled the boy to his chest, holding him by his hair and the threat of the blade.

Quill clung to the arm holding the knife to his throat with both hands, trying to steady his own wobbly stance and keep the weapon from digging deeper into his flesh. He could feel the warmth of his blood trickling down the side of his neck, the sharp burn like the first blazing flare of a match being lit. Nausea rolled in his stomach and his vision blurred with tears.

"Let go! Please!" The soft plea slipped out before Quill realized it was his own voice.

Crowe tightened his grip and dug the edge of the knife deeper. Quill gasped and pushed himself back against Crowe to try and widen the non-existent gap between his throat and the blade of the knife.

"Let go." The demanding voice echoing Quill's was deeper, familiar and not the least bit pleading.

Crowe swung Quill around to face the source of the voice, gripping Quill more tightly to him. He made sure Quill was between himself and Burke.

Quill squirmed and called out. "Da!"

Daniel Burke edged toward his son, gun raised and ready, his face calm and relaxed. "I could say 'please' too, if it would help."

Crowed snorted. "Don't think so, *Colonel*. You and this little alley bastard has cost me too much as it is. Nothing anyone says will change what happens here tonight."

"Da!" Quill gasped and jerked back against Crowe as the knife dug into his neck.

A delighted glint appeared in Crowe's eyes, a sneered parody of a grin on his twisted lips. "'Da' is it? Well fancy that."

Crowe looked from Quill to Burke, taking in the fiercely protective expression the older man wore.

"I've been plotting all week on the best way to make the big 'hero' here pay for making me look the incompetent fool last time around." Crowe pulled Quill a few paces to one side, maneuvering toward the missing back door and escape.

"Now it looks like just completing my original mission will be the best payback I could give." His tightened his grip until Quill grunted in distress.

"How many sons will that leave you with, Hero? Got anymore bastard whelps in this fancy palace of yours?" Crowe kicked aside debris and continued backing away. Burke matched him step for step.

Muffled gunfire came from the front of the house. The noise was growing closer.

"No Crowe, just have the one." Burke raised his gun a little higher and gripped the trigger a fraction tighter.

Crowe recognized the preamble to taking a shot and pulled Quill up higher against his chest. The blade sliced into the vulnerable flesh near Quill's windpipe.

Quill reacted instinctively, pushing a hand under the sudden source of intense pain. Crying out as the edge of the knife entered his palm, Quill wriggled and kicked, pulling frantically at Crowe's arm. By chance, the boy's flailing hand hit the raw wound in Crowe's biceps.

With a grunt of pain, Crowe's arm dropped uselessly to his side. The knife clattered to the floor.

Quill twisted and pulled, trying to tear his hair from the man's other fist, mindless of the blood flowing from his own wounded hand.

Thrown off balance by pain and the boy's wild movements, Crowe fought one-handed to keep his advantage, using a leg to try and drag the boy back against him again.

Taking the opening, Burke rushed them. Crowe used the only weapon available to him. He heaved Quill away from him.

Burke automatically reached for the injured boy.

He caught Quill with one arm, keeping him from slamming into a kitchen counter. Burke spun and shoved Quill down behind the protective shield of the kitchen island counter.

"Stay down!"

Crowe pull a second handgun and aimed the weapon at Burke, then swerved to track Quill as the boy ducked for cover.

Burke managed to get off two shots first. Both bullets caught the assassin in the upper torso. Crowe's body jerked from the impact and blood splattered the wall, but his Kevlar vest took most of the damage.

"You're losing a lot of blood, Crowe. Give it up before you bleed to death!"

"Not likely! Your aim's off, Hero! If you want to stop me, you're going to have to do better than that." Hidden behind the over-turned breakfast table, Crowe returned fire.

Burke rolled behind the counter, ending up a few feet from a trembling, wide-eyed Quill. "Give it up, Crowe. It's over! You can't win."

"Says who?" Having crept closer while Burke went for cover, Crowe's voice came from a point much nearer. Too near. Crowe rolled over top of the counter, leaving a bloody path across the white tile surface. He landed on the opposite side of Quill, bodily pulling the stunned boy with him as he rolled across the floor.

Hooking an arm around Quill's bleeding neck, Crowe applied pressure, unfazed by the boy's frantic tugging on his arm as it crushed down on Quill's windpipe. He jammed the end of his gun against Quill's temple.

Burke froze in place, his own weapon pointed at

Crowe's head. He hesitated, his shot partially blocked by his son's bruised and blood-smeared face.

"Guess maybe I haven't lost the game just yet." Crowe tightened his arm.

"This isn't a game, Crowe." Burke looked at Quill as his son fought against the suffocating hold. A faint tinge of bluish-gray coloring had crept into the boy's pale face.

"It's a boy's life you're willing to destroy. An innocent boy whose biggest crime is trying to get to know his absent father." Burke's expression hardened, growing fiercer and less controlled. "You want the real person responsible for this mess, look at me. The whole thing was my fault from the beginning."

Quill gasped and blindly reached out for Burke, his bloodstained hand grabbing at the empty air between them. Crowe tightened his grip.

"Sorry, Burke, but I've already lost my reputation and any chance at rank advancement in a career I've dedicated my whole bloody life to because of your brat." Crowe ground the barrel of his gun harder against Quill's face. "I think it's only fair you lose your future, too."

Blood ran down the side of Quill's face to drip sluggishly from the corner of his jaw onto the tile floor. Crowe wrenched upright, dragging Quill with him.

"Time to pay for fucking around where you weren't wanted, Hero, both last week," Crowe spared a quick glance at Quill then sneered, "and about seventeen years ago, apparently."

Quill sagged heavily, forcing Crowe to lose his hold. Blood loss and pain slowed Crowe's reactions. He struggled with the dead weight and for a brief moment, he was fully exposed. A brief moment was more than enough for Burke.

A single bullet sliced through the side of Crowe's forehead, leaving a neat, unimpressive dark hole in his temple. Behind him, the wall transformed into an abstract splatter of dripping blood embedded with bits of bone and tissue.

Crowe's head snapped back and his face froze into a startled, faintly confused expression before going lax. His body slumped, still on his knees, then slowly crumpled to the floor, landing in an ungainly heap.

Quill was pulled backward by Crowe's momentum, but strong hands scooped him up and away. With his ability to breathe restored, reflex kicked in and he gasped for air.

"You okay?" Burke grabbed a kitchen towel from off the counter by their heads and tightly wrapped Quill's injured hand in it. Expecting a relieved and thankful child, Burke was unprepared for the explosion that burst to life in his arms.

"You bloody bastard! You lying arse! You're supposed to be safe!" His voice strained and unnaturally rough, Quill pounded his fists on Burke's chest and shoulders. The hysteria-driven blows were weak and ineffective as an attack, but each one was a direct hit to Burke's heart. "You're supposed to be *safe*! *I'm* supposed to be safe with you!"

"Slow down! You *are* safe. Crowe's dead." Burke pulled his struggling son closer. "He's dead, Quill. He won't hurt you again!"

"Liar! You promised that before!"

Quill tried to push out of Burke's restraining arms. Twisting violently to one side, he caught his first glimpse of Crowe's body and he froze. Blood had soaked through

271

the dead man's clothing, forming a growing puddle on the floor, his previous wounds reopening during the struggles. Quill's gaze involuntarily followed the trail of blood splatter from the small bullet wound in Crowe's ashen face up to the kitchen wall plastered gore.

"Holy Jesus! Just like Kev and Liam. Just like...just...just..." Quill's strained voice rose and fell in an eerie rasp, losing volume every few syllables and ending in a hoarse squeak.

Feeling Quill tense up, Burke wrapped his arms around his son and grimly held on. "It's over, Quill. It's done. He can't hurt you anymore."

"Don't want to do this again! I don't!" Quill buried his face in Burke's shirt. "Can't, can't, can't."

Riding out the storm of another burst of frenzied struggles, Burke held on until Quill collapsed against him, exhausted and completely spent. Burke threaded a hand through the boy's sweaty hair, holding him closer and murmuring reassurances. The battle-scarred room became eerily still, except for the low, deep murmur and an occasional muffled gasp from Quill.

One part of Burke's covert-ops trained mind had been keeping track of the noise and activity level from the front of the house. Little could be heard through the thick walls and the number of rooms separating the kitchen from the rest of the house, but the occasional flurry of gunfire had been heard near the hallways.

Burke felt certain Burr, James, and Weston had taken care of the frontal assault team. It was what they had done for the last fourteen years. In uniform or out, they were very, very good at it. He hoped the remainder of his household had fared better than he and Quill.

Cautious footsteps in the hallway forced Burke to

raise his gun. At the sight of an unscathed James, Burke let out a relieved sigh. Marcus Plant followed close behind the big Texan, armed and healthy. Burke nodded a greeting and lowered his weapon again.

At the same moment Weston sprang through the missing back doorway, weapon ready. Taking in the level of carnage in the room, the newly-arrived men lowered their weapons, visibly relaxing.

"You two okay?" James knelt on one knee in front of Burke.

Burke shrugged and glanced down. The dark bruises were emerging on the boy's throat, and blood still oozed from the wound on his temple, but pink had replaced the dusky blue on his lips. Coughing occasionally, Quill was breathing easier; wheezing slightly as air was drawn past swollen, abused passages. "I think we will be."

"Good to hear. The police are coming. Jackson stayed out front to deal with them." James looked around the room. "There's gonna be a whole passel of questions about this one, Daniel."

Burke nodded and resumed the slight rocking motion he had unconsciously started. He was surprised to find it was as comforting for him as it seemed to be for Quill. He ignored the sardonic, questioning lift of Plant's eyebrow.

"How many?" Burke asked.

Gesturing with his gun at the hallway, James tapped it in the air three times. "Counting the three in the hallway you musta took out on the way here, there were nine in the primary team. Two are still breathing, but I can't say for how long." He tilted his head towards Crowe. "Surprised to see that one. Thought he'd be out of

273

commission for a lot longer."

Burke nodded. "Me too. I think he was being given the chance to redeem himself for his earlier failure." A larger piece of matter made a wet, sucking sound when it fell to land beside Crowe. Burke tracked its path down the wall. "Fortunately for us, he was...unredeemable."

Crouching down, Plant pressed a dishcloth to a jagged wound on Burke's head. Burke flinched away, frowning. He acquiesced when the irritated man wordlessly showed him the bloodied towel. Plant returned the cloth to the wound, pressing extra hard.

Burke silently tolerated the first aid with the air of someone long-suffering and accustomed to the older man's attentions.

Raising his chin to point in the direction of the pantry, Burke motioned to Weston. "Ray, would you check in the back? I haven't seen Ramona. She was with Quill when this all started."

Weston moved to the dimly-lit pantry, then disappeared. After a brief moment he called out. "She's here. Looks like she took a good punch in the jaw, but she coming around. Don't worry."

Burke nodded to no one in particular and relaxed against the cabinets behind him. He could hear a number of heavy footsteps trampling through the house, growing nearer.

He flexed his numb, tingling fingers, burying one deeper into the matted waves on his son's head and shifted the clinging boy closer, physically contradicting his next words to James.

"Ethan, will you take him for me? I need to get up off this floor before I stick to it permanently."

James took Quill from Burke, maneuvering the

lanky, boneless body with ease, gracefully rising to his feet in one smooth display of power and strength.

Plant rose as well, handing Burke the bloodied cloth to hold. "I'll go and help Ray." He patted Burke on the arm. "You've got other things to look after." He left to join Weston in the pantry.

James lifted his burden higher. "I'll take this one up to his room and stay with him while you handle things. Might wanna get a doc over here first thing, though. The boy looks like he was pulled through a knothole and back out again."

"I will. Thanks, Ethan. I appreciate it."

Burke patted his son on the back and squeezed his shoulder. "I'll be up to see you as soon as I can. I promise."

Quill looked at his father, nodded, then closed his eyes. One hand rested protectively on his bleeding neck while the other gripped James' shirt in a white-knuckled fist. It appeared that all of his energy was going into breathing evenly.

James gave a curt nod and left, shouldering his way past a group of police officers in the hallway, none of which even considered stopping the large man.

Burke laid his gun on the counter and leaned back, resting his weight against it. Four uniformed officers and the plainclothes detective who had interviewed them in Dr. Ivanov's office entered the room. Burke remembered the detective's name as the man approached.

There was a resigned expression on the older man's haggard face and his boxy frame was dressed in a suit and overcoat more rumpled than last time.

"Evening, Lt. Christopher. Welcome to my home. Or what's left of it." Burke's tone was lighter and more carefree than he felt. He waited for the other man's response.

The officers with Christopher fanned out, marking off the crime scene. Silent, Christopher glanced around the room slowly taking in the shattered windows, missing door, gore-stained walls and finally, Crowe's bloody body. The detective turned back to face Burke.

"Kinda like dejá vu, huh, Colonel?" He gestured vaguely with one hand at the scene surrounding them. "This gonna happen on a regular basis, now that you're a more permanent resident?" The question was a mix of wariness and anticipation, the detective's voice oddly congenial, considering the circumstances.

Burke took a deep breath and pushed off the counter's edge. He clapped Christopher on the shoulder and the man jumped. "As a matter of fact, Detective, there *are* a couple of small things you and your men might want to be aware of. In the event of similar...déjà vu moments."

Christopher glanced down at Burke's friendly, bloodied hand still resting on his shoulder and grimaced. "I'll take that as a 'yes'."

* * * * *

Rolling his head to ease the stiffness settling into his neck, Burke shifted in the bedroom chair and stretched his legs out in front of him. On the bed beside him, Quill lay on his side, huddled under a mound of blankets.

Quill had still been awake, but very subdued when Burke had relieved James. Burke's family physician, Dr. Asher, had paid a house call after the situation was explained. He sutured Quill's wounds, examined his bruised airway, and talked with him about his ordeal.

Afterwards, Asher had recommended medicating Quill to ensure a few hours of needed rest. Burke had agreed. Quill had been indifferent to the suggestion, barely acknowledging the doctor's presence throughout the visit.

Burke was concerned by his distant behavior, but Asher assured him it was a normal reaction and not to be too surprised if Quill was reluctant to be around strangers for a time. For now, he needed to feel safe and it was Burke's job to make sure he did.

Drawing a chair up close to the bedside, Burke sat down and reassured the dazed boy he would remain with him until he fell asleep.

Quill's only response had been to turn on his side so he faced his father and then he closed his red-rimmed, bloodshot eyes. Every few seconds he would open them to stare at Burke, then they would flutter closed again. Finally, the medication took effect and sleep claimed him.

Four hours later, Burke was still at his son's side, stretching muscle kinks from weary limbs. There were still a lot of problems needing attention, but his son was alive and safe for the moment and his extended family was intact. The rest would be dealt with in time.

Burke rose from his seat to answer a soft knock on the door, utilizing stealth skills he had acquired over his years as a black ops agent to remain noiseless. In all those years, he had never imagined them helping him function as a parent.

Burr stood on the other side of the door, a white plastic cylinder in his arms. "Hey. The pharmacy in town delivered the humidifier the doctor wanted Quill to have. I filled it up. All you have to do is plug it in." Burr peered around Burke to catch a glimpse of Quill. "How's the kid?"

"Getting restless. Breathing a little easier, but not by much. This will help." Burke took the machine. "Thanks for bringing it, Jack."

Burke placed it on the bedside table and plugged it in. The machine made a hissing noise and a fine mist began to drift through the air. Burke pointed the outlet toward Quill and sat back down in his chair.

"How you holding out, Bossman?"

They'd known each other too long for Burke to hide his weariness for pride's sake. "Tired. Sore. I'll get some rest later, after I know Quill's all right. I've talked to some people about what went down here tonight."

Restless, Quill coughed and moved around in his sleep. Both men turned toward the sound.

Burr waved a hand through the mist, then rubbed his hands together to dry it. "Doc Asher said the kid was going to be fine. Sore and achy, and his voice would take a couple of days to get back to normal, but fine."

Nodding, Burke stared at his son's profile, seeing the boy's mother in the fine, chiseled bone structure. "I know. I just want to talk to him, hear him tell me he's okay."

"He doesn't blame you for this, Daniel. It wasn't your fault. Any of it."

Giving a derisive snort, Burke glanced up at Burr. "I guess I need to hear that from him, Jack."

Burr shrugged, clapped Burke on the shoulder, then left the room. Burke tracked his movements with his hearing, never taking his gaze off his son's face. He was startled when he realized he had been staring at half-lidded eyes that were staring back at him.

He watched as his son's eyes fluttered and opened.

Quill swallowed several times before speaking. "Don't blame you, Da. Really. Just was scared." Quill's soft voice dipped and wavered, losing volume on half of the words. "Sorry I said those things. Didn't really mean them. Just...scared."

Moving to the bed, Burke rested his hand on Quill's shoulder. His thumb rubbed at the edge of the bright, white dressing covering the knife wound on Quill's neck.

"Just so you know, Quill, you weren't the only one scared back there."

Burke could feel the burn of tears in the back of his eyes. "I was afraid I'd lose you. Lose the chance to get to know you. Lose the only part of your mother I'll ever have. Lose a part of me I want to keep near forever." Burke managed a small, twisted smile. "That is, if you'll have me."

Tears leaked from the corners of Quill's eyes as he nodded. Burke gathered his son to his chest and let the shirt covering his shoulder absorb the fallout.

It would be rocky, but he was sure this corner of his world was going to be all right in time. If nothing else, the court order forced them to be together for the next seven years, didn't it? They would work it out, even if they had to destroy half the state of New York to do it.

Chapter Twenty-six

"I don't think you've been as honest as you could be, Lord Davenport." Burke caught himself pacing and forced himself to sit at his desk chair. Davenport was a tricky, savvy man. Burke needed to proceed with care, old family friend or not. The stakes were higher than ever before for Burke–his son's life and welfare.

"I've told you everything you need to know, Daniel."

Davenport's condescending tone irritated Burke. "My sources indicate Crowe's assault on your home was a rogue effort fueled by his insane outrage over having been thwarted by you the first time. He was trying to regain the respect of his superiors. It wasn't a government-sanctioned mission."

"You don't believe that any more than I do, Sir. Crowe didn't have the resources or the contacts to pull off an attack of this size on his own."

"You should let the matter rest, my boy. It's over. You have bigger problems ahead of you. Like exploring that amazing memory of that boy of yours. He holds the futures of an untold number of men and women in his young head. Along with a fair bit of highly secret information, I might add. A heavy burden for an adolescent."

"He's getting help. I'm sure you know General Weiss has assigned a professional therapist to help out. Quill likes her and he's willing to work with her. She has a high enough security clearance that anything he remembers regarding the files will be relayed to General Weiss directly."

Burke decided Davenport needed to be reminded of whose child they were talking about. "After it goes through me, of course."

"Of course, dear boy, of course." Davenport's tone was thoughtful.

Burke wondered what the old fox was up to.

"Congratulations, by the way. He looks like his mother. Fine boned with delicate features. Good looking lad, too. Almost pretty, some would say."

Burke leaned forward in his chair and concentrated on Davenport's conversation. The older man's tone had become harder, almost threatening. Burke listened for a message hidden in the words.

"Pretty?"

"If a man was into such things. Like young boys." Davenport's inflection changed.

Burke felt like he was being let in on a dirty secret, one that was important to him.

"Apparently," Davenport politely cleared his throat, "there is a lot of that making the news lately. Even one of your own government's cabinet members has been caught with his hand in the cookie jar. Or the school playground, as it were. Seems Cabinet Member Michael Gerund's last trip to the Middle East, involved a side visit to what has since been unearthed as his own personal estate. Apparently, he kept a stable of unwilling young boys for his private enjoyment. Video tapes by the truck load." Davenport paused, then added, "Young boys, your son's age. He likes them pretty. But they don't remain that way long. Has a thing for torture, evidently, by all reports from those who had a strong enough constitution to watch the tapes."

Burke reviewed the past few days of his sporadic CNN viewing. He knew none of this had been on the news or in the papers. Quill's e-mail tracer program had uncovered Gerund's name days ago, linked to the assassination plot. Burke would have latched onto that name in connection to anything reported recently.

Cautious not to ask the wrong question and shut down the conversation Burke asked, "Where's Gerund now? I must have missed it in the reports. It's been a bit hectic here. I'm sure you can understand."

"Indeed, my boy, I can." Davenport was jovial and very casual, confident he was being understood. "Alas, the crafty bastard, or should I say bugger, slipped his leash and fled the country. I hear he was sighted in both Argentina and Amsterdam. Left behind a very shocked young wife."

Bile rose to the back of Burke's throat. He forced it down and sipped from the glass of brandy at his elbow, and waited a moment to calm himself. "How unfortunate for everyone."

"Yes. But I feel certain we can be certain he won't pop up again. Scoundrels like that have a way of running afoul of the most interesting people when they least expect them. People should take extra precautions in the meantime."

"Lock their doors." Burke played the game.

"And know where their children are at all times, and whom they are with." The warning note was back in Davenport's tone. "Even old friends can be suspects, if the payoff is large enough."

Burke replied, "I think I just proved I can take care of my own."

"True, but you might consider drawing that circle of friends and family a little tighter, my boy. Gerund was known to have powerful friends in high places all over the world. Not all of whom believe the idiotic blather Gerund privately recruited with either, Daniel. Accomplices haven't been revealed as of yet, but he wasn't alone."

"And this means what to me?"

"Your son's memory is remarkable but the information stored there is of little consequence now. These people have abandoned their plans. The conspirators will never be discovered." Davenport sounded weary, as if every one of his sixty-six years rested on his shoulders. "It's over."

Burke settled back into his chair and tried to read between the lines again. Was Davenport warning him or reassuring him? Or both? Burke really couldn't decide.

"Have you been able to debrief the lad in any manner?"

Burke considered his answer for a moment then decided a lifetime of trust in the man called for the truth.

"There's a problem with that. Quill has only a limited amount of control over his memories. Seems they're triggered by other things, a sound, a word, an object, or even a color. He can't just call them up and recite things." Burke sighed and ran a hand through his hair. "Using the words of Dr. Gray, this is going to take some time."

"I see. Well, I'm sure you'll do what's best for the boy, Daniel. I wish you the best of luck with it."

"I'll keep you informed."

"I was hoping you would. You're a fortunate man, my boy. Give your mother my best when you see her."

"I will sir, and thank you. I appreciate the...news

update."

"You're most welcome. British news coverage is so much more detailed than what you Americans get."

"If you say so, Sir. Good evening."

"Take care, my boy."

Burke stared at the phone before replacing it in its cradle. He picked up his forgotten glass and sipped the alcohol. He enjoyed the burn of the liquor as it slid down his dry throat.

The future held a lot of unanswered questions, but the retired Colonel was looking forward to it. After all, how hard could parenting really be? Quill was a teenager, almost grown. The tough years were over, right?

* * * * *

Burke stood in the middle of his foyer and surveyed the remaining damage to his home. Carpenters and masons had been laboring for days to replace the broken windows, twisted iron security grates, and restore the damage of the outer walls to their former state. Another group of workers labored in the back of the house, repairing the kitchen area.

Early that morning, Burke had stood in the once warm and cheerful room looking out over the expansive flower garden that bordered the back porch. The high, open bank of leaded windows that ran the length of the eating area was one of his favorite places in the house. Or was, until he realized this was how Crowe's team had timed their assault.

The open expanse of windows had provided the invaders with a clear view of the household activities in the back of the house. He had sent Quill off to the kitchen to help Ramona put together a quick meal, thinking to distract the boy for a period of time.

The assault team had taken advantage of the moment when Quill was alone with only an older woman to protect him. They hadn't needed to wait for the cover of darkness. They only needed to wait for Burke to screw up.

And he had. He'd failed his son again, and it had almost cost the boy his life a second time.

Burke immediately ordered blinds and window coverings to be installed within the week. His once secure home was going to have to become an impenetrable fortress. It sheltered more than just a priceless art collection now. A lot more.

All that was left of the massive oak front door was a section of shattered wood still attached to the heavy metal hinges. Bits and pieces of the splintered wood were embedded in the room's fine furniture and the singed remains of the curtains and tapestries still hung on the walls.

Feeling the need to contribute to the salvage efforts, he bent down to help the workman sweep the debris into a large dustpan. Crouched low to the scarred marble floor, a pair of navy linen heels came into his line of vision.

Following the low pumps to a trim ankle, Burke's gaze traveled from stocking legs to a modest navy skirt over well-curved hips. His gaze lingered there, then wandered past a narrow waist cinched under the clean lines of a tailored navy jacket, and over an interesting, but average bust line.

This led to a long neck decorated with a single strand of gray pearls. Porcelain smooth skin over a high-cheeked face framed by waves of dark brown hair topped off the five-foot, six-inch tall vision. Burke felt the stirrings of genuine attraction for a woman for the first time in years.

Scooping the last of the splintered wood into the pan, Burke turned the dustpan over to the laborer, who nodded his thanks. Burke wiped off his hands on his jeans as he stood. "May I help you, Ms....?"

He extended a hand in greeting, and smiled. The woman was preoccupied with taking in the overwhelming destruction of the once elegant room.

She started at the sound of Burke's voice, spinning around to face him. She stepped over a small pile of stone rubble, transferred her clutched notebooks to her left arm, and shook Burke's hand. "Gray. Dr. Juliet Gray, child psychologist. I'm here at the request of General Weiss and the court order."

Dr. Gray's gaze continued to wander around the room, taking in the singed fabrics and smoke-damaged walls.

"Daniel Burke, owner and current remodeler of this estate." Burke followed her gaze and saw the room from a stranger's point of view for the first time.

Gray forced her attention back to Burke. "I know. I've been assigned to review a young man in your custody, one Quillan Tarquin. I'll be providing counseling, too, if I decide it's needed."

A loud shriek of metal split the air as two men pried the fused door hinges from the charred threshold.

"This may not be the best time, Dr. Gray." Burke took her arm and guided her several more paces away from the work area to stand at the bottom of the grand staircase.

Gray eased her arm from Burke's hand, and straightened her shoulders. Her pale red lips set into a prim line and she tilted her chin up just a touch.

Burke caught himself admiring her full lips and long neck.

"From what I've read in the file, which admittedly isn't much, therapy and counseling should have been provided to this child days ago. Waiting is not in his best interest, Colonel Burke."

"You can drop the Colonel, I'm retired. Call me Daniel instead. And believe me, I've been trying to protect his best interests, Doctor."

"By neglecting his mental and emotional health?"

"No, by trying to make sure he lived long enough to benefit from your expert services." Burke waved one hand at the surrounding destruction. "You may have noticed a subtle coarseness to the present décor."

The screech of ripped wood interrupted them as a worker tore a fire-scarred length of wood from the hall entry.

Dr. Gray's voice was suddenly flat. "Your door's been blow off."

Burke nodded and shrugged. "Plastic explosives. It was only a small charge. The foundation wasn't affected."

Dr. Gary turned around, hesitant, and touched a crack in the wall beside them. "The holes in the walls are *bullet* holes."

"Submachine guns." Burke's tone was casual and light, like he was discussing the wallpaper.

"Machine guns?" Gray's face paled.

"The bullets ricocheted like a b–, like crazy off these stone walls. But at least stone doesn't burn. The fires didn't last long."

"The fires?"

"From the flame thrower." Burke pointed to the

singed threads of an old tapestry draped over the end of the banister. "Didn't expect that one."

"Mr. Burke–" Her expression turned grim.

"Daniel, please." Burke's easy smile and amused look only seemed to make her face pinch tighter.

"Mr. Burke, I'm not sure this young man should remain in your custody. I'm sure others can be found who–."

"He's not just 'in my custody', Dr. Gray. He's my son, biologically and legally. Papers were filed to ensure both his rights and my own in the New York State Superior Court three days ago."

"His file contains–" Gray tapped one manicured fingertip against her attaché notebook.

"Very little of the truth, I'm afraid. Security reasons." Burke took her elbow and walked her toward a less affected area of the house.

Over the noise of power saws and hammering, the racket of dogs barking and people yelling could be heard nearing the house.

Burke paused in front of the gaping hole in the front of the entryway. "If you know General Weiss, I know you understand the circumstances surrounding Quill."

"I know all I really need to know. He was witness to his two best friends being murdered. I know he was almost murdered himself. I know he's a helpless child, alone, far from home and left in the care of strangers in a house that just got blown up."

"It was only a little explosion, Doctor. And this is his home now."

"Mr. Burke!"

The barking of the dogs grew closer.

"And we're not strangers. Quill's–"

Burke broke off his sentence as a blur of red fur attached to sharp, white teeth leapt through the front opening. It raced between Gray's legs and up the stairs, ignoring Gray's shriek.

Behind it came the teenager in question, hobbling as fast as his braced leg would allow him. His face showed fresh bruises and cuts. There was a crooked twist to his lips and a twinkle in his eyes that belied the seriousness of his state. A stark, white bandage engulfed his one hand.

"Bloody Hell! Come back here! Damn little wanker's too fuck–!"

"Quill!" Burke sliced a hand through the air at neck level, and glanced at Dr. Gray to gauge her reaction.

Reaching the bottom of the stairs, the boy collapsed. Breathing hard, Quill gave his father his most innocent look, eyes wide and hands gesturing vaguely up the steps in the direction of the speeding furball. "I swear, Da, I didn't know it was for training the dogs. I thought it was caught in a trap!" Quill gasped for breath in between each sentence.

Before Burke could respond, two very large dogs burst over the threshold and rocketed up the stairs, pushing between Burke and Gray and running over Quill in the process. One of the two animals bayed the entire way, the mournful howl echoing off the smooth, stone walls. Both dogs disappeared from sight.

"Ow! Damn it, that hurt, you heavy-arsed barker!" Quill rubbed at his side where the larger of the dogs, a huge, male, two hundred pound Tosa Inu, had stepped.

Burke stuck his hand in his pocket and snorted. "Dr. Gray, meet my son, Quill."

Burke watched her stare at the lively array of black and blue marks across the boy's chin and forehead, taking in the split lip and the bruises that dotted his neck like fingerprints. Her gaze dropped to the brace on his right leg, then the thick bandage on his left hand.

She turned on her heel and glared at Burke. "This is taking care of him?"

Grimacing, Burke looked at his son and crossed his arms over his chest. "Considering he had a gun pressed to his head and someone tried to cut his throat a few days ago, he looks pretty good."

He smiled at Quill. "He's still breathing." The smile evaporated. "The other guy isn't."

Gray stiffened and sucked in a gasp of air. "This is too much. I–"

Weston and Burr ran into the room, their cheeks red from being in the cold. James ambled in after them. Burr was breathing hard from the extended chase. Weston smiled at the doctor, but stayed by Burr's side.

"Daniel, did you see Ruby and Brutus come through here? Chasing a little red fox, *somebody*," Burr glared at Quill, "let out of its pen?"

"By mistake. *By. Mis-take!*" Quill appealed to Burke. "I swear, Da', I thought it was trapped! I didn't know Jackson was using it to train the dogs for scent! I didn't!"

A mournful howl followed by the crash of breaking glass came from the second story. Burr transferred his attention to the ceiling above. He followed the trail of destruction as it moved from room to room and took off up the stairs, pausing only long enough to land a warning thump to the top of Quill's head as he passed him.

"I'll be talking to you later, boy." Burr growled, then sprinted up the remaining stairs.

Weston winked at Quill's startled face and took the

stairs two at a time. James sauntered past Burke and Gray, giving the doctor a small bow. He drawled, honey smooth, "Morning, ma'am," then reached down and pulled an unresisting Quill to his feet. He steadied the boy with one big hand.

"Here to visit a spell?" This he said to Gray as he heaved Quill up over one shoulder.

Quill grunted a short-lived, "Fu–!"

James punctuated the aborted curse with a swat to the boy's conveniently presented backside. "There's a lady present, son."

"Bloody Texas Ranger!" Quill muttered.

James grinned and ignored the comment, turning so he could face Gray. "Looks like Jack forgot something. I'd best take it to him."

Gray said, "I'm here to review the care this boy is receiving in this...'environment' and to help him with the trauma he's been through."

"So, you'll be around for a right long spell then." James began to walk up the stairs, jiggling Quill into a more comfortable carrying position on his shoulder. The boy grunted in protest.

Gray cast a startled glance from James to Burke and back again. "I don't know. I'm here for however long it takes to help him."

James snorted a laugh and continued up the stairs. "In that case, Daniel, you'll need to get a bedroom ready for the lady. Sorting out *this* papoose is going to take a heap of time."

Quill's head shot up and he called out as James bounded up the steps. "Lady, if you're really wanna help me, *you* explain to Jackson about the fox pen. I swear it was a mistake!"

The two were soon out of sight, but not hearing range. A loud thump was followed by an outraged, "Bloody hell! What a blooming mess! Christ, Ethan let me go. Jack's going to murder me!"

Burke shook his head and just grinned.

Chaos having moved to the next level of the house, the workmen returned to their jobs and the sounds of the restoration buzzed in the background.

Dr. Gray stood with her mouth hanging open.

Burke touched her elbow, drawing her attention back to the empty foyer. "Doctor, would you like to join us for lunch?"

Gray glanced back up the stairs. "I *would* like to see how this family interacts in a more normal setting."

Burke snorted, a soft chuckling sound. "That, Doctor, *was* 'normal interaction' for around here."

"Oh." Gray blinked and turned to face her host.

Burke pointed to the rooms to their left. "Would you like to accompany me to the den? We can talk in private there."

"Yes. Yes, I would. I think we have a lot to discuss, Mr. Burke." Dr. Gray let him guide her toward the living space, her gaze wandering over the shattered foyer one last time. "I think this may take some time."

Burke smiled and touched her hand where it rested on his arm. "Strange, but I was hoping you would say that. May I call you Juliet?"

The End

Flight of the Sparrows

Laura Baumbach